Friends, Lovers, Chocolate

Also by Alexander McCall Smith

The *No. 1 Ladies' Detective Agency* Series
THE NO. 1 LADIES' DETECTIVE AGENCY
TEARS OF THE GIRAFFE
MORALITY FOR BEAUTIFUL GIRLS
THE KALAHARI TYPING SCHOOL FOR MEN
THE FULL CUPBOARD OF LIFE
IN THE COMPANY OF CHEERFUL LADIES

THE 2½ PILLARS OF WISDOM
THE SUNDAY PHILOSOPHY CLUB
44 SCOTLAND STREET

These titles are also available as
Time Warner AudioBooks

Friends, Lovers, Chocolate

ALEXANDER
McCALL SMITH

LITTLE, BROWN

LITTLE, BROWN

First published in Great Britain in September 2005 by Little, Brown
Reprinted 2005

A CIP catalogue record for this book
is available from the British Library

HARDBACK ISBN 0 316 72780 6
C FORMAT ISBN 0 316 72977 9

Typeset in Bembo by M Rules
Printed and bound in Great Britain
by Clays Ltd, St Ives plc

Little, Brown
An imprint of
Time Warner Book Group UK
Brettenham House
Lancaster Place
London WC2E 7EN

www.twbg.co.uk

For Angus and Fiona Foster

1

The man in the brown Harris tweed overcoat –
double-breasted with three small leather-covered
buttons on the cuffs – made his way slowly along the street
that led down the spine of Edinburgh. He was aware of the
seagulls which had drifted in from the shore and which were
swooping down onto the cobblestones, picking up fragments
dropped by somebody who had been careless with a fish.
Their mews were the loudest sound in the street at that
moment, as there was little traffic and the city was unusually
quiet. It was October, it was mid-morning, and there were
few people about. A boy on the other side of the road,
scruffy and tousle-haired, was leading a dog along with a
makeshift leash – a length of string. The dog, a small Scottish
terrier, seemed unwilling to follow the boy and glanced for
a moment at the man as if imploring him to intervene to

stop the tugging and the pulling. There must be a saint for such dogs, thought the man; a saint for such dogs in their small prisons.

The man reached the St Mary's Street crossroads. On the corner on his right was a pub, the World's End, a place of resort for fiddlers and singers; on his left, Jeffrey Street curved round and dipped under the great arch of the North Bridge. Through the gap in the buildings, he could see the flags on top of the Balmoral Hotel: the white-on-blue cross of the Saltire, the Scottish flag, the familiar diagonal stripes of the Union Jack. There was a stiff breeze from the north, from Fife, which made the flags stand out from their poles with pride, like the flags on the prow of a ship ploughing into the wind. And that, he thought, was what Scotland was like: a small vessel pointed out to sea, a small vessel buffeted by the wind.

He crossed the street and continued down the hill. He walked past a fishmonger, with its gilt fish sign suspended over the street, and the entrance to a close, one of those small stone passages that ran off the street underneath the tenements. And then he was where he wanted to be, outside the Canongate Kirk, the high-gabled church set just a few paces off the High Street. At the top of the gable, stark against the light blue of the sky, the arms of the kirk, a stag's antlers, gilded, against the background of a similarly golden cross.

He entered the gate and looked up. One might be in Holland, he thought, with that gable; but there were too many reminders of Scotland – the wind, the sky, the grey stone. And there was what he had come to see, the stone which he visited every year on this day, this day when the

2

poet had died at the age of twenty-four. He walked across the grass towards the stone, its shape reflecting the gable of the kirk, its lettering still clear after two hundred years. Robert Burns himself had paid for this stone to be erected, in homage to his brother in the muse, and had written the lines of its inscription: *This simple stone directs Pale Scotia's way / To pour her sorrows o'er her poet's dust.*

He stood quite still. There were others who could be visited here. Adam Smith, whose days had been filled with thoughts of markets and economics and who had coined an entire science, had his stone here, more impressive than this, more ornate; but this was the one that made one weep.

He reached into a pocket of his overcoat and took out a small black notebook of the sort that used to advertise itself as waterproof. Opening it, he read the lines that he had written out himself, copied from a collection of Robert Garioch's poems. He read aloud, but in a low voice, although there was nobody present save for him and the dead:

> *Canongait kirkyaird in the failing year*
> *Is auld and grey, the wee roseirs are bare,*
> *Five gulls leem white agin the dirty air.*
> *Why are they here? There's naething for them here*
> *Why are we here oursels?*

Yes, he thought. Why am I here myself? Because I admire this man, this Robert Fergusson, who wrote such beautiful words in the few years given him, and because at least somebody should remember and come here on this day each year.

And this, he told himself, was the last time that he would be able to do this. This was his final visit. If their predictions were correct, and unless something turned up, which he thought was unlikely, this was the last of his pilgrimages.

He looked down at his notebook again. He continued to read out loud. The chiselled Scots words were taken up by the wind and carried away:

Strang, present dool
Ruggs at my hairt. Lichtlie this gin ye daur:
Here Robert Burns knelt and kissed the mool.

Strong, present sorrow
Tugs at my heart. Treat this lightly if you dare:
Here Robert Burns knelt and kissed the soil.

He took a step back. There was nobody there to observe the tears which had come to his eyes, but he wiped them away in embarrassment. *Strang, present dool.* Yes. And then he nodded towards the stone and turned round, and that was when the woman came running up the path. He saw her almost trip as the heel of a shoe caught in a crack between two paving stones, and he cried out. But she recovered herself and came on towards him, waving her hands.

'Ian. Ian.' She was breathless. And he knew immediately what news she had brought him, and he looked at her gravely. She said, 'Yes.' And then she smiled, and leant forward to embrace him.

'When?' he asked, stuffing the notebook back into his pocket.

4

'Right away,' she said. 'Now. Right now. They'll take you down there straightaway.'

They began to walk back along the path, away from the stone. He had been warned not to run, and could not, as he would rapidly become breathless. But he could walk quite fast on the flat, and they were soon back at the gate to the kirk, where the black taxi was waiting, ready to take them.

'Whatever happens,' he said as they climbed into the taxi, 'come back to this place for me. It's the one thing I do every year. On this day.'

'You'll be back next year,' she said, reaching out to take his hand.

On the other side of Edinburgh, in another season, Cat, an attractive young woman in her mid-twenties, stood at Isabel Dalhousie's front door, her finger poised over the bell. She gazed at the stonework. She noticed that in parts the discoloration was becoming more pronounced. Above the triangular gable of her aunt's bedroom window, the stone was flaking slightly, and a patch had fallen off here and there, like a ripened scab, exposing fresh skin below. This slow decline had its own charms; a house, like anything else, should not be denied the dignity of natural ageing – within reason, of course.

For the most part, the house was in good order; a discreet and sympathetic house, in spite of its size. And it was known, too, for its hospitality. Everyone who called there – irrespective of their mission – would be courteously received and offered, if the time was appropriate, a glass of dry white wine in spring and summer and red in autumn and winter. They would then be listened to, again with courtesy, for Isabel believed in giving moral attention to everyone. This made her profoundly egalitarian, though not in the non-discriminating sense of many contemporary egalitarians, who sometimes ignore the real moral differences between people (good and evil are *not* the same, Isabel would say). She felt uncomfortable with moral relativists and their penchant for non-judgementalism. But of course we must be judgemental, she said, *when there is something to be judged.*

Isabel had studied philosophy and had a part-time job as general editor of the *Review of Applied Ethics*. It was not a demanding job in terms of the time it required, and it was badly paid; in fact, at Isabel's own suggestion, rising production costs had been partly offset by a cut in her own salary. Not that payment mattered; her share of the Louisiana and Gulf Land Company, left to her by her mother – *her sainted American mother*, as she called her – provided more than she could possibly need. Isabel was, in fact, wealthy, although that was a word that she did not like to use, especially of herself. She was indifferent to material wealth, although she was attentive to what she described, with characteristic modesty, as her minor projects of giving (which were actually very generous).

'And what are these projects?' Cat had once asked.

Isabel looked embarrassed. 'Charitable ones, I suppose. Or eleemosynary if you prefer long words. Nice word that – *eleemosynary* . . . But I don't normally talk about it.'

Cat frowned. There were things about her aunt that puzzled her. If one gave to charity, then why not mention it?

'One must be discreet,' Isabel continued. She was not one for circumlocution, but she believed that one should never refer to one's own good works. A good work, once drawn attention to by its author, inevitably became an exercise in self-congratulation. That was what was wrong with the lists of names of donors in the opera programmes. Would they have given if their generosity was not going to be recorded in the programme? Isabel thought that in many cases they would not. Of course, if the only way one could raise money for the arts was through appealing to vanity, then it was probably worth doing. But her own name never appeared in such lists, a fact which had not gone unnoticed in Edinburgh.

'She's mean,' whispered some. 'She gives nothing away.'

They were wrong, of course, as the uncharitable so often are. In one year, Isabel, unrecorded by name in any pro-gramme and amongst numerous other donations, had given eight thousand pounds to Scottish Opera: three thousand towards a production of *Hansel and Gretel*, and five thousand to help secure a fine Italian tenor for a *Cavalleria Rusticana* performed in the ill-fitting costumes of nineteen thirties Italy, complete with brown-shirted Fascisti in the chorus.

'Such fine singing from your Fascisti,' Isabel had remarked at the party which followed the production.

'They love to dress up as fascists,' the chorus master had responded. 'Something to do with only being in the chorus, I suspect.'

This remark had been greeted with silence. Some of the Fascisti had overheard it.

'Only in the most attenuated way,' the chorus master had

added, looking into his glass of wine. 'But then again, perhaps not. Perhaps not.'

'Money,' said Cat. 'That's the problem. Money.'

Isabel handed Cat a glass of wine. 'It invariably is,' she said.

'Yes,' Cat went on. 'I suppose that if I were prepared to offer enough I would be able to get somebody suitable to stand in for me. But I can't. I have to run it as a business, and I can't make a loss.'

Isabel nodded. Cat owned a delicatessen just a few streets away, in Bruntsfield, and although it was successful, she knew that the line between profitability and failure was a narrow one. As it was, she had one full-time employee to pay, Eddie, a young man who seemed to be on the verge of tears much of the time, haunted, thought Isabel, by something which Cat could not, or would not, speak about. Eddie could be left in control for short periods, but not for a week it seemed.

'He panics,' said Cat. 'It gets too much for him and he panics.'

Cat explained to Isabel that she had been invited to a wedding in Italy and wanted to go with a party of friends. They would attend the wedding in Messina and then move north to a house which they had rented for a week in Umbria. The time of year was ideal; the weather would be perfect.

'I have to go,' said Cat. 'I just have to.'

Isabel smiled. Cat would never ask outright for a favour, but her intention was transparent. 'I suppose . . .' she began. 'I suppose I could do it again. I rather enjoyed it last time.

And if you remember, I made more than you usually do. The takings went up.'

This amused Cat. 'You probably overcharged,' she said. And then a pause, before she continued: 'I didn't raise the issue to get you to . . . I wouldn't want to force you.'

'Of course not,' said Isabel.

'But it would make all the difference,' Cat went on quickly. 'You know how everything works. And Eddie likes you.'

Isabel was surprised. Did Eddie have a view on her? He hardly ever spoke to her, and certainly never smiled. But the thought that he liked her made her warm towards him. Perhaps he might confide in her, as he had confided in Cat, and she would be able to help him in some way. Or she could put him in touch with somebody: there were people who could help in such circumstances; she could pay for it if necessary.

They discussed the details. Cat would be leaving in ten days' time. If Isabel came for a hand-over day before then, she could be shown the current stock and the order book. Consignments of wine and salamis were expected while Cat was away and these would have to be attended to. And then there was the whole issue of making sure that the surfaces were cleaned – a fussy procedure subject to an entire litany of regulations. Eddie knew all about that, but you had to watch him; he was funny about olives and often put them in containers marked down for coleslaw.

'It will be far more difficult than editing the *Review of Applied Ethics*,' said Cat, smiling. 'Far more difficult.'

Which might have been true, thought Isabel, although she

did not say it. Editing a journal was largely repetitive work: sending letters to reviewers and assessors; discussing deadlines with copy editors and printers. All that was mundane work; reading the papers and dealing with authors was a different matter. That required insight and a large measure of tact. In her experience, the authors of papers which were turned down almost invariably proved resentful. And the more incompetent or eccentric the paper – and there were many of those – the more truculent the disappointed author became. One such author – or his paper – lay on her desk before her at the time. 'The Rightness of Vice': a title which reminded her of a recent book she had reviewed, *In Praise of Sin*. But while *In Praise of Sin* had been a serious investigation of the limits of moralism – and ultimately claimed to be in favour of virtue – 'The Rightness of Vice' had no truck with virtue. It was about the alleged benefits for character of vice, provided that the vice in question was what a person really wanted to do. That was defensible – just – thought Isabel, provided that the vice was a tolerable one (drinking, gluttony, and so on), but how could one possibly argue in favour of the sorts of vices which the author of the paper had in mind? It was impossible, thought Isabel. Who could defend . . . She went over in her mind some of the vices explored by the author, but stopped. Even by their Latin names, these vices barely bore thinking about. Did people really do *that*? The answer, she supposed, was that they did, but she very much doubted that they would expect a philosopher to spring to their defence. And yet here was an Australian professor of philosophy doing just that. Well, she had a responsibility to her readers. She could not defend the

10

indefensible. She would send the article back with a short note, something like: *Dear Professor, I'm so sorry, but we just can't. People feel very strongly about these things, you know. And they would blame me for what you say. They really would. Yours sincerely, Isabel Dalhousie.*

Isabel put the thought of vice behind her and turned her attention back to Cat. 'It may be difficult,' she said. 'But I think I'll manage.'

'You can say no,' said Cat.

'Can, but shall not,' said Isabel. 'You go to the wedding.'

Cat smiled. 'I'll reciprocate some day,' she said. 'I'll be you for a few weeks and you can go away.'

'You could never be me,' said Isabel. 'And I could never be you. We never know enough about another person to be him or her. We think we do, but we can never be sure.'

'You know what I mean,' said Cat. 'I'll come and live here and reply to your letters and so on while you get away.'

Isabel nodded. 'I'll bear that in mind. But there's no need to think of reciprocation. I suspect that I shall enjoy myself.'

'You will,' said Cat. 'You'll enjoy the customers – or some of them.'

Cat stayed, and they ate a light supper in the garden room, enjoying the last of the evening sun. It was June – close to the solstice – and it never became truly dark in Edinburgh, even at midnight. The summer had been slow to come, but had now arrived and the days were long and warm.

'I've been feeling lazy in this weather,' Isabel remarked to Cat. 'Working in your shop is exactly what I need to wake me up.'

'And Italy is exactly what I need to wind me down,' said Cat. 'Not that the wedding itself should be quiet – anything but.'

Isabel enquired who was getting married. She knew few of Cat's friends, and tended to get them mixed up. There were too many Kirstys and Craigs, Isabel thought; they had become interchangeable in her mind.

'Kirsty,' said Cat. 'You've met her with me once or twice, I think.'

'Oh,' said Isabel. 'Kirsty.'

'She met an Italian last year when she was teaching English in Catania. Salvatore. They fell for one another and that was it.'

For a moment Isabel was silent. She had fallen for John Liamor in Cambridge all those years ago, and that had been it too. She had gone so far as to marry him and had tolerated his unfaithfulness until it had been too much to bear. But all these Kirstys were so sensible; they would not make a bad choice.

'What does he do?' Isabel asked. She half expected Cat not to know; it always surprised her that her niece seemed uninterested in, or unaware of, what people did. For Isabel, it was fundamentally important information if one were even to begin to understand somebody.

Cat smiled. 'Kirsty doesn't really know,' she said. 'I know that'll surprise you, but she says that whenever she's asked Salvatore he's become evasive. He says that he's some sort of businessman who works for his father. But she can't find out exactly what this business is.'

Isabel stared at Cat. It was clear to her – immediately clear – what Salvatore's father did.

'And she doesn't care?' Isabel ventured. 'She's still prepared to marry him?'

'Why not?' said Cat. 'Just because you don't know what happens in somebody's office doesn't mean that you shouldn't marry them.'

'But what if this . . . this office is headquarters of a protection racket? What then?'

Cat laughed. 'A protection racket? Don't be ridiculous. There's nothing to suggest that it's a protection racket.'

Isabel thought that any accusations of ridiculousness were being made in exactly the wrong direction.

'Cat,' she said quietly. 'It's Italy. In the south of Italy if you won't disclose what you do, then it means one thing. Organised crime. That's just the way it is. And the most common form of organised crime is the protection racket.'

Cat stared at her aunt. 'Nonsense,' she said. 'You have an overheated imagination.'

'And Kirsty's is distinctly underheated,' retorted Isabel. 'I simply can't imagine marrying somebody who would hide that sort of thing from me. I couldn't marry a gangster.'

'Salvatore's not a gangster,' said Cat. 'He's nice. I met him several times and I liked him.'

Isabel looked at the floor. The fact that Cat could say this merely emphasised her inability to tell good men from bad. This Kirsty was in for a rude awakening, with her handsome young mafioso husband. He would want a compliant, unquestioning wife, who would look the other way when it came to his dealings with his cronies. A Scotswoman was unlikely to understand this; she would expect equality and consideration, which this Salvatore would not give her once

13

they were married. It was a disaster in the making and Isabel thought that Cat simply could not see it, as she had been unable to see through Toby, her previous boyfriend; he of the Lladró porcelain looks and the tendency to wear crushed-strawberry corduroy trousers. Perhaps Cat would come back from Italy with an Italian of her own. Now that would be interesting.

2

When it came to a Queen's Hall concert, Isabel Dalhousie had a strategy. The hall had been a church, and the upstairs gallery, which ran round three sides of the hall, was designed to be uncomfortable. The Church of Scotland had always believed that one should sit up straight, especially when the minister was in full flow, and this principle had been embodied in its Scottish ecclesiastical architecture. As a result, the upstairs seats prevented any leaning back, and indeed were inimical to too much spreading out in any direction. For this reason, Isabel would attend concerts in the Queen's Hall only if she could arrange a ticket for downstairs, where ordinary seats, rather than pews, were set out in the main body of the kirk, and only in the first few rows which afforded a reasonable view of the stage.

Her friend Jamie had arranged the ticket for her that evening, and he knew all about her requirements.

'Third row from the front,' he assured her on the telephone. 'On the aisle. Perfect.'

'And who'll be sitting next to me?' Isabel asked. 'Perfection implies an agreeable neighbour.'

Jamie laughed. 'Somebody wonderful,' he said. 'Or at least, that's what I asked for.'

'Last time I was in the Queen's Hall,' Isabel observed, 'I had that strange man from the National Library. You know, the one who's the expert on Highland place names, and who fidgets. Nobody will sit next to him normally, and I believe he was actually hit over the head with a rolled-up programme at a Scottish Chamber Orchestra concert – out of sheer irritation. No excuse, of course, but understandable. I have, of course, never hit anybody with a programme. Not once.'

Jamie laughed. This was a typical Isabel comment, and it delighted him. Everybody else was so literal; she could turn a situation on its head and render it painfully funny by some peculiar observation. 'Maybe it's the way the music takes him,' he said. 'My pupils fidget a lot.'

Jamie was a musician, a bassoonist who supplemented his earnings as a member of a chamber orchestra with the proceeds of teaching. His pupils were mostly teenagers, who traipsed up the stairs of his Stockbridge flat once a week for their lessons. For the most part they were promising players, but there were several who attended under parental duress, and these were the ones who fidgeted or looked out of the window.

Isabel enjoyed a close friendship with Jamie – or at least as close a friendship as could flourish across an age gap of fifteen years. She had met him during the six months that he had spent with Cat, and she had been disappointed when her niece and this good-looking young man, with his sallow complexion and his *en brosse* haircut, had separated. It was entirely Cat's doing, and it had taken all of Isabel's self-restraint not to upbraid her niece for what she saw as a disastrous mistake. Jamie was a gift: a wonderful, gentle gift from the gods – sent straight down from Parnassus – and Cat was walking away from him. How could she possibly do it?

Over the months that followed, the torch which Jamie continued to carry for Cat had been kept alight by Isabel. She had barely discussed the matter with him, but there was an unspoken understanding that Jamie was still part of the family, as it were, and that by remaining in contact with Isabel, the chance of a resumption of the affair was at least kept alive. But the bond between them had gone deeper than that. It appeared that Jamie needed a confidante, and Isabel fulfilled that role with instinctive sympathy. And for her part, she enjoyed Jamie's company immensely: he sang while she accompanied him on the piano; she cooked meals for him; they gossiped – all of which he appeared to enjoy as much as she did.

She was content with what she had in this friendship. She knew that she could telephone Jamie at any time and that he would come up from his flat in Saxe-Coburg Street and share a glass of wine and talk. From time to time they went out for dinner together, or to a concert when Jamie had spare tickets. He took it for granted that she would be at

17

every performance of his chamber orchestra, in Edinburgh or in Glasgow, and she was, although Isabel did not enjoy going through to Glasgow. Such an unsettling city, she confessed. And Jamie smiled: what was unsettling about Glasgow was that it was *real*; there was a meatiness about life in Glasgow that was quite different from the rarefied atmosphere of Edinburgh. And of course he liked that: he had studied at the Royal Scottish Academy of Music and Drama and remembered a student life of late-night parties and bars and dinners in cheap Indian restaurants off the Byres Road, all against the smell of the river and the sound of the ships and the factories.

Now, sitting in her seat in the third row – as promised – Isabel studied the programme for that evening's concert. It was a charity concert in aid of a Middle East relief fund, and an eclectic selection of local musicians had offered their services. There was a Haydn cello concerto, a ragbag of Bach, and a selection of anthems from the Edinburgh Academy Chorus. Jamie's chamber orchestra was not performing that night, but he was playing the contrabassoon in an impromptu ensemble that was to accompany the singers. Isabel ran her eye down the list of performers: almost all of them were known to her.

She settled back in her seat and glanced up towards the gallery. A young child, the younger sister perhaps of one of the members of the Academy Chorus, was gazing down over the parapet, met her eye, and lifted a hand in a hesitant wave. Isabel waved back, and smiled. Behind the child, she saw the figure of the man from the National Library – he went to every concert, and fidgeted at them all.

The hall was now almost full, and only a few latecomers were still to find their way to their seats. Isabel looked down at her programme and then, discreetly, glanced at her neighbour on the left. She was a middle-aged woman with her hair tied back in a bun and a vaguely disapproving expression on her face. A thin-faced man, drained of colour, sat beside her, staring up at the ceiling. The man glanced at the woman, and then looked away. The woman looked at the man, and then half turned to face Isabel on the pretext of adjusting the red paisley shawl she had about her shoulders.

'Such an interesting programme,' whispered Isabel. 'A real treat.'

The woman's expression softened. 'We hear so little Haydn,' she said, almost conspiratorially. 'They don't give us enough.'

'I suppose not,' said Isabel, but she wondered: precisely who took it upon themselves to ration Haydn?

'They need to wake up,' muttered the man. 'When did they last do *The Creation*? Can you remember? I can't.'

Isabel looked back at her programme, as if to assess the quota of Haydn, but the lights were dimmed and the members of a string quartet appeared from the door at the back of the stage to take their places. There was enthusiastic applause led, it seemed to Isabel, by her neighbours.

'Haydn,' whispered the woman, transformed. And the man nodded.

Isabel suppressed a smile. The world, she supposed, was full of enthusiasts and fans of one kind or another. There were people who loved all sorts of extraordinary things and lived for their passions. Haydn was a perfectly respectable

19

passion, as were trains, she supposed. W. H. Auden, or WHA as she called him, had appreciated steam engines, and had confessed that when he was a boy he had loved a steam engine which he thought 'every bit as beautiful' as a person to whom his poem was addressed. You are my steam engine, one might say, in much the same way as the French addressed their lovers as *mon petit chou*, my little cabbage. How strange was human passion in its expression.

The quartet tuned up and then began their Haydn, which they played with distinction and which in due course prompted rapturous applause from Isabel's row. This was followed by the Bach, which took them up to the interval. Isabel often remained in her seat during intervals, but it was a warm evening and thirst drove her into the bar, where she joined a line of people waiting for drinks. Fortunately the service was efficient and she did not have to wait long. Nursing her white wine spritzer, she made her way to one of the small tables under the mezzanine.

She looked at the milling crowd. A few people greeted her from the other side of the room – with nods of the head and smiles. Where was Jamie? she wondered. He would be playing immediately after the interval and might be in the green room, preparing his bassoon reed. She would see him after the concert, she imagined, and they might enjoy a drink together, discussing the performance.

Then she saw him, standing in a knot of people in the corner of the bar. One of them she recognised as another member of the chamber orchestra, a young man called Brian, who came from Aberdeen and who played the viola. And then, immediately next to Jamie, a tall girl, with blond hair and wearing a strappy red dress, who was holding a drink in her left hand and talking, and who now turned and leant up against Jamie. Isabel watched. She saw Jamie smile at the girl and place a hand on her shoulder, lightly, and then his hand moved up and brushed the hair from her forehead, and she returned his smile and slipped her free arm round his waist.

Isabel saw the intimacy of the gestures and felt immediately empty, a sensation so physical and so overwhelming that she felt for a moment that she might stop breathing, being empty of air. She put down her glass and stared at the table for a few moments before she raised her eyes again and looked in their direction. Jamie was looking at his watch and saying something to the viola player, and to the girl too, and then he unwound himself from her clasp and moved off towards the green-room door and the girl looked at one of the paintings on the wall – amateurish, characterless landscapes that the Queen's Hall was trying in vain to sell.

Isabel stood up. Making her way back to the hall she had to walk past the girl, but she did not look at her. Back in her seat she sat down heavily, as if dazed, and stared at the programme. She saw Jamie's name and the name of the viola player, and her heart was beating hard within her.

She watched as the players assembled, and then the Academy Chorus, young singers between the ages of fourteen and eighteen, the boys in white shirts and dark trousers and the girls in their white blouses and navy blue pleated skirts. Then the conductor came on, and she watched him rather than look directly at Jamie, who seemed to be looking for her now, to smile discreetly at her in the audience as he often did.

They began with Howells, which Isabel hardly heard. Who was this girl? There was no girlfriend – not since Cat – and she had simply assumed that there would not be one. He had always made it clear that he wanted Cat back, and would wait for as long as it took. And she, Isabel, had gone along with this, and all the time what was happening was that she was becoming increasingly possessive of Jamie without ever having to acknowledge it. Now there was another woman, a girl really, and there was an obvious intimacy between them which would exclude her, as it would have to do, and that would be the end of everything.

When the Howells finished, she stole a glance at Jamie, but looked away again quickly because she fancied that he was looking at another part of the hall, where perhaps the girl was sitting. The chorus moved on to a Taverner motet, grave and echoing, and then to a John Ireland anthem, 'Many Waters Cannot Quench Love'. Isabel listened now. *Many waters cannot quench love, neither can floods drown it.* No they cannot; they cannot. *Love is as strong as death*; it is stronger; it is stronger.

At the end of the concert, she stood up as soon as the applause had abated. Normally she would have left by the back door, through the bar, where she would have seen Jamie coming out of the green room, but not this evening. She was one of the first out, into the busy night street where there were people about with business other than concerts. Then she walked briskly towards the Meadows, following the path beside the traffic, walking quickly, as if in a rush to get home; though nothing awaited her at home but the solace of the familiar.

The night sky was still light, a glow to the west, and it was warm. *Many waters cannot quench love*: the anthem's setting remained in her ears, repeating itself; a tune so powerful that it might gird one against the disappointments of life, rather than make one aware that our attempts to subdue the pain of unrequited love – of impossible love, of love that we are best to put away and not to think about – tended not to work, and only made the wounds of love more painful.

She stopped at the crossing light and waited for the signal to walk. A young woman, of student age, was at her side, waiting too. She looked at Isabel, hesitated for a moment, and then reached out to touch her gently on the arm.

'Are you all right?' she asked. She had seen the tears.

Isabel nodded. 'Thank you,' she said. 'Thank you.'

3

Of course it was much better in the clear light of day.
When she went downstairs the following morning,
Isabel might not have forgotten about her momentary weakness, but at least she was back in control of herself. She
knew that what she had experienced the previous evening
was a sudden rush of emotion – the emotion in question
being jealousy, no less. Emotional states of this sort came on
quickly and were difficult to manage when first experienced,
but the whole point about being a rational actor was that one
could assert control. She, Isabel Dalhousie, was quite capable
of holding negative emotions in check and sending them
back to where they belonged. Now, where was that? In the
dark reaches of the Freudian id? She smiled at the thought.
How well-named was the id – a rough, un-house-trained,
shadowy thing, wanting to do all those anarchic deeds that

24

the ego and super-ego frowned upon. Much Freudian theory was scientifically shaky, even if it was such a literary treat to read, but Isabel had always thought that of all the Freudian conceits the id was probably the most credible. The bundle of urges and wants that went with being a physical being: the need for food, the need to reproduce – those two alone were enough to cause any amount of difficulty, and indeed were at the bottom of most disputes between people. Arguments over space, food, and sex: id business. This is what humanity's conflicts were eventually reduced to.

By the time she had prepared her coffee, the whole affair had been sorted out and defused. It was natural to feel jealousy over those for whom one had a particular affection, and so it was perfectly natural that she should have felt the way she had when she saw Jamie with that girl. The sight had brought it home to her that Jamie was not hers; she may feel strongly about him, but that feeling could never be allowed to change the fact that there was between them nothing more than friendship.

She had hoped that Jamie and Cat would get together again, but she knew full well how unrealistic that hope was. Jamie must come to understand this sooner or later, and that meant that he would look for somebody else, as any young man would do. That girl at the concert, with her posture of adoration for Jamie, would probably be ideal. It would probably mean the loss of the comfortable intimacy which Isabel and Jamie currently enjoyed. That was to be regretted, of course, but the right thing for her to do would be to take pleasure in whatever happiness it brought Jamie. It would be like freeing a bird that one had temporarily held captive.

The bird catcher may feel sad at the loss of his companion, but he must think only of the happiness of the released creature. That is what she must do: it was obvious. She must try to like that young woman and then let Jamie go with her blessing.

Isabel had finished her first cup of coffee and eaten her morning allocation of two slices of toast and marmalade by the time that her housekeeper, Grace, arrived. Grace, who was a woman of roughly Isabel's age, had kept house for Isabel's father and now did the same for her. She was a woman of clear views, who had never married – in spite of what she described as *innumerable offers* – and Isabel often used her as a sounding board for ideas and opinions. On many issues they tended not to agree, but Isabel enjoyed Grace's perspective, which was almost always a surprising one.

'I may not be a philosopher,' Grace once pointed out, 'but I have no difficulty in knowing where I stand. I cannot understand all this doubt.'

'But we have to doubt,' said Isabel. 'Thinking is doubting. It amounts to the same thing.'

Grace's retort had come quickly. 'It certainly does not. I think about something, and then I make up my mind. Doubt doesn't come into it.'

'Well,' said Isabel, 'people differ. You're lucky that you're so certain. I'm more given to doubt. Maybe it's a question of temperament.'

That morning, Isabel was not in the mood for an exchange of this nature, and so she confined herself to a question about Grace's nephew, Bruce. This young man was a Scottish nationalist, who believed firmly in the independence of Scotland. Grace herself had at times been influenced by his fervour, and muttered darkly about London, but this had never lasted. She was by nature a conservative, and the Union was something too settled to do anything radical about.

'Bruce is off to some political rally,' she answered. 'They go up to Bannockburn every year and listen to speeches. They get all whipped up, but then they come home again and go off about their business like everybody else. It's a hobby for him, I suppose. He used to collect stamps, and then he took up nationalism.'

Isabel smiled. 'Such a striking-looking boy, in his kilt and his bonnet. And Bruce is such a good name, isn't it, for a patriot? Could one be a convincing Scottish nationalist if one were called, say, Julian?'

'Probably not,' said Grace. 'Did you know, by the way, that they're also talking about a boycott of the railways until they stop referring to English breakfasts in their restaurant cars?'

'So much for them to do,' mused Isabel. 'Such a constructive contribution to national life.'

'Of course they do have a point,' said Grace. 'Look at the way Scotland's been treated. How does the song go? *Such a parcel of rogues in a nation . . .*'

Isabel steered the conversation away from the subject of Bruce.

'I saw Jamie with a girl last night,' she said simply, watching for Grace's reaction as she spoke.

'Another girl?'

'Yes,' she said. 'A girl at a concert.'

Grace nodded. 'Well, that doesn't surprise me,' she said. 'I've seen them too.'

Isabel was silent for a moment; the pronounced beating of the heart the physical manifestation of the emotion. Then: 'With a blond-haired girl? Tall?'

'Yes.'

Of course it would be the same girl and she should not have felt any surprise. But she asked for details, nonetheless, and Grace explained.

'It was near the university. There's a café there near the back of the museum. They put tables out in the good weather and people sit out and drink coffee. They were there, at a table. They didn't see me as I walked past. But it was Jamie and a girl. This girl.'

'I know the place you're talking about,' said Isabel. 'It has a strange name. Iguana, or something like that.'

'Everything has a strange name these days,' said Grace.

Isabel said nothing. The feeling of the previous evening had momentarily returned – a feeling of utter emptiness and of being alone. It was not an unfamiliar feeling, of course. She remembered that when she had first realised that John Liamor was being unfaithful to her, with a girl who had come to Cambridge from Dublin to talk to him about his research, this is what she had felt. It was the feeling of having something taken away from her, *out* of her, like being winded. But John Liamor was her past, and she was getting over him. For years she had been in his thrall, bound to thoughts of him, unable to trust men as a result. Should she now allow herself to be caught up in something

28

which had the same risk of pain and rejection? Of course not.

Grace was watching her. She knows, thought Isabel. She knows. It is that transparent, the disappointment of the woman who has learnt that her young lover is behaving exactly as a young lover should be expected to behave – except that Jamie and I are not lovers.

'It had to happen,' said Grace suddenly, looking down at the floor as she spoke. 'He would have gone back to Cat if she would have had him, but she wouldn't. So what is he to do? Men don't wait any more.'

Isabel was staring out of the window. There was a clematis climbing up the wall that divided her garden from next door, and it was in full flower now, large blossoms of striated pink. Grace thought that she was concerned about Cat; she had not worked out that this was personal distress. And indeed there was every reason for Grace to think that, Isabel reflected, because otherwise she would have to conclude that this was a case of an aunt – yes, an *aunt* – falling for the boyfriend of the niece, which was an altogether unseemly thing to do, and not the sort of thing that happened in Grace's Edinburgh. But aunts have ids, she thought, and then smiled at the thought. There would be no emptiness any more, because she would again will herself to be pleased.

'You're quite right,' said Isabel. 'Jamie could hardly be expected to wait for ever. I despair of Cat.' She paused before adding, 'And I hope that this girl, whoever she is, is good for him.' The sentiment sounded trite, but then didn't most good sentiments sound trite? It was hard to make goodness – and good people – sound interesting. Yet the good were worthy of note, of course, because they *battled* and that battle was a great story, whereas the evil were evil because of moral laziness, or weakness, and that was ultimately a dull and uninteresting affair.

'Let's hope,' said Grace, who had now opened a cupboard and was extracting a vacuum cleaner. As she brought it out and began to unwind the electric cord, she half turned to look at Isabel.

'I thought that you might be upset,' she said. 'You and Jamie are so close. I thought that you might be . . .'

Isabel supplied the word. 'Jealous?'

Grace frowned. 'If you put it that way. Sorry to think that, it's just that when I walked past that table the other day that's how I felt. I don't want her to have him. He's ours, you see.'

Isabel laughed. 'Yes, he is ours, or so we like to think. But he isn't really, is he? *I had a dove.* Do you know that line? The poet has a dove, and the sweet dove dies. But it could equally well fly away.'

'Your Mr W. H. Auden?'

'Oh no, not him. But he did write about love quite a lot. And I suppose he must have felt very jealous, because he had a friend who went off with other people and all the time Auden was waiting in the background. It must have been very sad for him.'

'It's all very sad,' said Grace. 'It always is.'

Isabel thought about this. She would not allow herself to be sad; how sad to be sad. So she stood up briskly and rubbed her hands. 'I'm going to have a scone with my coffee,' she said. 'Would you like one too?'

4

Isabel had arranged with Cat that she would call in at the delicatessen that afternoon and go over various matters. Cat was leaving for Italy the following day and she wanted to make sure that Isabel knew how everything worked. Eddie knew most of the food-handling regulations and could see that everything was in order from that point of view, but Isabel would have to be shown the special customer list which gave the details of who needed what. And there was also the business of the burglar alarm, which was unduly complicated, and which must not be allowed to go off in error.

The delicatessen was only ten minutes' walk from Isabel's house. She made her way along Merchiston Crescent, past the line of Victorian flats that snaked along the south side of the road. Work was being done on the long building's stonework, and several masons were standing on a scaffolding platform while below them, at the foot of the structure, a stone-cutting machine whined and threw up dust. Isabel looked up and one of the men waved. Immediately to the side of the scaffolding, a woman stood at a window, looking out. Isabel knew who this woman was: the wife of a scholarly man who wrote obscure books about pyramids and sacred geometry. This was one of the reassuring things about Edinburgh; if a person wrote about pyramids and sacred geometry, then the neighbours would know about it. In other cities even such an original might be anonymous.

She arrived at the delicatessen in Bruntsfield Place and found Cat standing be-aproned in the doorway.

'You look just like an old-fashioned grocer,' remarked Isabel. 'Standing there, waiting to welcome your customers.'

'I was thinking about a wedding present,' said Cat. 'I suppose that they have everything they need, as everybody does these days.'

Much of it ill-gotten, Isabel said to herself, remembering the conversation about the gangster father. Though so much was ill-gotten, when one came to think of it. How did anybody become rich other than by exploiting others? And even those who did not exploit could enjoy the fruits of exploitation. Rich Western societies were wealthy because of imperialism, which had been a form of theft, and now the poor in those rich societies strove to obtain more generous payments from the state, which could only pay them because of the position of relative economic advantage which past plunder had set up. Living, just living, it seemed, meant that one had to participate in a crime; unless, of course, one changed one's definition of a crime to include only those things that one did oneself. And surely this was the only practical way of looking at it. If we were all responsible for the misdeeds of the governments that represent us, thought Isabel, then the moral burden would be just too great.

With these burdens on her mind, she went inside, where Eddie, wearing the same style of apron as Cat, was opening a large new hessian sack of wholewheat flour, leaving the unpicked neck open for customers to dig into with a scoop. He looked up at Isabel and smiled, which she thought was progress. She walked over to him and held out her hand to shake his; Eddie lifted up his hand, which was covered in flour, and grinned.

Cat led the way into the small office which she kept at the back. It was a room which Isabel had always liked, with its shelves of samples and its well-thumbed Italian food producers' catalogues. Her eye was caught by a large poster on the wall advertising Filippo Berio olive oil: a man riding an old-fashioned bicycle down one of those dusty white roads which meander across the Tuscan countryside. Underneath the poster, Cat had pinned a leaflet from a Parmesan cheese factory which showed great rounds of cheese, hundreds of them, stacked up in a warehouse. She had been there, she thought, to that very factory, some years ago when she had been visiting a friend in Reggio Emilia, and they had gone to buy cheese direct from the factory. There had been a mynah bird in a cage in the front office, where they cut and wrapped the cheese for visitors, and the bird had glared at the visitors before screeching, scatologically, *bagno, bagno!* Later she had heard that the bird had been relegated to a cage outside after a visiting Brussels bureaucrat had complained that the hygiene regulations of the European Union, that vast petti-foggery, were being flouted by the juxtaposition of bird and cheese.

'You don't have a sliver of Parmesan, do you?' she asked. 'I have a sudden urge. Inexplicable.'

Cat laughed. 'Of course. I've got a magnificent cheese which we're working through at the moment. It's just the right age and it's delicious.' She stepped over to the door and called out to Eddie, asking him to bring in a small piece of the cheese. Then she took down a bottle from a shelf, uncorked it, and poured a small quantity of Madeira into a glass.

'Here,' she said. 'This will be perfect with the Parmesan.'

Isabel sat down with Cat at her desk and went over the list which her niece had prepared for her. As she did so, she sipped at the Madeira, which was strong and nutty, and savoured the generous portion of cheese which Eddie had put on a plate for her. The cheese was rich and crumbly, a good cheese-mile away from the cardboard-like powder which people assumed was real Parmesan but which was nothing to do with Italy. Then, when everything had been explained, Cat passed over to her a small bunch of keys. Eddie would lock up that night and the following morning Isabel would be in charge.

'I feel very responsible,' said Isabel. 'All this food. The shop. Locks and keys. Eddie.'

'If anything goes wrong, just ask Eddie,' said Cat reassuringly. 'Or you can call me in Italy. I'll leave a number.'

'I won't do that,' said Isabel. 'Not at your wedding.'

Not yours, she thought, but you know what I mean; and then, unbidden, there came into her mind a picture of Cat at the altar, in full bridal dress, and a Sicilian bridegroom, in dark glasses, and outside one of those raggedy brass bands that seem to materialise out of nowhere in Italian towns, playing old saxhorns and tubas, and the sun above, and olive trees, and Mr Berio himself laughing as he tossed rice into the air.

She raised her almost-drained glass of Madeira in a toast to Cat. 'To the wedding,' she said with a smile.

She walked back, conscious of the keys in the pocket of her jacket. Grace had left by the time she arrived at the house and everything looked neat and tidy, as Grace always left it: *The house has been graced*, she thought. Grace was a most atypical professional housekeeper, a woman whose interests ran well beyond the domestic, who read novels and took a close interest in politics (even if her allegiances were notoriously shifting in that respect); a woman who could have had much more of a career had she chosen but who had been put to this work by an unambitious mother. Isabel would not have had a housekeeper had she been given the choice, but there had been no choice; on the death of Isabel's father Grace had assumed that she would remain in office, and Isabel had not the heart to question this. Now she was glad that Grace had remained, and could not imagine what life would be without Grace and her views. And Isabel, who did good by stealth, had quietly placed money in an account for Grace's benefit, but had not yet revealed the fund's existence. She assumed that Grace would retire one day, even if there had been no mention of this. Still, the money was there, ready for her when she needed it.

She went into the kitchen. Grace left notes for her on the kitchen table – notes about household supplies and telephone messages. There was a large brown envelope waiting for her, and a piece of paper with a few lines in Grace's handwriting. Isabel picked up the envelope first. It had not arrived with the normal morning delivery because it had been misdelivered to a neighbour, who had dropped it off. Isabel lived at number 6 while the neighbour lived at number 16, and a harassed postal official could easily make a mistake; but it was never bills that were misdelivered, Isabel reflected – bills always found their target. The envelope was simply addressed to the editor, and by its weight it was a manuscript. She always looked at the stamp and postmark first, rather than at the name and address of the sender: an American stamp, an aviator looking up into the clouds with that open-browed expression that befits aviators, and a Seattle postmark. She set the envelope aside and looked at the note which Grace had left. There had been a telephone call from her dentist, about a change in the timing for her check-up, and a call from the author of a paper which the *Review* had accepted for publication: Isabel knew that this author was troublesome and that there would be some complaint. Then, at the bottom of the list, Grace had written: *And Jamie called too. He wants to talk to you, he says. Soon.* This was followed by an exclamation mark – or was it? Grace liked to comment on the messages she took for Isabel, and an exclamation mark would have been an eloquent remark. But was this an exclamation mark or a slip of the pencil?

Isabel picked up the envelope and walked through to her study. Jamie often telephoned; this was nothing special, and yet she was intrigued. Why would he want to talk to her soon? She wondered whether it was anything to do with the girl. Had Jamie sensed that there was something wrong? It was possible that he had waited for her after the Queen's Hall concert and he might even have seen her sneaking away. He was not an insensitive person who would be indifferent to the feelings of others, and he could well have understood precisely why she had left without speaking to him. But of course if he had realised that, then that could change everything between them. She did not want him to think of her as some hopeless admirer, an object of pity.

She moved towards the telephone, but stopped. The hopeless admirer would be eager to call the object of her affections. She was not that. She was the independent woman who happened to have a friendship with a young man. She would not behave like some overly eager spinster, desperate for any scrap of contact with the man on whom her affections had settled. She would not telephone him. If he wanted to speak to her, then he would be the one to do the calling. She immediately felt ashamed; it was a thought worthy of a moody, plotting teenager, not of a woman of her age and her experience of life. She closed her eyes for a moment: this was a matter of will, of *voluntas*. She was not enamoured of Jamie; she was pleased that he had found a girlfriend. She was in control.

She opened her eyes. Around her were the familiar

surroundings of her study: the books reaching up to the ceiling, the desk with its reassuring clutter, the quiet, rational world of the *Review of Applied Ethics*. The telephone was on the desk, and she picked up the receiver and dialled Jamie's number.

Isabel, said a recorded Jamie. *I am not in. This is not me you're talking to; well it is, actually, but it's a recording. I need to talk to you. Do you mind? May I see you tomorrow? I can call round any time. Phone me later.*

She replaced the receiver in its cradle. Messages from people who were not there were unsettling, rather like letters from the dead. She had received such a letter once from a contributor to the *Review* whose article had been turned down for publication. *I cannot understand why you are unwilling to publish this*, he had written. And then, a few days later, she had heard that he was dead, and she had reflected on how her act had made his last few days unhappy; not that she could have reached any other decision, but the imminence of death might make one ponder one's actions more carefully. If we treated others with the consideration that one would give to those who had only a few days to live, then we would be kinder, at least.

She picked up the envelope from Seattle and slit it open, carefully, gently, as if handling a document of sacramental significance. There was a covering letter – the University of Washington – but she put this to one side, again gently, and looked at the title page of the manuscript. 'The Man Who Received a Bolt in the Brain and Became a Psychopath.' She sighed. Ever since Dr Sacks had written *The Man Who Mistook His Wife for a Hat* there had been a flurry of similar titles. And had not this whole issue of brain and personality disorder been explored by Professor Damasio, who had dealt with this precise case of the ironworker and his bolt in the brain? But then she remembered: she would give this article her full attention.

She began to read. Twenty minutes later she was still sitting with the manuscript before her, mulling over what she had read. That is what she was doing when the telephone interrupted her. It was Jamie.

'I'm sorry that I wasn't in when you called.'

'You wanted to see me.'

'Yes, I do. I need to see you.'

She waited for him to say something more, but he did not. So she continued: 'It sounds important.'

'It isn't really. Well, I suppose it's important to me. I need to discuss something personal.' He paused. 'I've met somebody, you see. I need to talk about that.'

She looked at the shelves of books. So many of them were about duty, and obligation, and the sheer moral struggle of this life.

'That's very good news,' she said. 'I'm glad.'

'Glad?'

'Yes, of course,' she said. It was so easy to do the right thing, when the right thing involved just words; deeds might be more difficult. 'I'm glad that you've met somebody. In fact, I think I saw her at the Queen's Hall. She looked . . .' She paused. 'Very nice.' The simple words were difficult.

'But she wasn't there,' said Jamie.

Isabel frowned. 'That girl in the interval . . .'

'Friend,' said Jamie.

39

5

She was there at the delicatessen the next morning a few minutes before Eddie arrived. One of the locks seemed stiff, and she had to struggle with it before it opened. Her fumblings triggered the alarm and by the time she was inside, the first shrill braying of the klaxon could be heard. She rushed through to the office, where the system's control panel was blinking in the half-light. She had committed the number to memory but now, faced with the keypad and its array of numbers, only the mnemonic remained: *the date of the fall of Constantinople.* That was a date which she would never forget, of course, but now she did, remembering only Miss Macfarlane, the history teacher, in the black bombazine which she occasionally wore, perhaps out of deference to the headmistress, who wore nothing else, standing in front of the class of small girls in the room overlooking George Square and saying, *A fatal year for the West, girls, a fatal year. We must not forget this date.*

Isabel thought: We must not forget this date, girls, and it came back to her and promptly silenced the alarm. 1492. She felt relief, but then doubt, and confusion. Constantinople had fallen not in 1492, but in 1453 when Sultan Mehmed had defeated the defenders. *Remember, girls, that the Turk had more than one hundred thousand men,* said Miss Macfarlane, *and there were only ten thousand of us.* Isabel had looked at Miss Macfarlane and wondered, but only for a moment. Miss Macfarlane was Scottish and yet she claimed affinity with the defenders of Constantinople. Us? And who was *the Turk*?

'In fourteen hundred and ninety-two,' she muttered, 'Columbus sailed the ocean blue.'

'And something happened in a place called Constantinople,' said a voice behind her. 'That's what Cat said. That's how we're meant to remember the number.'

Isabel spun round. Eddie had entered, quietly, and was standing behind her. His suddenly announced presence had given her a fright, but it had at least solved the mystery. Cat had given her the number, written it down on her list, and at the same time had given the mnemonic that she used. And Isabel dutifully had committed the wrong mnemonic to memory, not thinking to correct it.

'That's how errors are made,' she said to Eddie.

'You fed in the wrong number?'

'No, but Constantinople did not fall in 1492. It fell in 1453. The Turk had over one hundred thousand men and we had only . . .' She paused. Eddie was looking confused.

41

Of course he might never have been taught any history, she thought. Would he know who Mary, Queen of Scots, was? Or James VI? She looked at him, at the quiet, rather frightened young man whose life, she realised, had been ruined by something traumatic and who had done nothing to deserve that.

'You're going to have to be patient with me,' she said to him. 'I really don't know what I'm doing. And setting the alarm off like that was not very clever of me.'

He smiled at her, nervously, but still it was a smile. 'It took me a long time to learn how to do this job,' he ventured. 'I couldn't remember the names of the cheeses for ages. Cheddar and Brie were all right – I knew those – but all those others, that took me ages.'

'Not your fault,' said Isabel. 'I'm not bad on cheeses, and wines too, I suppose, but when it comes to spices, I always get them mixed up. Cardamom and all those things. I always forget the names.'

Eddie moved to switch on a light. The office had no outer window and the only light filtered in through the shop, past the coffee tables and the open-topped sacks of muesli and basmati rice.

'I usually start by getting the coffee going,' said Eddie. 'We get a few people coming in for a coffee on the way to work.'

The delicatessen had three or four tables at which people could sit, purchase a cup of coffee, and read out-of-date Continental newspapers. There was always a copy of *Le Monde* and *Corriere della Sera*, and sometimes *Spiegel*, which Isabel found interesting because of its habit of publishing articles about the Second World War and German guilt. It

42

was important to remember, and perhaps some Germans felt that they could never forget, but would there be a point at which those awful images of the past could be put away? Not if we want to avoid a repetition, said some, and the Germans took this very seriously, while others perhaps preferred to forget. The Germans deserved great credit for their moral seriousness, which is why Isabel liked them so much. Anyone – any people – was capable of doing what they did in their historical moment of madness – and their goodness lay in the fact that they later faced up to what they had done. Did the Turks go over their history with a moral fine-tooth comb? She was not aware of it, if they did, and nobody seemed to mention the genocide of the Armenians – an atrocity which was virtually within living memory – except the Armenians, of course.

And the Belgians, she suddenly remembered, who had passed a resolution in their Senate only a few years previously noting what had happened in Armenia. Some had said that was all very well, but then what about what Leopold did in the Congo? And were there not islanders, somewhere in the Pacific, whose ancestors stood accused of eating – yes, *eating* the original inhabitants of the lands they occupied? Most unfortunate. And then there were the British who behaved extremely badly in so many parts of the world. There was the woeful story of the extinction of the Tasmanian aboriginals and so many other instances of cruelty and theft under the bright protection of the Union Jack. When would British history books face up to the appalling British contribution to slavery, which involved the Arabs, too, and numerous Africans (who were not just on the receiving end)? We were all as bad as one another, but at some point we had to overlook that fact, or at least not make too much of it. History, it seemed, could so quickly become a matter of mutual accusation and recrimination, an infinite regress of cruelty and oppression, unless forgetfulness or forgiveness intervened.

All of this was very interesting, but nothing to do with the running of a delicatessen. Isabel reminded herself of this and opened the safe with the code which Cat had noted down for her: 1915. The year that the Turks fell upon the Armenians, Isabel noted, though Cat could hardly have intended that. She had never heard Cat mention the Armenians – not once. Nineteen fifteen were the last four digits of Cat's telephone number, an altogether more prosaic choice.

She heard Eddie tipping the coffee beans into the grinder and savoured the smell of the grounds. Then she busied herself with putting the float in the till, and checked that there was an adequate supply of plastic bags for the packing of purchases. Now we are ready, Isabel thought, with some satisfaction. Trading begins. She looked at Eddie, who gave her a thumbs-up signal of encouragement. We feel the common feeling of employees, she thought; that peculiar feeling of involvement with those with whom one works. It was not like friendship; it was a feeling of being together in something which afflicts all humans – work. We are working together, and hence there exist between us subtle bonds of loyalty and support. That is why trade unionists addressed one another as brother and sister. We are together in our bondage, each lightening the load of another; somewhat extreme, she reflected, for a middle-class delicatessen in Edinburgh, but nonetheless something to think about.

The morning was busy, but everything went well. There was one rather difficult customer who brought in a bottle of wine – half consumed – and claimed that the wine was corked and should be replaced. Isabel knew that Cat's policy was to replace or refund in such circumstances, and to do so without question, but when she sniffed at the neck of the offending bottle what she got was the odour of vinegar and not the characteristic mustiness of a corked wine. She poured a small amount of the wine into a glass and sipped at it gingerly, glared at by the customer, a young man in a rainbow-coloured woolly hat.

'Vinegar,' she said. 'This wine has been left opened. There's been oxidation.'

She looked at the young man. The most likely explanation, in her view, was that he had drunk half the bottle and then left it open for a day or two. Any wine would turn to vinegar in warm weather like this. Now he thought that he could get a fresh bottle of wine without paying. He must have read about corked wine in a newspaper.

'It was corked,' he said.

'Then why is so much of it drunk?' asked Isabel, pointing to the level in the bottle.

'Because I poured a large glass,' he said. 'Then, when I tasted it I had to throw that out. I poured another glass just to be sure, but that was as bad.'

Isabel stared at him. She was sure that he was lying, but

there was no point in persisting. 'I'll give you another bottle,' she said, thinking: This is exactly how lies prevail. Liars get away with it.

'Chianti, please,' said the young man.

'This isn't Chianti,' said Isabel. 'This is an Australian Shiraz. Our Chianti is more expensive than this.'

'But I've been inconvenienced,' said the young man. 'It's the least you can do.'

Isabel said nothing, but crossed to a shelf and took down a bottle of Chianti, which she handed to the young man.

'If you don't finish it,' she said, 'make sure you put the cork back in and keep it in a cool place. That should slow down oxidation.'

'You don't need to tell me that,' he said truculently.

'Of course not,' said Isabel.

'I know about these Spanish wines,' he went on.

Isabel said nothing, but caught Eddie's glance and his suppressed look of mirth. It was going to be fun, she thought. Running a delicatessen was different from running the *Review of Applied Ethics*, but, in its own way, might be every bit as enjoyable.

Being busy, she had little time to think about the impending arrival of Jamie, who had agreed over the telephone to meet her for lunch at the neighbouring coffee bar and potted plant shop. Eddie ate his lunch in the delicatessen and did not need time off, he said, and so she was able to slip out at one o'clock when Jamie arrived.

The coffee bar was uncrowded and they had no difficulty finding a couple of seats near the window.

'This is rather like eating in the jungle,' Isabel said, pointing to the palm fronds at her back.

'Without the bugs,' said Jamie, glancing at the palm and the large *Monstera deliciosa* behind it. Then: 'I'm very glad you could see me. I didn't want to discuss this over the telephone.'

'I don't mind,' said Isabel. And she did not. It was good to see him, and now that he was here, in the flesh, her *inappropriate* feelings seemed a thing of the past, virtually forgotten. This was Jamie, who was just a friend, although he was a friend of whom she was very fond.

Jamie looked down, seeming to study the tablecloth. Isabel looked at his cheekbones, and at the *en brosse* hair. When he looked up, she caught his gaze, and held it – eyes which were almost grey in that light; kind eyes, she thought, which was what made him so beautiful in her view.

'You've met somebody,' she prompted.

'Yes.'

'And?'

'And I'm not sure what to do. I'm happy, I suppose, but I'm all mixed up. I thought that you being . . .'

'The editor of the *Review of Applied Ethics*,' she supplied.

'And a friend,' Jamie went on. 'Perhaps my closest friend.'

No woman likes to hear that from a man, thought Isabel. Men may think about women in those terms, but it's certainly not what most women want to hear. But she nodded briefly and Jamie continued: 'The difficulty is that this person, this woman I've met, is not somebody I thought I would fall for. I hadn't planned it. I really hadn't.'

'Which is exactly what Cupid's arrows are all about,' said

Isabel gently. 'Very inaccurate. They fly about all over the place.'

'Yes,' said Jamie. 'But you usually have a general idea of what sort of person you're going to go for. Somebody like Cat, for instance. And then somebody else comes along and wham!'

'Yes,' said Isabel. 'Wham! That's the way it happens, isn't it? But why fight it? Just accept that it's happened and make the most of it. Unless it's impossible, that is. But that doesn't happen much these days. Montague and Capulet difficulties. Social barriers and all the rest. Even being the same sex is not a problem today.'

'She's married,' Jamie blurted out, and then looked down at the tablecloth again.

Isabel caught her breath.

'And she's older than me,' said Jamie. 'She's about your age, actually.'

She had not been prepared for this and her dismay must have shown. Jamie frowned. 'I knew that you would disapprove,' he said. 'Of course you would disapprove.'

Isabel opened her mouth to say something, to deny the disapproval, but he cut her short. 'I shouldn't have bothered you with this. It would have been better not to tell you.'

'No,' she said. 'I'm glad you told me.' She paused, gathering her thoughts. 'It is a bit of a shock, I suppose. I hadn't imagined . . .' She trailed off. What offended her was that it was a woman of her age. She had accepted that he would want somebody of his own age, or younger, but she had not prepared herself for competition from a coeval.

'I didn't ask for it to happen,' Jamie went on, sounding

quite miserable. 'And now I don't know what to do. I feel . . . what do I feel? I feel, well I feel as if I'm doing something wrong.'

'Which you are,' said Isabel. Then she paused. 'I'm sorry, I don't mean to be unsympathetic, but . . . but don't you think you're doing something wrong if you're participating in deception, which adultery usually involves? Not always, but often. There's somebody whose trust is being abused. Promises are being broken.'

Jamie looked down at the tablecloth, tracing an imaginary pattern with a finger. 'I've thought of all that,' he said. 'But in this case the marriage is almost over. She says that although they're still married, they lead separate lives.'

'But they're still together?'

'In name.'

'In house?'

Jamie hesitated. 'Yes, but she says that they would prefer to live apart.'

Isabel looked at him. She reached out and touched him gently on the arm. 'What do you want me to say, Jamie?' she asked. 'Do you want me to tell you that it's perfectly all right? Is that what you want?'

Jamie shook his head. 'I don't think so. I wanted to talk to you about it.'

The milky coffee which Isabel had ordered now arrived and she picked up the large white cup in which it was served. 'That's understandable,' she said. 'But you should bear in mind that I can't tell you what to do. You know the issues perfectly well. You're not fifteen. You may want me to give you my blessing, to say that it's perfectly acceptable,

49

and that's because you're feeling guilty, and afraid.' She paused, remembering the line from WHA's poem: *Mortal, guilty, but to me/The entirely beautiful.* Yes, that spoke to this moment.

The misery had not left Jamie's voice. 'Yes, I do feel guilty. And yes, I suppose I did want you to tell me that it was all right.'

'Well, I can't do that,' said Isabel, gently. And she reached across and took his hand, and held it for a moment. 'I can't tell you any of that, can I?'

Jamie shook his head. 'No.'

'So what can I say?'

'You could let me tell you about her,' said Jamie quietly. 'I wanted to do that.'

Isabel understood now that he was in love. When we love others, we naturally want to talk about them, we want to show them off, like emotional trophies. We invest them with a power to do to others what they do to us; a vain hope, as the lovers of others are rarely of much interest to us. But we listen in patience, as friends must, and as Isabel now did, refraining from comment, other than to encourage the release of the story and the attendant confession of human frailty and hope.

6

The next day it was Eddie who opened the deli-catessen. By the time that Isabel arrived, he had already prepared the coffee and was pouring her a cup as she entered the shop.

'Everything's ready,' he said, handing her the cup. 'And I've spoken to the delivery people about coming this after-noon. They can do it.'

'Such efficiency,' said Isabel, smiling at him over the rim of her coffee cup. 'You don't really need me, I think.'

Eddie's face showed his alarm. 'No,' he said. 'I do.'

'I wasn't entirely serious,' Isabel said quickly. She had noticed that Eddie was very literal, and it crossed her mind that he might have Asperger's. These things came in degrees, and perhaps he suffered from a mild version of the condition. It would certainly explain the shyness; the withdrawal.

51

Isabel sat at Cat's desk, her coffee before her. The morning's mail, which had been retrieved by Eddie, contained nothing of note, other than an inexplicable bill for which payment was demanded within seven days. Isabel asked Eddie about it, but he shrugged. Then there was a letter from a supplier saying that a consignment of buffalo mozzarella had been delayed in Italy and would be delivered late. Eddie said that this did not matter, as they still had plenty.

Then the customers began to drift in. Isabel dispensed small tubs of olives and sun-dried tomatoes. She cut cheese and wrapped bread and reached for tins of mackerel fillets from the shelves. She exchanged views with customers – on the weather, on the contents of that day's copy of the *Scotsman*, and, with questionable authority, on a local planning issue. So the morning drifted by, and not once, she reflected, had she had the opportunity to think about moral philosophy. This was cause for thought: most people led their lives this way – doing rather than thinking; they acted, rather than thought about acting. This made philosophy a luxury – the privilege of those who did not have to spend their time cutting cheese and wrapping bread. From the perspective of the cheese counter, Schopenhauer seemed far away.

If there was no time to think about the affairs of the *Review of Applied Ethics*, there was time enough to think about Jamie. The entire previous evening, when Isabel had been catching up with *Review* work, she had found her mind wandering back to her conversation with Jamie. The news of his involvement with Louise – that being the only name he had revealed to her – had initially upset Isabel, and after a while she had found herself depressed by what he told her.

There was nothing romantic in the situation, she felt, no matter how Jamie might wish to portray it. He was clearly infatuated, and Isabel doubted very much that Louise would reciprocate. Her picture of Louise was of a bored and rather hard woman, living with a husband who was probably unfaithful to her but staying with him because he provided material security. She would not leave her husband, and indeed Jamie might have been a way of her getting back at a man who paid her little attention. It was exactly the strategy which some people urged on ignored wives: make him jealous. And Jamie would be perfect for that – a younger man, handsome, and, as a musician, slightly exotic.

Isabel ate her lunch at one of the tables in the delicatessen. While Eddie attended to the customers, she picked up a copy of *Corriere della Sera* and flicked through the news. Much of it was of the internecine battles of Italian politicians; the shifting of coalitions, the pursuit of narrow advantage, the accusations by liars of lying by others. There was a statement from the Pope about the importance of papal statements.

Isabel looked up from her paper and reached for her sandwich. A man was standing at the table, a plate in his hand, gesturing at the vacant seat.

'Would you mind?'

Isabel noticed that while she had been reading the other tables had filled up. She smiled at the man. 'Not at all. In fact, I shouldn't be sitting here much longer. I'm staff, you see.'

The man sat down, placing the plate in front of him. 'I'm sure that you need a break, just as everyone does.'

Isabel smiled. 'It's not as if I'm real staff,' she said. 'I'm standing in for my niece.' She looked at his plate, which had on it a small portion of tomato salad, a few hazelnuts, and a sardine. He was on a diet, and yet there seemed to be no need. He was a man in his mid-fifties, she thought, not at all overweight – the opposite, in fact. She noticed, too, that he had that look about him which her housekeeper Grace described as distinguished, but which she herself would have described as intelligent.

He noticed Isabel's glance at his plate. 'Not very much,' he said ruefully. 'But needs must.'

'Looking after your heart?' Isabel asked.

The man nodded. 'Yes.' He paused, moving the sardine to the centre of the salad. 'It's my second.'

'Sardine?' she asked, and then immediately realised what he meant.

She felt herself blush, and began to explain, but he raised a hand. 'Sorry, I didn't make myself clear. I've had a heart transplant, and I have fairly strict instructions from my doctors. Salads, sardines, and so on.'

'Which can be made to taste perfectly nice,' she said, rather weakly, she thought.

'I don't complain about this new diet of mine,' said the man. 'I feel much better. I don't feel hungry, and' – he paused, touching the front of his jacket, at the chest – 'and this, this heart – *my* heart I should call it now – seems to thrive on it, and on the immunosuppressants.'

Isabel smiled. She was intrigued. 'But it is your heart,' she said. 'Or now it is. A gift.'

'But it's also *his* heart,' he said. 'And at least I know that it was a he. If it had been a woman, then that would be a bit odd, wouldn't it? Then I'd be a man with the heart of a woman. Which would make me very much of a new man, wouldn't you say?'

'Perhaps,' said Isabel. 'But I'm interested in what you said about it being *his* heart. Things that we own remain ours, don't they, even when we pass them on. I saw somebody driving my old car the other day, and I thought, That woman's driving my car. Perhaps there are echoes of owner-ship that persist well after we lose possession.'

The man lifted his knife and fork to begin his meal. Noticing this, Isabel said: 'I'm sorry. You have your lunch to eat. I should stop thinking aloud.'

He laughed. 'No, please go on. I enjoy a conversation which goes beyond the superficial. Most of the time we exchange banalities with other people. And here you are launching into linguistics, or should I say philosophical specu-lation. All over a plate of salad and a sardine. I like that.' He paused. 'After my experience – my brush with death – I find that I have rather less time for small talk.'

'That's quite understandable,' said Isabel, glancing at her watch. There was a small line of customers building up at the cash desk and Eddie had looked over at her table, as if to ask for help.

'I'm very sorry,' she said. 'I have to get back to work.'

The man smiled at her. 'You said you don't really work here,' he said. 'May I ask: what is it you do normally?'

'Philosophy,' said Isabel, rising to her feet.

'Good,' said the man. 'That's very good.'

He seemed disappointed that she was leaving the table,

and Isabel was disappointed to go. There was more to be said, she thought, about hearts and what they mean to us. She wanted to know how it felt to have an alien organ beating away within one's chest; this bit of life extracted from another, and still living. And how did the relatives of the donor feel, knowing that part of their person (Isabel refused to use the expression *loved one*, because it was so redolent of the world of its original coiners, American undertakers) was still alive? Perhaps this man – whoever he was – knew about this and could tell her. But in the meantime, there was cheese to be cut and sun-dried tomatoes to measure out; matters of greater immediate importance than questions of the heart and what they meant.

She would have liked to do nothing that evening, but could not. It had been a demanding day, with many more customers than usual, and she and Eddie had been kept busy until almost seven o'clock. Now, back at the house, the sight of her unopened mail, neatly stacked on her desk by Grace and containing several very obvious manuscripts, dispirited her. What she would have liked to do was to have a light dinner in the garden room, and follow that with a walk in the garden, with a glimpse, perhaps, of *Brother Fox*, her name for the urban fox who lived part of his cautious, hidden life there, and then a long, warm bath. But this was impossible, as the mail would stack up and it would begin to haunt her, reproaching her every time she entered her study. So she had no alternative but to work, and had resolved to do so when the telephone rang and Jamie announced that he and Louise would be passing by on their way to Balerno (not en route,

Isabel thought, but did not say), and would she mind if they called in for a quick cup of something. Isabel wanted to say yes she would mind, but even with the pile of mail in view she said no, she would not mind. This made her think of *akrasia*, weakness of the will, by which we do that which we really want to do in the full knowledge that we should be doing something else. But why should she want to see Jamie and Louise? Curiosity, she assumed.

After the telephone call she could settle to nothing. She was no longer interested in dinner, and although she tried to deal with the mail, she could not concentrate on that and gave up. There were already more than twenty outstanding items; tomorrow there would be five or six more – sometimes it was many more than that – and so on. But even the thought of the numbers (over a hundred and fifty letters in one month, three hundred in two) failed to motivate her, and she ended up sitting in the drawing room at the front of the house, paging through a magazine, waiting for Jamie to arrive. They were going to Balerno, were they? Balerno was a suburb in the west of Edinburgh, a place of well-set suburban homes, each planted squarely in a patch of garden, and each staring out on the world with windows that looked to all intents and purposes like two rectangular eyes. Balerno was somnolent, a respectable place in which nothing out of the ordinary happened.

Then she remembered something else which had been said to her by somebody a long time ago, perhaps when she was a schoolgirl or a very young woman. Somebody had said – or whispered, perhaps – that the suburbs of Edinburgh had a reputation for adultery, and that Balerno was a great place for that. Yes, somebody had said that and sniggered, as a schoolgirl might snigger; and of course it was easy to imagine. If you were tucked up in a suburb, then might you not feel the need to take some risks? And that would lead to the adventure of adultery committed after parties in insurance offices in town, on company training weekends in Perthshire hotels; snatched moments of excitement, lived out against the emptiness of a predictable life.

Jamie had been drawn into that world, and that was why he was going to Balerno. The thought made Isabel grimace. There was no romance there; only tawdry shame. And poor Jamie had been entrapped by this Louise person, this older woman, who probably cared nothing for his music or for his moral qualities, and for whom he was something to toy with.

One might work oneself up into a state of anger just thinking about Louise, and what she stood for. But Isabel would not allow this to happen; it was always a mistake, she thought, to dwell on the cause of one's anger, like Tam O'Shanter's wife, *Nursing her wrath to keep it warm*, as Burns put it. No, thought Isabel, I must *like* Louise, because that is my duty; not because one has a moral duty to like people in general – an impossibility for those short of sainthood – but because I know that Jamie will be hoping that I should like her.

She was thinking of friendship and its duties when the bell rang. When she opened the door, she saw immediately from Jamie's expression that she had been right about how he would feel: there was a strange look on his face, one in which anticipation was mixed with concern. She wanted to

lean forward and whisper to him, *Don't worry. Don't worry.*
But could not, of course, because standing behind him was
Louise, who seemed to be looking up at the evening sky.

She invited them in and the introductions took place in
the hall. Jamie did not give Louise's other name, an endemic
social failing which Isabel had stopped remarking upon; so
many people now gave only their first names. In this case,
though, there might be a reason. Was Louise openly in
Jamie's company, or was discretion still required?

Isabel looked at Louise and smiled. She saw more or less
what she had expected to see – a woman in her late thirties,
of average height, wearing a longish red skirt and a soft
padded green jacket of the sort which became perversely
fashionable in the West in the days of Madame Mao – peas-
ant chic. The skirt and the jacket were expensive, though,
and overall there was a feel to this woman, Isabel thought,
which suggested that she was accustomed to wealth and
comfort. Material security brought a particular form of self-
assurance – an easy confidence that things would simply be
there if one wanted them, and this woman had that assurance. The wealthy, thought Isabel, fit in. They are never out
of place.

And as for the face – high cheekbones and wide, dark
eyes – it was a face which she had seen used in the faux
nativities which artists painted when they tried to capture the
spirit of Renaissance Italy. It was unarguably a beautiful face,
and it could beguile any man, even a young man, thought
Isabel. This was not a charitable thought, and she reminded
herself to smile as she shook hands with Louise, who looked
back at her, smiling too, and undoubtedly performing her

own calculations as to who Isabel was and what she meant to Jamie. Was she a threat? Well Isabel was attractive too, but she was a philosopher, was she not, buried in her books, a bit above all that sort of thing (young men, affairs, and the rest).

They went into the drawing room and Isabel offered them white wine. Jamie said he would pour it, and Isabel noticed that Louise had picked up this sign of familiarity. Isabel found herself pleased at this: it would do her no harm to know that she and Jamie had been friends for years.

'Your health,' said Isabel, raising her glass to Jamie first and then to Louise. They sat down, Louise choosing the sofa, where she patted a cushion beside her, discreetly, almost as one would give a secret signal, for Jamie to sit beside her, which he did.

Isabel sat opposite them and looked at Jamie. Nothing was said, but Louise noticed the exchange of glances and frowned, almost imperceptibly, which was noticed by Isabel.

'I have to go out to Balerno to look at a bassoon,' said Jamie. 'One of my pupils lives out there and he has been offered an instrument which he can't bring into town. I'm going to tell him if it's worth buying. It's a bit complicated.'

Isabel nodded. Jamie was always looking at bassoons. 'I thought perhaps Louise lived out there.'

Louise looked up sharply. 'Balerno?'

Isabel smiled disarmingly. 'My mistake,' she said. 'Do you live in town?'

Louise nodded, and although Isabel waited for her to say something else, no further information was forthcoming.

'Louise has a job with the National Gallery,' Jamie said. 'Part-time, but quite interesting, isn't it, Louise?'

'Most of the time,' said Louise.

'Well, you get around with it,' said Jamie. 'Didn't you have to accompany a painting to Venice the other day? Sitting on the seat beside you, in its little crate?'

'Yes,' said Louise. 'I did.'

Jamie looked nervously at Isabel, who said, 'I suppose you can't put paintings in the hold when you're lending them for an exhibition.'

'We can't,' said Louise. 'The small ones travel with us in the plane. They get tickets.'

'But no meal,' said Jamie, weakly.

For a few moments there was silence. Isabel took a sip of her wine. She wanted to say to Louise, *And what does your husband do?* It was a delicious thought, because it was such a subversive, tactless thing to ask in the circumstances – to bring up the husband, the ghost at this banquet. She could ask the question disingenuously, as if she had no idea of the nature of the relationship between Jamie and this woman, but of course Jamie would know that she had asked it mischievously, and would be mortified. But then he could hardly complain if he brought her here, to flaunt her. Could he not understand that this whole meeting would be painful for her? Was it too much to expect that he should sense her unhappiness over all this?

Isabel raised her wineglass and took another sip. Opposite her, Louise had begun to fiddle with a button on her jacket. This, thought Isabel, is because she is uncomfortable. She does not want to be here. She has no interest in me. In her eyes she is the adventuress, the passionate one, fashionable, a woman who can get a young man so very easily while this

61

other woman, this philosopher woman, has nothing. She watched her, and she saw the eyes go to the mantelpiece and to the pictures with a look on her face that was utterly dismissive, though she had no idea that Isabel would see it. I am nothing to her, she told herself; I am beneath her notice. Well, in that case . . .

'What does your husband do?' asked Isabel.

7

She had decided to apologise, of course, at least to
Jamie, but the next day she had neither the time to
feel guilty nor to make the telephone call that would assuage
her guilt. Shortly after she arrived in the morning to open up,
a consignment of cheeses was delivered from a cheesemaker
in Lanarkshire, and they had to be unwrapped by hand,
priced, and put on display. Isabel did this while Eddie prepared the coffee, and then there was a spate of talkative
customers who took up her time with long-drawn-out conversations. There was an elderly customer who thought that
Isabel was Cat, and addressed her accordingly, and a shoplifter
whom she saw eating a bar of chocolate, unpaid for, while he
stuffed a can of artichoke hearts into a pocket. At least we
have discerning thieves, she thought, as she watched him run
down the street; artichoke hearts and Belgian chocolate.

At one o'clock she signalled to Eddie that he should take over at the till while she took a break. Then she helped herself to a bagel and several slices of smoked salmon before moving over to the table area. The tables were busy, with all the chairs taken, except for one, where her lunching companion of the previous day sat, a frugal tub of salad before him, reading a newspaper. He had not seen her, and she hesitated. She was not sure if she wanted to sit at his table uninvited, and was about to go back to the office, to eat her lunch amongst the calendars and the catalogues, when he looked up and smiled at her, gesturing to the unoccupied chair.

He put the newspaper to the side. 'You're busy.'

She looked about her. 'I prefer it that way. I find that I quite like being busy.'

'I used to,' he said. 'I used to be busy and now I mark time, reading the papers, doing the shopping for my wife.'

She had not anticipated the reference to a wife; men who sat by themselves in delicatessens were likely to be single.

'She works?'

'Like me, a psychologist. Or at least, I used to be a psychologist. I gave it up just before the operation.'

Isabel nodded. 'A good idea, I suppose, if one has been very ill. There's no point—'

'In hastening one's appointment at Mortonhall Crematorium,' he interjected. 'No, I stopped, and found that I didn't miss it in the least.'

Isabel broke her bagel in two and took a bite out of one of the pieces.

'I still read the professional journals,' he said, watching

her eat. 'It makes me feel that I'm on top of the subject, not that there is anything completely new and suprising to be said in psychology. I'm not at all sure that our understanding of human behaviour has progressed a great deal since Freud – awful admission though that is.'

'Surely we know a bit more. What about cognitive science?'

He raised an eyebrow. Her reference to cognitive science was clearly not what he expected of a woman working in a delicatessen, but then he remembered that she was a philosopher. Perhaps one should expect to be attended to by philosophers in Edinburgh delicatessens, just as one might be waited upon by psychoanalysts in the restaurants of Buenos Aires. *Is the braised beef really what you want?*

He picked at a lettuce leaf. 'Cognitive science has helped,' he said. 'Yes, of course, we know much more about how the brain works and how we see the world. But behaviour is rather more than that. Behaviour is tied up with personality and how our personalities make us do what we do. That stuff is all very messy and not just a simple matter of neural pathways and the rest.'

'And then there's genetics,' said Isabel, taking another bite of her bagel. 'I thought that behavioural genetics might explain a great deal of what we do. What about all those twin studies?'

'My name's Ian, by the way,' he said, and she said: Isabel *Dalhousie*, with an emphasis on the Dalhousie. 'Yes, those twin studies. Very interesting.'

'But don't they prove that whatever the environmental influences, people behave as they do because of heredity?'

'They do not,' Ian said. 'All that they show is that there is a genetic factor in behaviour. But it's not the only factor.'

Isabel was not convinced. 'But I read somewhere or other about these pairs of separated twins that keep turning up in America. And when they look at them they discover that they like the same colours and vote the same way and say the same sort of thing to the researchers.'

Ian laughed. 'Oh yes, it's wonderful stuff. I've read some of the papers from Minnesota. In one of them they found that twins who had been separated at birth had actually both married women of the same name, divorced them at roughly the same time, and then remarried. And the second wives of each man had the same name. Two Bettys or whatever to begin with, and then two Joans.' He paused. 'But then, Middle America's full of Bettys and Joans.'

'Even so, the odds are very much against it,' said Isabel. 'Two Bettys is not too unlikely, but then to pick two Joans. I'm no statistician, but I should imagine that would be astronomically unlikely.'

'But the unlikely can happen, you know,' said Ian. 'And that, of course, can change everything we believe in. Single white crow, you see.'

Isabel looked at him blankly, and he continued: 'That's something said by William James. The finding of a single white crow would disprove the theory that all crows are black. It's quite a pithy way of making the point that it won't take much to disprove something which we take as absolutely firmly established.'

'Such as the proposition about black crows.'

'Precisely.'

Isabel glanced at Ian. He was looking away from her, out through the window of the shop. Outside, in the street, a bus had stopped to disgorge a couple of passengers: a middle-aged woman in a coat which looked too warm for the day, and a young woman in a T-shirt with a legend bleached out in the wash.

'You're looking worried,' she said. 'Are you all right?'

He turned back to face her. 'I came across that quote from William James in an article recently,' he said. 'Something rather close to home.'

She waited for him to continue. He had picked up his newspaper and folded it again, running a finger down the crease. 'It was used as an introduction to an article about the psychological implications of transplant surgery, a subject obviously of some interest to me.'

Isabel felt that she should encourage him. 'Well, I can imagine that these are major. It must be a massive disturb-ance for the system. All surgery is to some degree.'

'Yes, of course it is. But this article was about something very specific. It was about cellular memory.'

She waited for him to explain, but instead he looked at his watch. 'Look,' he said, 'I'm very sorry, but I'm going to have to dash. I agreed to meet my wife ten minutes ago, and she has to get back to her office. I can't keep her.'

'Of course,' said Isabel. 'You'd better go.'

Ian rose to his feet, picking up his newspaper and the empty salad tub. 'Could I speak to you about this? Could I discuss it with you later? Would you mind?'

There was something in his tone which spoke of vulner-ability, and Isabel thought that she could not refuse his request, even if she had wanted to. But, in fact, her curiosity had been aroused; curiosity, her personal weakness, the very quality which had led her into such frequent interventions in the lives of others and which she simply could not resist. And so she said: 'Yes, by all means.' And she scribbled her telephone number on the top of his newspaper and invited him to call her and arrange a time to come round to the house for a glass of wine, if his regime allowed for that.

'It does,' he said. 'A minuscule glass of wine, almost invisible to the naked eye.'

'The sort they serve in Aberdeen,' said Isabel.

'Very appropriate,' he said, smiling. 'I'm from Aberdeen.'

'I'm sorry,' said Isabel hurriedly. 'I've always found Aberdonians very generous.'

'Perhaps we are,' he said, adding, 'in a frugal sort of way. No, wine is all right, in small quantities. But I have to avoid chocolate apparently. And that's very hard. Even the thought of chocolate is difficult for me. It sets up such a yearning.'

Isabel agreed with this. 'Chocolate involves major philosophical problems,' she said. 'It shows us a lot about temptation and self-control.' She thought for a moment. There was a lot that one might say about chocolate, if one thought about it. 'Yes,' she concluded, 'chocolate is a great test, isn't it?'

The afternoon passed as the morning had, in a flurry of business. Again Isabel was tired by the time she locked the front door and drew down the shutters. Eddie had left a few minutes early for some reason – he had mumbled an explanation which Isabel had not quite caught – and Isabel had

68

shut everything up herself. She glanced at her watch. It was seven o'clock, and she had still to call Jamie. But she thought that if she did so now, then there would be a chance that Louise might be there and it would be difficult for him to talk, if he wanted to talk to her, of course. The previous evening had been a social disaster. After Isabel had brought up the issue of the husband, with her inexcusably mischievous question, Louise had become more or less silent, and had not responded to the question. The tactic had worked, though, Isabel realised, and although Louise persisted with her air of studied boredom, it was obvious that she had a new understanding of her hostess. Jamie had been flustered and had gulped down his wine before suggesting that it was time that they went on to Balerno. The farewells at the front door had been perfunctory.

Isabel had almost immediately regretted her rudeness, for it was simple rudeness to embarrass a guest, no matter what provocation the guest had offered. It had been a petty action, and not one from which she was likely to benefit. The bonds of friendship might appear strong, but she understood that there was nothing easier to break than friendship, with all its expectations. One might ignore a friend, or let him down, but you could not do something deliberate to hurt him.

An apology could not be put off. Isabel remembered her father making this point when he considered Japan's apology to China for what it did in Manchuria. Forty years is slightly late, he had observed, adding, but I suppose one doesn't want to rush these things.

'Jamie?'

There was a slight hesitation at the other end of the line,

which is always a sign of resentment. This was the *so it's you* pause.

'Yes.'

She took a deep breath. 'You can guess why I'm calling.' Another moment of silence. Of course he could guess.

'No,' he said.

'About last night, and my bad behaviour. All I can say is that I'm sorry. I don't know what came over me. Jealousy, maybe.'

He came in quickly. 'Why should you be jealous?'

He doesn't know, she thought. He has no idea. And this should not surprise her.

'I value your friendship, you see,' she said. 'One can see other people as a threat to a friendship, and I thought . . . well, I'm afraid I thought that Louise was not in the slightest bit interested in me and that she would cut me out of your life. Yes, I suppose that's what I felt. Do you think you can understand that?'

She paused, and she heard Jamie's breathing. Now there was silence, each uncertain whose turn it was to speak.

'Nobody is going to cut anybody out,' Jamie began. 'Anyway, things did not go well last night. It had nothing to do with you. We had an argument even before we came to see you. Then things got worse and I'm afraid that's more or less it.'

Isabel looked up at the ceiling. She had not dared to hope for this, but it was exactly what she had wished for, subconsciously perhaps, and it had occurred much sooner than she would have thought possible. People fell in and out of love rather quickly, of course; it could happen within minutes.

'What a pity,' whispered Isabel. 'I'm so sorry.'

'You're not,' said Jamie sharply.

'No,' said Isabel. 'I'm not.' She paused. 'You'll find some-body else. There are plenty of girls.'

'I don't want plenty of girls,' Jamie retorted. 'I want Cat.'

8

'And Salvatore?' asked Isabel. 'Tell me all about Salvatore.'

'Charming,' said Cat, meeting Isabel's eye. 'Exactly as I told you he was.'

They were sitting in the gazebo in Isabel's back garden that Sunday afternoon, shortly after Cat's return from Italy. It was an unusually warm day for Edinburgh, where summer is unpredictable and where the occasional warm day is something to be savoured. Isabel was used to this, and although she bemoaned, as everybody did, the tendency of the sky to disappear behind sheets of fast-moving cloud, she found a temperate climate more to her taste than a Mediterranean one. Weather was a test of attitude, she felt: had Auden not pointed that out? Nice people, he observed, were nice about the weather; nasty people were nasty about it.

Cat was a heliophile, if there was such a word for a sun-worshipper, she thought. Italy in the summer must have suited her perfectly; a climate of short shadows and dry breezes. Cat liked beaches and warm seas, while Isabel found such things dull. She could think of nothing worse than sitting for hours under an umbrella, an open invitation to sandflies, looking out to sea. She wondered why it was that people did not talk on beaches; they sat, they lay prone, they read, but did they engage in conversation? Isabel thought not.

She remembered, years before, at the end of her spell at Georgetown, a visit she had paid to the Bahamas with her mother's sister, the one who lived in Palm Beach. This aunt had bought, almost on impulse, an apartment in Nassau, to which she travelled once or twice a year. She had made there a group of bridge-playing friends, bored and unhappy tax exiles, and Isabel had met these people at drinks parties. They had little to say, and there was little to be said about them. And on one occasion, visiting the house of one of these bridge couples, she had been seized with a sudden existential horror. The house had white carpets and white furniture and, most significantly, no books. And they sat on the terrace, which was just above a small private beach, and looked out towards the ocean, and nothing was said, because nobody could think of anything to speak about.

'Beaches,' said Isabel to Cat.

'Beaches?'

'I was thinking about Italy, and the weather, and beaches came into my mind.' She looked at Cat. 'And I suddenly remembered going to the Bahamas and meeting some people who lived on a beach.'

73

'Beach people?'

Isabel laughed. 'Not in that sense. Not people who had a tent or whatever and let their hair get full of salt and all the rest. No, these people had a house on a beach and sat on a marble terrace, which must have cost heaven knows what to import, and they looked out at the sea. And there were no books in their house, not a single book. Not one.

'He had lived in England and had left the country because he couldn't bear to pay taxes to a socialist government, or to any government, I suspect. And there they were on their Caribbean island, sitting on their terrace, with their heads full of nothing very much.

'They had a daughter, who was a young teenager when I saw her. She was as empty-headed as the parents and although they tried to do something about her education, nothing much got in. So they withdrew her from her expensive school in England and brought her back to the island. She took up with a local boy whom the parents wouldn't let into the house, with its white carpets and all the rest. They tried to stop her, but they couldn't. She had a baby, and the baby had nothing much in its head either. But they didn't want their daughter's baby and I later heard that they just pretended that the baby didn't exist. It crawled around on the white carpets, but they didn't really see it.'

Cat looked at Isabel. She was used to her relative's musings, but this one surprised her. Usually Isabel's stories had a clear moral point, but she was not sure what the moral point of this one was. Emptiness, perhaps; or the need for a purpose in life; or the immorality of tax havens. Or even babies and white carpets.

'Salvatore was quite charming,' said Cat. 'He took us all out for a meal at a restaurant in the hills. It was one of the places where they give you very little choice but just bring course after course.'

'They're generous people, the Italians,' Isabel remarked.

'And his father was very kind, too,' went on Cat. 'We went to their house and met all the relatives. Aunts, uncles and so on. Crowds of them.'

'I see,' said Isabel. There was still the question of Salvatore's father's occupation. 'And did you find out what the family business was?'

'I asked,' said Cat. 'I asked one of the uncles. We were sitting under the pergola in the garden, having lunch – a large table with about twenty people at it. I asked Salvatore's uncle.'

'And?' She imagined the uncle saying that he was not sure what his brother did; or that he had forgotten. One could not forget such a thing, just as one could not forget one's address, as a Russian once claimed to Isabel when she asked him where he lived. He was frightened, poor man; those were times when one might not want one's address in a foreigner's address book, but it might have been better for him to say so, rather than to claim that he had forgotten it.

'He said it was shoes.'

Isabel was silent. Shoes. Italian shoes: elegant, beautifully designed, but always, always too small for Isabel's feet. My Scottish-American feet, she thought, so much larger than Italian feet.

Cat smiled at her; she had dispelled the suspicions which

her aunt had expressed over Salvatore's family business. Perhaps it had been embarrassment over shoes, which were, after all, somewhat prosaic items.

'And what else did you do?' asked Isabel at last. 'Apart from these lunch parties with Salvatore and the Salvatore family. *Turismo?*'

'We went to see Etna.'

'*On the day of Sicilian July, with Etna smoking*,' said Isabel. 'Lawrence wrote that in his curious snake poem. You know the one, where a snake comes to his water trough, and he's in his pyjamas for the heat, and he throws a rock at the snake. Auden never threw rocks at snakes, and that's the crucial difference, isn't it: writers who would throw rocks at snakes and those who wouldn't. Hemingway would, wouldn't he?' She smiled at Cat, who was shading her eyes against the afternoon sun, and looking at her with what Isabel always described as her patient look.

'I digress. I know,' Isabel went on. 'But I always think of Etna smoking. And of Lawrence in his pyjamas.'

Cat took control of the conversation. Isabel could talk for hours about anything, unless stopped. 'That was with a cousin of Salvatore's, Tomasso. He's from Palermo. They live in a large Baroque palazzo. He's fun. He took me to all sorts of places I wouldn't have seen otherwise.'

Isabel sat quite still. When Cat talked like this, about men being fun, it meant that she was interested in them, as she had been interested in Toby, with his crushed-strawberry trousers and his tedious skiing talk; as she had been interested in Geoff, the army officer who drank too much at parties and engaged in childish pranks, such as gluing people's hats

76

to the hatstand; as she had been interested in Henry, and David, and perhaps others.

'Tomasso's a rally driver,' said Cat. 'He drives an old Bugatti. It's a beautiful car – red and silver.'

Isabel was noncommittal. At least Tomasso was at a safe distance . . .

'And he's bringing the car over to Scotland soon,' said Cat. 'It's being brought over by train and ferry. He wants to drive it around the Highlands and see a bit of Edinburgh. He thought he might stay in Edinburgh for a few weeks.'

'When?' asked Isabel. There was resignation in her voice.

'Next week, I think,' said Cat. 'Or the week after that. He's going to call me and let me know.'

There was little more to be said on the subject. As they talked about the delicatessen and about what had happened there over the week, Isabel's thoughts returned to one of the central issues of her moral life. She had determined long ago not to interfere in Cat's affairs, no matter what the temptation to do so was. It was very easy to see what was best for one's family, particularly when one did not have many relatives, but she understood how this offended the principle of autonomy, which holds, so stubbornly, that we must each be left to live our own lives as we see fit. This did not mean that we could do anything we liked – far from it – but it did mean that we had to make our own decisions as to what to do. And if this meant that we made bad choices, then we would have to be left with the making of those choices. Cat saw her destiny in men who would make her unhappy, precisely because they were inconstant, and selfish, and narcissistic. That was what she wanted to do, and she had to be allowed to do it.

'You're fond of him?' Isabel asked quietly, and Cat, know-ing what the question was about, was guarded in her response. Perhaps she was fond of him. She would see.

Isabel said nothing. She wondered for a moment what Tomasso would be like. Of course, if one bore in mind that he drove an old Bugatti and lived in a Baroque palazzo, then the answer was clear. He would be stylish, raffish no doubt, and he would make Cat unhappy, as she had been unhappy with the other men. And Jamie would be unhappy too, and would spend hours anxiously imagining Cat and Tomasso together, in the silver and red Bugatti; somewhere in Fife or Perthshire, on narrow, exhilarating roads.

9

She had suggested to Ian that they meet at her house, but when he telephoned her it was with a counter-invitation. He would like to take her to lunch, if he might, at the Scottish Arts Club in Rutland Square.

'They do mackerel fillets for me,' he said. 'Mackerel fillets and lettuce. But you can have something more substantial.'

Isabel knew the Arts Club. She had friends who were members and she knew the club president, a dapper antiques dealer with an exquisitely pointed moustache. She had even thought of joining, but done nothing about it, and so her visits to the club were restricted to the occasional lunch and the annual Burns Supper. The Burns Supper, which took place on or about the anniversary of Robert Burns's birth, was of variable quality. In a year when there was a good speaker, the address to the Immortal Memory could be moving. But the occasion could rapidly drift into maudlin reflections on the ploughman poet and his carousing in Ayrshire, nothing of which Scotland could be proud, she thought. There was nothing edifying in the profound consumption of whisky, she felt. Every Scottish poet, it seemed, had drunk too much, or written about drink, or written nonsense while under its influence. How much had been lost as a result – great screeds of unwritten poetry, whole decades of literature; lives unsung, hopes unrealised. And the same could be said of Scottish composers, or at least some of them – the sixth Earl of Kellie, for example, who had composed such fine fiddle music but who had often been drunk and who, it was said, laughed so much at his own jokes that he would turn purple. That, of course, was a marvellous social detail; one could forgive a great deal in a man who turned purple in such circumstances. One might even love such a figure.

Not that she laid the blame at the door of the Arts Club, before which she now stood, awaiting admission by one of the staff. Members had their own keys, but guests must wait until a member arrived or the secretary heard the bell. Isabel pressed the bell again and then looked back, over her shoulder, at the Rutland Square Gardens. Rutland Square was one of the finest squares in Georgian Edinburgh, tucked away at the west end of Princes Street, behind the great red sandstone edifice of the Caledonian Hotel. The gardens in the centre were not large, but had a number of well-established trees, which shaded the stone of the surrounding buildings. In spring the grass was covered with a riot of crocuses, impossible purples and yellows, and in summer, at lunchtime, it was lain upon during brief moments of sun by people from the nearby offices, pale secretaries and clerks in their shirtsleeves, just as Isabel and her friends at the Ladies' College in George Square had stretched out on the grass and watched the students from the university, the boys in particular, and waited for their real lives to start.

Every part of Edinburgh had memories for Isabel, as any resident of any city remembers the places where things happened, the corners where there had been a coffee bar a long time ago, or the building in which she had had her first job, the scene of an assignation, a disappointment or triumph. While she waited for the door to be opened, Isabel looked across the square to the corner where her friend Duncan had lived in his bachelor days. Behind an unassuming, black door was a common stone stair, winding and well-trodden over the years, that led up to four separate flats, one of them Duncan's. And what parties had been conducted under that roof: parties that only started when everything else had finished; evenings of long conversations, one of which she remembered had ended with the arrival of the fire brigade when a spark from a log in the fireplace had started a smouldering fire in the floorboards – not anybody's fault, as the firemen had pointed out as they stood in the kitchen later on and accepted a glass of whisky, and then another, and one after that, and had ended up singing with Duncan and his guests: *My brother Bill's a fireman bold/He pits oot fires*. At the end, when the six firemen had made their way down the stair, one had remarked that it was a fine class of fire that one attended in Rutland Square, which was undoubtedly true. And another, the one who had proposed to Isabel in the kitchen, only to withdraw the offer ten minutes later on the grounds that he thought that he might already be married, had waved at her as he disappeared downstairs and doffed his fire helmet.

The door was opened. Inside the club, Isabel made her way upstairs to the large L-shaped sitting room – the smoking room – where members congregated. It was a room filled with light, with two large ceiling-to-floor windows at the front, overlooking the square and its trees, and another large window at the back, looking down onto the mews behind Shandwick Place. There were two fireplaces, a grand piano, and comfortable red leather bench seats running along one wall, like the seats of an old parliament somewhere, in some forgotten corner of the Commonwealth.

The Arts Club usually had an exhibition of paintings hanging in the smoking room, sometimes by members, many of whom were artists. This exhibition was by a member, and Isabel picked up the explanatory sheet and examined the works. They were a mixture of small portraits and watercolours of domestic scenes. She recognised the subjects of a number of the portraits, and was impressed by the likenesses: Lord Prosser, a brilliant, good man standing against a background of the Pentland Hills; Richard Demarco in an empty theatre, smiling optimistically. And then there was another one, a large picture that dominated the wall behind the piano, a portrayal of pride, an actor whom Isabel knew very slightly but who was well known in general, standing with a self-satisfied sneer on his face, a curl of the lip, pure arrogance. Did he recognise himself in the likeness, she wondered, or did he not see himself as others saw him? Burns had said that, of course, and it had been repeated at the last but one Burns Supper downstairs, in a bucolic address given by a former moderator of the Church of Scotland: *the gift to gie us/to see ourselves as ithers see us.*

'Yes,' said a voice at her shoulder. 'That's him, isn't it? She's really summed him up, hasn't she? Look at the eyebrows.'

Isabel turned round to see Ian standing behind her.

'One might have to keep one's voice down,' said Isabel. 'He could be a member here.'

'Not grand enough for him,' said Ian. 'The New Club is more his territory.'

Isabel smiled. 'Look at this portrait here,' she said, pointing to another of the pictures. A man sat in his study, one hand on a pile of books and the other resting on a blotter. Behind him was a window in which a steep hillside of rhododendrons was visible.

'That's a very different person altogether,' said Ian. 'I know that man.'

'As it happens,' said Isabel, 'so do I.'

They looked at the picture together. Isabel leant forward to examine the painting more closely. 'Isn't it extraordinary how experience writes itself on the face?' she said. 'Experience and attitude – they both reveal themselves in the physical. One can understand people turning leathery, as Australians sometimes do, and one can understand how the pleasures of the table lead to fleshy jowls, but what is it that makes the spiritual face so different from the face of the venal? Especially with the eyes – how can the eyes be so different?'

'It's how we read the face,' said Ian. 'Remember that

83

you're talking to a psychologist. We like to think about things like that. It's a question of numerous little signals that create the overall impression.'

'But how do internal states show themselves physically?'

'Very easily,' said Ian. 'Think of anger. The knitted brow. Think of determination. The gritted teeth.'

'And intelligence?' asked Isabel. 'What's the difference between an intelligent face and an unintelligent one? And don't tell me that there isn't a difference – there is.'

'Liveliness and engagement with the world,' said Ian. 'The vacuous face shows neither of these.'

Isabel gazed at the painting of the good, and then looked at the painting of the proud. In an earlier age, it might have been possible to believe that goodness would prevail over pride, but not any more. The proud man could be proud with impunity, because there was nobody to contradict him in his pride and because narcissism was no longer considered a vice. That was what the whole cult of celebrity was about, she thought; and we fêted these people and fed their vanity.

They went down to lunch, choosing one of the few private tables at the rear of the dining room. The main tables, both round, were filling up. One was presided over by a *Scotsman* journalist who held court in the club three days a week; at the other table a gaggle of lawyers sat, chuckling over some misfortune.

'It was good of you to accept my invitation,' said Ian, as he poured Isabel a glass of water. 'After all, I was a perfect stranger when we bumped into one another the other day.'

'That's what you thought,' said Isabel. 'But I know more about you than you think.'

He raised an eyebrow. 'How?'

'You told me that you were a psychologist,' Isabel explained. 'I telephoned a psychologist friend and found out all I needed to know.'

'Which was?'

'That you had a distinguished career. That you were almost given a personal chair here in Edinburgh. That you published a lot. That's about it.'

He laughed. 'And I know about you,' he said.

Isabel sighed. 'Scotland is a village.'

'Yes,' went on Ian. 'But so is everywhere. New Yorkers say that about New York. And of course now we have the global village.'

Isabel thought about that for a moment. If we lived in a global village, then the boundaries of our responsibility were greatly extended. The people dying of poverty, the sick, the dispossessed, were our neighbours even if they were far away. And that changed a great deal.

'I asked our mutual friend Peter Stevenson about you,' Ian continued. 'He can tell you just about anything. And he said that you were, well, who you are. He also said that you had a reputation for discreetly looking into things.'

'That's a polite way of putting it,' said Isabel. 'Some would call it indecent curiosity. Nosiness, even.'

'There's nothing wrong with taking an interest in the world,' said Ian. 'I'm curious about the world too. I like to speculate as to what lies behind the surface.'

'If anything,' interjected Isabel. 'Sometimes the surface is all there is.'

'True, but not always true. Those pictures up there, for

instance, the ones we've just been looking at: there's so much behind each of them. But one would have to enquire. One would have to be a bit of a John Berger. You've seen his *Ways of Seeing*? It changed the way I look at things. Completely.'

'I picked it up a long time ago,' said Isabel. 'Yes, it makes scales drop from the eyes.'

The waitress arrived at their table, placing a small plate of bread and butter before them. Ian reached out and pushed it over towards Isabel.

'We had a conversation the other day,' he said. 'Or we started it, rather. I told you about how it felt to have heart surgery. But I didn't get very far.'

Isabel watched him. She had decided that she liked him, that she appreciated his openness and his willingness to engage with issues, but now she found herself wondering whether this was to be an operation conversation. People liked to talk about their medical problems – for some it was the most interesting of all subjects – but surely Ian could not have sought her out purely as a sympathetic ear for an operation saga.

It was as if she had given voice to her reservations. 'Don't worry, I don't intend to burden you with the details,' he said quickly. 'There's nothing worse than hearing about the medical problems of others. No, that's not the issue.'

Isabel looked at him politely. 'I don't mind,' she said. 'A friend told me about her ingrown toenail the other day. It was quite a saga. It took her half an hour. Do you know that once the toenail starts to . . .' She stopped, and smiled.

Ian continued. 'I wanted to tell you about something

quite . . . well, quite unsettling I suppose is the word. Would you mind?'

Isabel shook her head. The waitress had returned with their plates and had placed a helping of mackerel fillets and salad in front of Ian. He thanked her and gazed, with resignation, Isabel thought, at the meal before him. She listened as he began to talk, telling her briefly that he had become ill suddenly, after a massive viral attack, and that his heart, quite simply, had given out. He told of receiving the news that he would need a heart transplant and of his feeling of calm, which surprised even him.

'I found that I really didn't mind,' he said. 'I thought it highly unlikely that a donor would be found in time and that I would be going. I felt no great regrets. I just felt this extraordinary sense of calm. I was astonished.'

The call for the operation came suddenly. He had been out for a walk, at the Canongate Kirk, in fact, and had been fetched. They told him later that he had travelled over to Glasgow with the donor heart, which was in a container beside him, as the donor had come from Edinburgh. That was all that they said about that, as the donor's family had wished to remain anonymous. All he knew was that it was a young man, because they had used the male pronoun when they spoke to him about it and they had said that the heart was young.

'I don't remember a great deal of the next few weeks,' he said. 'I lay there in my bed in Glasgow, not knowing what day it was. I drifted in and out of sleep. And then, I slowly came back to life, or that's what it seemed like. I thought I could feel my new heart, beating within me. I lay and listened to its rhythms, echoed in a machine that they had linked me to. And I felt a curious sadness, a feeling of disjointedness. It was as if my past had been taken away from me and I was adrift. I found that I had nothing to say to anybody. People tried to coax me into conversation, but I just felt this great emptiness. There was nothing for me to say.

'I am told that all of this is quite normal. People feel like that after major heart surgery. And it did get better – once I was home I recovered my sense of who I was. I felt more cheerful. The emptiness, which was probably some form of depression, disappeared and I began to read books and see friends. At that point I began to feel gratitude – just immense gratitude – to the doctors and the person whose heart I had been given. I wanted to thank the family, but the doctors said that I should respect their desire for anonymity. Sometimes I thought of the donor, whoever he was, and just wept. I suppose that in a sense I was mourning him – I was mourning the death of somebody whom I didn't know, even whose name was unknown to me.

'I would have loved to have been able to speak to the family. I wrote a letter to them to thank them. You can imagine how difficult it was to do that – to find the words that could do justice to my feelings. When I read the letter over it sounded stilted to me, but there was nothing I could do about that. It had to be passed on through the doctors – I wonder if the family read it and thought that it sounded formal, and forced. I hate to think that they might have thought that I was writing out of a sense of duty – a formal thank-you letter. But what else could I do?'

He paused, as if expecting a response. Isabel had been listening intently. She had been intrigued by the idea of frustrated gratitude. Should one let people express their gratitude properly, even if one is embarrassed or reluctant to do so? There is an art in accepting a present, and indeed there is sometimes an obligation to let others give. Perhaps the family should have allowed him to meet them, and to thank them properly; one cannot put just any condition one wishes on a gift, a condition should not be unreasonable or demeaning. Isabel had always thought that legacies which stipulated that the beneficiaries should change their names were fundamentally offensive.

'You had no alternative,' she said. 'That's all you could do. But I think that they might have allowed you to speak with them. You could argue that they had no right to insist on anonymity, given the natural desire that you would have to express your gratitude.'

Ian's eyes widened. 'You think I have the right to know? To know who he was?'

Isabel was not prepared to go that far. 'No, I don't think so. But obviously you would know who he is once you spoke to them. Your right – if one can call it a right – is to be able to express your very natural and entirely understandable feelings of gratitude. You can't do that at the moment – or you can't do it properly.'

He was silent for a moment. 'I see.'

Isabel felt concerned. 'I'm not necessarily suggesting that you should pursue that. I don't have a particularly strong view about it. It's just a thought – that's all.' She paused. Was this what he wanted to speak to her about? Did he want her to trace the family for him? She would have to tell him that this was not what she did.

'You should know something,' she began. 'Whatever people have said about me, I'm not in the business of going round and finding things out. If you want me—'

He held up a hand. 'No, no. It's not that at all. Please don't think that—'

Isabel interrupted him. 'I suppose that in the past I've become involved in, how might one put it, issues in people's lives. But I'm really just the editor of the *Review of Applied Ethics*. That's all.'

He shook his head. 'I had nothing like that in mind. I felt that . . . well, one of the problems that I've had to face is not being able to talk. My wife is worried sick over me and I don't want to make it worse for her. And the doctors are busy and concerned with getting all the technical things right – the drug dosages and the rest.'

Isabel immediately felt guilty. She had not intended to inhibit him. 'Of course I'm happy to hear about all this,' she said quickly. 'I didn't mean to sound so abrupt.'

He was silent for a moment. He had not yet tackled his mackerel fillets, and now he tentatively cut off a slice. 'You see,' he said, 'I've had a most extraordinary thing happen to me, and I haven't been able to talk to anybody about it. I need somebody who will understand the philosophical implications of all this. That's why it occurred to me that I could talk to you.'

'People rarely consult philosophers for their advice,' said Isabel, smiling. 'I'm flattered!'

There was less tension in his voice as he continued. 'All

my life has been lived according to rational principles. I believe in scientific evidence and the scientific method.'

'As do I,' said Isabel.

He nodded. 'Psychology and philosophy view the world in the same way, don't they? So both you and I would take the view that unexplained phenomena are simply that and no more – things that we haven't yet explained but for which there is either a current explanation in terms of our existing understanding of things, or for which an explanation may emerge in the future.'

Isabel looked out of the window. He had simplified matters rather, but she broadly agreed. But was this the conversation that he had taken such pains to engineer: a discussion of how we view the world?

'Take memory, for example,' Ian went on. 'We have a general idea of how it works – that there are physical traces in the brain. We know where some of these are. Mostly in the hippocampus, but there are other bits in the cerebellum.'

'London taxi drivers,' interjected Isabel.

Ian laughed. 'Exactly. They found out that they had a larger hippocampus than the rest of us because they've had to memorise all those streets in order to get their licence.'

'At least they know how to get you there,' said Isabel. 'Unlike some places. I had to take control of a taxi in Dallas once and do the map-reading and direct the driver. I was visiting my cousin there. Mimi McKnight. And when I eventually arrived at her house, cousin Mimi remarked: "Every society gets the taxi drivers it deserves." Do you think that's true, Ian?' She answered her own question. 'No. The United States is a good country. It deserves better taxi drivers.'

'And better politicians?'

'Undoubtedly.'

He ate a bit more of his mackerel, while Isabel finished her potato salad.

'Could memory be located elsewhere?' he asked. 'What if we were wrong about the physical basis of memory?'

'You mean it might be located somewhere other than in the brain?'

'Yes. Bits of it might.'

'Unlikely, surely.'

He sat back in his chair. 'Why? The immune system remembers things. My immune system remembers, doesn't it? Worms that are fed other bits of worms have been shown to have absorbed the characteristics of the consumed worm. It's known as cellular memory.'

'Then why don't you show the characteristics of a mackerel?' Isabel asked. 'Why don't you start remembering how to do whatever it is that mackerel do?'

He laughed. Although he might not have, thought Isabel. And I should be more careful in what I say to him. He's trusting me in this conversation and I must not be flippant.

'I'm sorry,' she said. 'That was a rather silly thing to say.'

'It was very amusing,' he said. 'I've been surrounded by rather literal people recently. It's nice to have a change.' He paused, looking out of the window at the trees in Rutland Square. Isabel followed his gaze. There was a slight breeze and the branches of the trees were swaying against the sky.

'I'll get to the point,' Ian continued. 'Cellular memory theory – if you can call it that – would find it perfectly possible that the heart may be the repository of memory. So when I received the heart of another, I acquired some of that person's memories.'

Isabel was silent. Then: 'Did that happen?'

He looked down at the table, fingering the edge of the tablecloth. 'I don't know what to say. My instinct as a scientist – as a rationalist – is to say that it's complete nonsense. I know that there have been all these stories about people acquiring the characteristics of the donors who have given them an organ. People have made films about it. I would have dismissed all that as pure fantasy.'

'Would have?' asked Isabel.

Ian looked at his mackerel, moving it to the side of the plate. 'Yes. Would have. Now I'm not so sure.' He paused, searching her expression for signs of ridicule. And she watched him too. He is embarrassed, she thought, as any rational person might be in the face of the inexplicable.

'I'm not going to laugh at you,' she said quietly.

He smiled. 'Thank you,' he began. 'You see, I now have a recurring memory, one I didn't have before. It's very vivid. It's something which I think I remember, but which I never experienced, as far as I know.'

'You can tell me about it,' she said. 'Go on. Tell me.'

'Thank you,' he said again. 'It'll be a great relief just to talk about it. I'm actually feeling a bit desperate, you know. This thing that is happening to me is very unsettling, and I fear that it's going to hinder my recovery, unless I can sort it out.' He paused, staring down at his plate. 'In fact, I'm worried that it's going to kill me.'

10

Grace was early the following morning. 'A miracle,' she announced as she entered Isabel's kitchen. 'An early bus. Two, in fact. I had a choice.'

Isabel greeted her absent-mindedly. The *Scotsman*, open in front of her on the table, reported a bank robbery that had gone wrong when the robbers had inadvertently locked themselves in the vault. Isabel finished reading the report and then told Grace about it.

'That goes to prove it,' said Grace. 'There are no intelligent criminals.'

Isabel reached for the coffeepot. 'Surely there must be some,' she said mildly. 'These criminal masterminds one hears about. The ones who never get caught.'

Grace shook her head. 'They usually get arrested in the end,' she said. 'People don't get away with things for ever.'

94

Isabel thought for a moment. Was this true? She doubted it. There were unsolved murders, to start with: Jack the Ripper was probably never caught, and Bible John, the Bible-quoting murderer who had so terrified Glasgow, was probably still alive somewhere in the west of Scotland, a man now in early old age, leading a normal life. He appeared to have got away with it, as had various war criminals. Perhaps the bigger the crime the more one was likely to go unpunished. The dictators, the commissioners of genocide, the looters of the treasuries of nations – they often escaped, while the small fry, the non-commissioned officers, the small-scale fixers, were pursued and caught.

She was about to say something to this effect, but stopped herself. Grace could dig in over a position and the discussion would reach no conclusion. Besides, there was something else that she wanted to tell Grace about. Her discussion with Ian over lunch the previous day was still fresh in her mind; indeed, she had awoken in the early hours of the morning and thought about it, lying in bed, listening to the wind in the trees outside.

'I had the most extraordinary conversation yesterday,' she began. 'With a man who has had his heart replaced. Have you ever met anybody who's had a heart transplant?'

Grace shook her head. 'My mother could have done with one,' she mused. 'But they didn't work in those days. Or they didn't have enough hearts to go round.'

'I'm sorry,' said Isabel. There was a hinterland of unremitting hard work and suffering in Grace's life, and occasionally this became apparent in what she said.

'We all have to go,' said Grace. 'And it's only a question

95

of crossing over. It's nothing to be afraid of – the other side.'

Isabel said nothing. She was not sure about the other side, but was open-minded enough to accept that we could not say with certainty that some form of spiritual survival was impossible. It all depended, she thought, on the existence of a necessary connection between consciousness and physical matter. And since it was impossible to identify the location of consciousness, one could not rule out the persistence of consciousness in the absence of brain activity. There were some philosophers who thought of nothing but conscious-ness – 'the ultimate knotty philosophical problem', her old professor had said – but she was not one of them. So she simply said: 'Yes, the other side . . .' and then, 'But he never reached the other side, of course. His new heart saved him.'

Grace looked at her expectantly. 'And?'

'And then he started to have the most extraordinary experi-ences.' She paused, and gestured for Grace to help herself to a cup of coffee from the coffeepot. 'You see,' she went on, 'he's a psychologist. Or, rather, he was, and he had read articles about the psychological problems that people have after heart operations. It's very unsettling, apparently.'

'I can well imagine,' said Grace. 'A new heart beating away within you. I would feel very unsettled.' She shud-dered. 'I'm not sure I would like it, you know. Somebody else's heart. You might suddenly find yourself falling in love with the dead person's boyfriend, or whatever. Imagine that!'

Isabel leant forward. 'But that's precisely what he says hap-pened. He didn't exactly fall in love like that, but he has experienced some of the things that people are meant to experience in those circumstances. The most extraordinary things.'

Grace now sat down opposite Isabel. This was very much her territory – the vaguely chilling, the inexplicable. But I'm just as interested in this, reflected Isabel: let she who is without gullibility cast the first stone.

'He told me,' Isabel continued, 'that from time to time he experiences a sudden jolt of pain. Not in his heart, but all over the front of his body and his shoulders. And then he sees something. Every time. The pain is accompanied by a vision.'

Grace began to smile. 'But you don't believe in manifestations,' she said. 'You told me that. Remember? I had spoken to you about a manifestation that we saw at one of the meetings, and you said . . .'

It was reasonable enough, thought Isabel, for Grace to feel a certain triumph over this; but he had not said there was a manifestation. There was at least some rationalist ground to be defended. 'I didn't say anything about a manifestation,' she said. 'A vision and a manifestation are quite different things. One is outside you, the other inside.'

Grace looked doubtful. 'I'm not sure that there's much difference. But anyway, what did he see?'

'A face.'

'Just a face?'

Isabel took a sip of her coffee. 'Yes. Not much of a manifestation, that. But it is rather odd, isn't it? To see the same face. And to see it at the same time as the pain comes on.'

Grace looked down at the tablecloth. With an index finger she traced a pattern; Isabel watched, but realised that it was nothing special, just a doodle. Did Grace go in for spirit-writing? she wondered. Spirit-writing had its possibilities – if it existed. Had somebody not been in touch with Schubert and acted as amanuensis while Schubert had dictated a symphony? Isabel smiled as she wondered whether the composer had suggested a name for this symphony: *The Other Side* might be appropriate, perhaps. She glanced at Grace, who was still staring fixedly at the table, and she suppressed her smile.

Grace looked up. 'So who does he think it is? Is it somebody he remembers?'

Isabel explained that it was not. The face, Ian had said, was of nobody he knew, but was memorable: a high-browed face, with hooded eyes and a scar running just below the hairline.

'But here,' Isabel continued, 'here's the really interesting bit. As I told you, this person to whom I was talking is a psychologist. He looked up what has been written about the experiences of people who have had heart transplants. And he found that there was quite a bit. Some books. A few articles.

'Somebody wrote a book about it some years ago. It described how a woman who received the heart of a young man started to behave in a totally different way. She became much more aggressive, which I suppose anybody might after having their heart taken out of them and replaced, but she also started to dress in a different way and to eat different food. She started to like chicken nuggets, which she had never liked before. Of course they then found out that the young man who donated his heart had had a particular liking for chicken nuggets.'

Grace shook her head. 'I can't abide them,' she said. 'Tasteless things.'

98

Isabel agreed. But chicken nuggets were not the point of the story. 'He also looked at various articles,' she went on, 'and there he found something very interesting. He stumbled across an article by some psychologists in the United States who looked at ten cases in which there had been changes in behaviour by people who had received the hearts of others. One of them caught his eye.'

Grace was sitting almost bolt upright. Isabel reached for the coffeepot and poured her housekeeper another cup. 'With all this talk of the heart,' she said, 'can you feel your heart beating within you? And does coffee make it go faster?'

Grace thought for a moment. 'I don't like to think about that,' she said. 'You have to leave your heart to get on with it. It's rather like breathing. We don't have to remind ourselves to breathe.' She took a sip of coffee. 'But let's get back to these cases. He said that one caught his eye. Why?'

'They,' Isabel began, 'that is, the people who wrote the article, went to see a man who said that since he had received his new heart he had sudden pains in his face, saw flashes of light and then a face. He gave a good description of this face, just as my friend did.

'The researchers found that the person who had given the heart was a young man who had been shot – in the face. The police thought they knew who shot him, but could not prove anything. But the police showed the researchers a picture of the suspected gunman – and it was exactly like the face which the recipient described.'

Grace reached for her cup. 'In other words,' she said, 'the heart was remembering what happened.'

'Yes,' said Isabel. 'Or that's what appears to have happened.

The people who wrote the article are properly sceptical. All they say is that if there is such a thing as cellular memory, then this might be a case of it. Or . . .'

'Or?'

Isabel gestured airily. 'Or it can all be explained by the fact that the drugs which the patient was taking led to hallucinations. Drugs can make you see flashes of light and so on.'

'But what about the similarities in the faces?' Grace asked.

'Coincidence,' suggested Isabel. But she did not feel much enthusiasm for this explanation, and Grace realised it.

'You don't really think that it was sheer coincidence, do you?' Grace said.

Isabel did not know what to think. 'I don't know,' she said. 'Perhaps it's one of those situations where one simply has to say that one doesn't know.'

Grace rose to her feet. She had work to do. But there was an observation that she felt she needed to make. 'But I remember your saying to me – some time ago – that we either know something or we don't. You said that there could be no halfway houses. You did say that, you know.'

'Did I?' said Isabel. 'Well, maybe I did.'

'And perhaps what you meant to say is that there are some occasions when we must say that we just can't be sure,' said Grace.

'Perhaps,' said Isabel.

Grace nodded. 'If you'd like to come to one of the meetings some day you could see what I mean.'

For a moment Isabel felt alarmed. She had no desire to become involved in séances, but to refuse would seem churlish and would be interpreted as a recanting on the open-mindedness that Grace had just obliged her to acknowledge. But would she be able to keep a straight face while the medium claimed to talk to the other side? Would there be knocking on tables and low moans from the spirit world? It was a source of complete astonishment to her that somebody as down-to-earth, as straightforward, as Grace could have this peculiar interest in spiritualism. It just did not make sense; unless, of course, as she had seen suggested, we all have a weak point, an area of intellectual or emotional vulnerability that may be quite out of keeping with our character. The most surprising people did the most remarkable things. Auden, she remembered, had written a line about a retired dentist who painted nothing but mountains. That had interested her because of the juxtaposition of dentistry and mountains. Why was it that anything which a dentist would do would seem almost poignant? *My dentist collects toy trains*, she might say – because it was true. But why was that any funnier than saying that a bank manager kept toy trains? Or was that funny too?

'I can tell that you think it'll be funny,' said Grace, as she made her way to the cupboard where she kept her cleaning equipment. 'But it isn't, you know. It's serious. Very serious. And you meet some interesting people there too.' She was standing in front of the cupboard now, extracting a broom, but still talking. 'I've just met a rather nice man in our group, you know. His wife went over into spirit a year or so ago. He's very pleasant.'

Isabel looked up sharply, but Grace had started to leave the room. She glanced at Isabel as she did so, but only briefly, and it was a glance that gave nothing away. Isabel looked through the open door, at the place where Grace had been standing, and mulled over what she had said. But then her thoughts returned to Ian, and to their curious, unnerving conversation in the Arts Club. He had said that he was concerned that the images that he was seeing would kill him – a strange thing to say, she thought, and she had asked him to explain why he should feel this. Sadness, he had said. Sadness. 'I feel this terrible sadness when it happens. I can't tell you what it's like – but it's the sorrow of death. I know that sounds melodramatic, but that's just what it is. I'm sorry.'

11

Isabel did not like her desk to get too cluttered, but that did not mean that it was uncluttered. In fact, most of the time there were too many papers on it, usually manuscripts that had to be sent off for peer assessment. She was not sure about the term *peer assessment*, even if it was the widely accepted term for a crucial stage in the publishing of journal articles. Sometimes the expression amounted to exactly that: equals looked dispassionately at papers by equals and gave their view. But Isabel had discovered that this did not always happen, and papers were consigned into the hands of their authors' friends or enemies. This was unwitting; it was impossible for anybody to keep track of the jealousies and rivalries that riddled academia, and Isabel had to hope that she could spot the concealed agendas that lay behind outright antagonism or, more often, and more subtly, veiled antagonism: 'an interesting piece, perhaps interesting enough to attract a ripple of attention.' Philosophers could be nasty, she reflected, and moral philosophers the nastiest of all.

Now, seated at her cluttered desk, she began the task of clearing at least some of the piles of paper. She worked energetically and it was almost twelve when she glanced at the clock. She had done, she thought, enough work for the morning, and perhaps for the day. She stood up, stretched, and went over to her study window to look out on the garden. The display of pinks in the flowerbed that ran alongside the far garden wall was as bright as it ever had been, and the line of lavender bushes that she had planted a few years previously was in full flower. She looked down at the flowerbed immediately below her window. Somebody had been digging at the roots of an azalea and had kicked small piles of soil onto the edge of the lawn. She smiled. *Brother Fox.*

She very rarely saw Brother Fox, who was discreet in his movements, as befitted one who must have thought that he lived in enemy territory. Not that Isabel was an enemy; she was an ally, and he might just have sensed that when he found the chicken carcasses that she left out for him. Once she had seen him at close quarters, and he had turned tail and fled, but had stopped after a few paces and they had looked at one another. Their eyes met for only a few seconds, but it was enough for Brother Fox to realise that her intentions towards him were not hostile, and she saw his body relax before he turned and trotted off.

She was looking at the signs of his digging when the telephone rang.

'So,' said Cat, who always started telephone conversations abruptly. 'Working?'

Isabel looked at her desk, now half clear. 'I was,' she said. 'But have you any better ideas?'

'You sound as if you want an excuse.'

'I do,' said Isabel. 'I was going to stop anyway, but an excuse would be welcome.'

'Well,' said Cat. 'My Italian friend has arrived. Tomasso. Remember the one I told you about.'

Isabel was guarded. Cat was sensitive about Isabel's past interference in her affairs and she did not want to say anything that could be misconstrued. So she simply said, 'Good.'

There was a silence. 'Good,' said Isabel again.

'I thought that you might like to come and have lunch here,' said Cat. 'In the delicatessen. He's coming back once he's put his car away safely at the hotel. He's staying at Prestonfield House.'

'You don't think that I shall be . . . in the way?' she asked. 'Won't you want to . . . to have lunch by yourselves? I'm not sure if you'll want me there.'

Cat laughed. 'Don't worry,' she said. 'There's nothing between him and me. I'm not thinking of getting involved, if that's worrying you. He's good company, but that's as far as it goes.'

Isabel wanted to ask whether Tomasso thought that too, but said nothing. She was serious about not interfering and any remark like that could easily be seen as interference. At the same time, she felt relieved that Tomasso was not going to be Cat's new boyfriend. She knew that it was wrong to judge him on the basis of scanty evidence – no evidence at all, in fact – but surely there was good reason to feel concerned. A handsome young Italian – she assumed he was handsome: all of Cat's male friends were – with a taste for vintage Bugattis would hardly be the reliable, home-loving sort. A breaker of speed limits – and hearts, she thought, and almost muttered, but stopped herself in time.

'Will you come over?' said Cat.

'Of course,' said Isabel. 'If you really want me to.'

'I do,' said Cat. 'I've got a salad specially prepared for you. Extra olives. The ones you like.'

'I would have come anyway,' said Isabel. 'You know that.'

Upstairs, she looked at herself in the mirror. She was wearing the dove-grey skirt that she often wore when editing. It was complemented, if *complemented* were not too strong a term, by a loose, cream wool cardigan on which a small smudge of ink had appeared on the left sleeve. She smiled. This would not do. One could not meet a man with an interest in vintage Bugattis in such an outfit; indeed, one could not meet any Italian dressed like that.

She opened her wardrobe. *Guilty by Design*, she thought, looking at a black shift dress she had bought from the aptly named dress shop in Morningside, for there was a great deal of guilt involved in the buying of expensive dresses – delicious guilt; she had loved that dress and had worn it too often. Italians wore black, did they not? So something different – a red cashmere polo-neck would transform the skirt, and a pair of dangly diamanté earrings would add to the effect. There! Cat would be proud of her. Tomasso's own aunt would probably wear widow's weeds and have a moustache and— She stopped herself. Not only was that uncharitable, but it was probably also incorrect. Italian aunts *used* to run to fat and excessive hair, but things had changed, had they not, and now they were more likely to be slender, fashionable, tanned.

She called out a goodbye to Grace, who replied from somewhere deep within the house, and then made her way outside. The students from Napier University nearby had lined the street with their cars, which irritated the neighbours but which Isabel did not mind too much. Local people were never all that real to students; they were the backdrop for the student drama of parties and long conversations over cups of coffee and . . . Isabel paused. What else did students do? Well, she knew the answer to that, and why should they not, as long as they were responsible about it? She did not approve of promiscuity, which she thought made a mockery of our duty to cherish and respect others; an emotional fast food, really, which one would not wish on anybody. But at the same time one should not starve oneself.

As she turned into Merchiston Crescent, the road that wound its way towards Bruntsfield and Cat's delicatessen, Isabel imagined what it would be like to give to others the gift of love. Not from oneself – as that may be unwanted – but from those whose love the recipient yearned for. Such a power that would be, she thought. Here, my dear, is the girl whom you have admired for so long, and yes, she is yours. And here, for you, is that desirable boy whose eye you have so long tried to catch, in vain; well, try catching it now.

I do not even have a man myself, Isabel said to herself; I am in no position to give one to another. Of course, she had not over-exercised herself in the obtaining of a man, not since John Liamor. For some years after that, a long time, she had not even been sure that she wanted one. But now, she thought, she was ready again to take the risk that men brought with them – the risk of being left, cheated upon, made unhappy. She could get one if she wanted, she imagined. She was young enough and attractive enough to compete. Men found her interesting; she knew that, because they showed it in the way they reacted to her. It would be good to go out to dinner with the right man. She could see herself sitting at a table in the window at Oloroso, looking out over the roofs of George Street to Fife in the distance, and a man on the other side of the table, a man who was a good conversationalist, with a sense of humour, who would make her laugh, but who could make her cry, too, when he spoke of the more important, moving things. A man just like . . . She racked her brain. What men like that were there? And, more to the point perhaps, where were they?

Jamie, of course. He came unbidden into her mind, sitting at that unreal table at Oloroso, watching her with those grey eyes of his, and speaking to her about exactly those things that they liked to speak about. She closed her eyes. It was too late. There had been a fatal, anachronistic error in the stars that had brought them together. Had she been born fifteen years later then it would have been a perfect match, and she could imagine herself fighting tooth and nail to possess him – he would have been all that she wanted; but now, it was inappropriate, and impossible, and she had decided not even to think about it. She had freed herself of those thoughts of Jamie in the same way in which an addict frees himself of thoughts of the bottle, or the racetrack, or the bedroom.

She was approaching the end of Merchiston Crescent, and she saw ahead the busy line of cars coming into town from Morningside and further south. Cat's delicatessen was in the middle of a block, with a jeweller on one side and an antiques shop on the other. A few doors further down, on the same side as the delicatessen, was the fishmonger from whom her father had bought his Loch Fyne kippers for all those years. She had seen the antiques dealer buying kippers himself, bending down to peer at the smoked fish on the slab. One of the pleasures of living in an intimate city, she thought, was that one could know so much about one's fellow citizens. This was what made those small Italian cities so comfortable: the fact that there was so little anonymity. She remembered visiting her friend who lived in Reggio Emilia, the same friend who had taken her to the Parmesan factory, and taking a stroll with her in the piazza. It seemed that they stopped every second minute to pass the time of day with somebody. That one was a cousin; that one was a friend of an aunt; that one had lived on the floor below for a year or two and had then gone to Milan, but must be back; that one had the cruellest nickname when he was at school, yes, they called him that, they really did. One could not stroll in quite the same way in Edinburgh – the weather was hardly perfect for *la bella figura* – but one could at least see people one knew buying kippers.

Cat's delicatessen was busy when she arrived. As well as employing Eddie full-time, Cat had now taken on a young woman, Shona, who worked several hours a day and who was now at the counter, slicing salami. Cat was weighing cheese and Eddie was at the cash register. Isabel wondered whether she should offer to help, but thought perhaps that she might just get in the way. So she sat down at a table and picked up a magazine that was lying on the floor, abandoned by some untidy previous customer.

She was immersed in an article by the time Cat came over to see her.

'He'll be here any moment,' Cat muttered. 'I'm sure you'll like him.'

'I'm sure I shall,' said Isabel mildly.

'No, I mean *really* like him,' Cat said. 'Just wait and see.'

Isabel was intrigued. 'But I thought you sounded a little bit . . . how shall I put it? A little bit lukewarm when you spoke about him, on the phone.'

'Oh,' said Cat lightly. 'If you mean I sounded as if he's not for me, yes, that's right. He isn't. But . . . But you'll see what I mean.'

'What's the snag?' asked Isabel.

Cat sighed. 'Age.'

'Age? How old is he? Seventy-five?'

'Not quite,' said Cat. 'About your age, I would have thought. Early forties.'

Isabel was taken aback. 'Over the hill in that case. You think.'

'I don't mean to be rude,' said Cat. 'Forty's nothing really. Forty is thirty these days, I know. I know. It's just that for me, from the perspective of twenty-something, forty-something is . . . I'm afraid I don't see myself falling for somebody who's almost twenty years older than I am. That's all. It's simply a question of sticking to one's contemporaries.'

Isabel touched her niece on the forearm in a gesture of reassurance. 'That's perfectly reasonable,' she said. 'You don't have to apologise.'

'Thank you.' Cat looked up. The door had opened and a man had entered. He cast a quick eye about the delicatessen and, spotting Cat, gave her a wave.

Tomasso came over to the table. Cat rose to her feet and gave him her hand. Isabel watched, and then he turned to her, and reached forward to shake hands with her. He was smiling, and she saw his eyes move across her, not very obviously or crudely, but move nonetheless.

He sat down with them and Cat went to fetch him the glass of mineral water for which he had asked. It was too late for coffee, he said, and he was not hungry. 'Water,' he said, 'will be perfect.'

He turned to Isabel and smiled. 'Your city is very beautiful,' he said. 'We Italians think of Scotland as being so romantic and here it is, just as we imagined it!'

'And we have our own ideas about Italy,' said Isabel.

He inclined his head slightly. 'Which are?'

'So romantic,' said Isabel.

Tomasso's eyes widened with mirth. 'Well,' he said. 'We are in the realm of cliché, are we not?'

Isabel agreed. But the clichés came from somewhere, and that was why they tended to have a measure of truth in them. If Italy was not romantic, then what country was? She looked at Tomasso, a bland look, she hoped, but one which concealed serious examination. He was tall and well built, and his features, which were strong, were . . . were familiar. He looked like somebody she knew, but who was it? And then, in a moment, she realised who it was. This was Jamie fifteen years on.

The realisation surprised her, and for a few moments she was sunk in thought. Jamie was the borderline-Mediterranean type, as she had often observed, and so it was perhaps not surprising that there should be some similarities between him and Tomasso, who was the real thing. But it went beyond that: there was something in the expression and in the way of speaking that made the two seem so similar. If you closed your eyes, briefly, which she now did, briefly, and if you factored out the Italian pronunciation, then it could be Jamie with her. But Jamie would never come into Cat's delicatessen – even now.

This unexpected comparison unnerved her and for a moment she floundered. The banal came to her rescue. 'You speak such beautiful English,' she said.

Tomasso, who had been about to say something, inclined his head. 'I'm glad you understand me. I've lived in London, by the way. I was there for four years, working in an Italian bank. You wouldn't have said that I spoke good English when I first arrived. They used to stare at me and ask me to repeat what I had just said.'

'They're ones to talk,' said Isabel. 'With their Estuary English and its words all run together. The language is being murdered daily.'

'The bank paid for me to have lessons with an elocution teacher,' said Tomasso. 'He made me hold a mirror in front of my mouth and say things like *The rain in Spain . . .*'

'*Falls mainly on the plain,*' supplied Isabel.

'And where's that ghastly plain?' asked Tomasso.

'In Spain,' Isabel answered.

They laughed. She looked at him, noticing the small lines around the edge of the mouth that told her that this was a man who was used to laughter.

'Is my niece going to show you Scotland?' Isabel asked.

Tomasso shrugged. 'I asked her if she would, but unfortunately she cannot. She is very tied up with this business. But I shall see what I can myself.'

Isabel asked him if he was going to Inverness. Visitors to Scotland made the mistake – in her view – of going to Inverness, which was a pleasant city, but nothing more. There were far better places to go, she thought.

'Yes,' he said. 'Inverness. Everybody tells me I must go there.'

'Why?'

'Because it's . . .' He trailed off, and then burst out laughing. 'I shall not go there. I shall not.'

'Good,' said Isabel.

Cat returned. She was not going to be able to show Tomasso Scotland, but she was able to get away to show him Edinburgh that afternoon. Would Isabel care to accompany them?

Isabel hesitated. She noticed Tomasso glance at Cat after the invitation had been extended; just a quick glance, but enough to tell her that he did not want her to go along.

'I'm sorry,' Isabel said, 'but duty calls. My desk is looking awful. In fact, I can't see the surface for papers.'

Cat looked at her. 'Are you sure you don't want to come?' she asked. 'Couldn't the work wait?'

There was a brief exchange of glances – a niece-to-aunt

113

exchange, a look between women, private, although in the presence of a man. Isabel interpreted it as a plea, and realised that Cat wanted her to be with her. Of course she would have to accede to the request, which she did.

'Yes, of course the work can wait,' she said. 'I'd love to come.'

Tomasso turned to face her. 'But I cannot put you out like that. No. No. Please: we shall do it some other time when nobody is busy.'

'It's no difficulty,' said Isabel. 'I have plenty of time.'

Tomasso was insistent. 'I cannot allow you to be inconvenienced. I have plenty to do myself. I have some business here in Edinburgh – there are people I must see.'

Isabel glanced at Cat. She felt a momentary sense of disappointment that he did not want her company; that was obvious. Cat, though, had her difficulties ahead. Tomasso was insistent, it seemed, and would not be put off that easily.

The Italian rose to his feet. 'I am keeping you both from your work,' he said. 'It's so easy, when one is on holiday oneself, to forget that everybody else has their work to do. Cat? May I telephone you tomorrow?'

'Of course,' said Cat. 'I'll be here. Working, I'm afraid, but I'll be here.'

He turned to Isabel. 'And perhaps we shall be able to meet too?'

'I'm here too,' said Isabel. 'And I'll be happy to show you round. I really would.'

Tomasso smiled at her. 'You are very kind.'

He bent forward and took Cat's hand in his; a lingering grasp, thought Isabel. Cat reddened. It was going to be difficult, Isabel thought, but Cat had to learn how to discourage men. And the easiest way of doing that, in Isabel's view, was to show excessive eagerness. Men did not like to be pursued; she would have to tell Cat that, tactfully, of course, but as explicitly as she could.

12

'Well, Miss Dalhousie. It is Miss Dalhousie, isn't it?'

Isabel nodded to the young man behind the enquiries desk at the library. 'It is. Well remembered.'

She looked at him, noticing the clean white shirt and the carefully knotted tie, the slightly earnest appearance. He was the sort who noticed things. 'How do you do it?' she asked. 'You must get so many people coming in here.'

The young man looked pleased with the compliment. He was proud of his memory, which came in useful profession-ally, but the reason why he remembered Isabel was that she had, on an earlier visit, explained to him that she was the editor of the *Review of Applied Ethics*. For a young librarian, fresh from a spell as a junior in the journals department, that was an exotic and exalted position.

He smiled at Isabel. 'Is there anything I can do for you?'

'I need to see copies of the *Evening News* for this past October,' said Isabel. She gave him the date and he told her that she was in luck; while the earlier issues were on microfiche, they still had bound volumes of the more recent months and he would bring these over to her personally. Isabel thanked him and took a seat near the window. As she waited she could look down into the Grassmarket and watch people window-shopping. It had changed so much, she reflected. When she had been young, the Grassmarket had been a distinctly insalubrious place, with winos slumped in the doorways and small knots of desolate people standing outside the entrance to the doss-houses. What had happened to the Castle Trades Hotel, which took through its doorway the homeless and destitute and gave them a bowl of soup and a bed for the night? It had become an upmarket hotel for tourists, its old clientele dispersed, vanished, dead. And a few doors away from it a glittering bank and a shop selling fossils. Money pushed people out of cities; it always had. And yet no matter how much the exterior of the city changed, the same human types were still there; wearing different clothes, more prosperous now, but with the same craggy faces that were always there to be seen on the streets of Edinburgh.

The young man returned with a large blue folder of bound newspapers. 'This is two months' worth,' he said. 'But it includes October.'

Isabel thanked him and opened the cover of the folder. The front page of the *Edinburgh Evening News* of the first of October greeted her eyes. There had been a fire in a nightclub, a large banner headline announced, and there was a picture of firemen directing a stream of water onto a

117

collapsed section of roof. Nobody had been hurt, she read, because the fire occurred after-hours when the building was empty. Isabel was suspicious. Fires in bars and nightclubs were a well-known way of dealing with shrinking profits. Occasionally there were arrests, but usually nothing could be proved, in spite of the best efforts of the loss adjusters. So the insurers paid up and another, better-positioned bar or night-club popped up in the place of the one that had gone.

She turned the page and began to read another story. A male teacher had been accused of making indecent remarks to a girl pupil. The teacher had been suspended and would face what was described as a rigorous inquiry into the inci-dent. 'This sort of thing cannot be allowed to happen,' said an official from the education department. Isabel paused. Who knew that it had happened? Surely the whole point of an inquiry was to find out whether anything happened at all, and yet here was the official prejudging the matter before a shred of evidence had been produced. And would it not be the easiest thing in the world for a streetwise teenage girl to make up an allegation of that sort in order to embarrass or destroy a teacher to whom she had taken a dislike?

There was a photograph of the suspended teacher, a man in his late thirties, Isabel thought, frowning at the camera. Isabel studied the photograph. It was a kind face, she decided, not the face of a predator. And here, she said to herself, is the victim of the witch-hunt, or its modern equiv-alent. Not much has changed. Witchcraft or sexual harassment: the tactics of persecution were much the same – the loathed enemy was identified and then demonised. And exactly the same emotions and energy that had gone into witch-hunting now went into the pursuit of our preferred modern victims. And yet, she thought: What if the girl had been telling the truth? What then?

She sighed. The world was an imperfect place, and our search for justice in it seemed an impossible task. But she had not come to the library to be immersed in such reports, and the speculations they provoked. She had come to find out about the events of a very particular week: the week during which Ian had had his heart transplant. That was in mid-October, which would be about a quarter of the way through the volume, she assumed. She slid a finger into the bound pages and turned over the heavy wad of paper. October the tenth: she had come in too early. She fingered the paper, preparing to turn another week's worth of papers. But before she did so, she saw the headline: 'Teacher Dies'. It was the same man, the one who had been suspended from duties pending the investigation of an allegation against him. He had been found dead at the edge of the Pentland Hills, just outside the city. A note had been recovered and the police were not treating the death as suspicious. He was survived by a wife and two children.

Isabel read the report with a heavy heart. A friend was quoted as saying that he was an innocent man who had been hounded to his death. The police confirmed that a teenager, who could not be named for legal reasons but who was connected with the case, had been charged with a separate offence of attempting to pervert the course of justice. That meant the making of a false allegation.

She made a conscious effort to put the case out of her mind. She had the moral energy, she thought, for one issue at a time. She could do nothing to help that schoolteacher and his sorrowing family. But she could help Ian, if he wanted her help – which was another matter. Now she was looking at the first newspaper in her targeted week, and she ran her eye over each column, scanning the pages for the headline that she wanted. 'Major Row Hits City Parks.' No. 'Lord Provost Defends Road Plans, Says Public Will Come to Welcome Them.' No. 'Police Dog Turns on Handler, Is Demoted.' No. (She avoided the temptation to read that one; she had to get on with the task in hand. Demoted?)

It was all the typical stuff of local papers: the planning disputes, the school prize-givings, the crimes great and small. It was immensely distracting, as local papers always are, but she persisted and, four days into her search (in newspaper terms), she came across the information for which she had been looking. A young man had been killed in what appeared to be a hit-and-run incident. There was his photograph, across two columns, a young man of twenty, wearing a white shirt and a plain tie, smiling into the camera. *Rory Macleod*, the caption read. *Former pupil of James Gillespie's School. Shortly after the celebration of his twentieth birthday.*

Isabel studied the face. He had been the sort of young man she had walked past every day in Bruntsfield, or George Street, or anywhere like that. He could have been a student or, with his white shirt and tie, a bank clerk from the Bank of Scotland in Morningside. In other words, he was unexceptional, as she had imagined he would be.

She turned to the report. He had played in a squash match in Colinton, the newspaper said, and had then gone with friends for a pint of beer at the Canny Man's. A friend had

120

walked with him as far as the post office and then had left him to go up to the Braids while he had turned left into Nile Grove. Possibly only five or ten minutes after the friend had said goodbye to him, he was found in Nile Grove itself, lying on the edge of the pavement, half hidden by a parked car. An ambulance was called and he was taken to the Infirmary, but he died later that night. He had been only twenty yards away from his front door. The newspaper then gave the address of that front door and a quote from an uncle, who spoke of the devastation of the family and the sense of loss at the ending of a life so full of promise. And that was all.

Isabel read through the report several times. She noted the number of the house in Nile Grove and the name of the uncle who had been interviewed. He had an unusual name, Archibald, which would make it comparatively easy to trace him, should she need to do so. She took a last look at the photograph, at the face of Rory Macleod, and then turned to the next day's *Evening News*. There was a further small item on the incident, confirming that Rory appeared to have been struck by a car and fatally injured. The police had appealed for anybody who had been in the vicinity of Nile Grove that night to come forward. 'Anything you saw may be important,' the police spokesman said. 'Any unusual behaviour. Anything out of the ordinary.'

She looked at the following day's paper, but there was nothing more on the incident. So she closed the folder and started to carry it back to the young man at the enquiry desk. He saw her coming and leapt to his feet.

'Miss Dalhousie,' he whispered. 'Please let me take that.'

She handed him the folder and thanked him.

'How is the *Review* going?' he asked her, as he took the folder from her.

'I'm almost putting the next issue to bed,' said Isabel. 'It's a busy time for me.'

He nodded. He would have liked to have asked her for a job, but he could not bring himself to do so. He would stay in the library service, he thought, and become old like those above him. And Isabel, looking at him, at his eager face, reflected on mortality. He could have been the young man in that photograph, but was not. Rory had died instead of this young man, because Rory had had the bad luck to be at that precise point in Nile Grove at the exact moment when the driver of the car had struck him. And then she thought of the driver. That could have been me, she reflected, or this young librarian, but it was not. That had been a man with a high brow and hooded eyes, and with that scar. Or it could have been. Just could have been.

She had arranged to meet Jamie at the Elephant House, a café farther down George IV Bridge. It was a spacious, L-shaped room, with windows at the back which looked down on Candlemaker Row. High-ceilinged and with exposed floorboards, it had a slightly cavernous feel to it – a cavern adorned with pictures and models of elephants on every wall. Isabel felt comfortable there, amongst its elephants and students, and regularly chose it as a place to meet her friends. And if her Sunday Philosophy Club were ever to meet again – it seemed to be impossible to find a date that suited the members – then this would have been a good place to sit and talk about the nature of good and our understanding of the world. For Jamie, who taught bassoon for six hours a week at George Heriot's School, it was less of a meeting place than a convenient place to go for a strong coffee after finishing with his pupils.

He was already there when she arrived, sitting at a table near a window in the back part of the room, a cup of coffee in front of him and immersed in one of the café's copies of the *Scotsman*. He looked up as she arrived and rose to his feet in welcome.

'You've been here for hours,' she said. 'I'm sorry.'

'Five minutes,' he said. 'Still on page three of the newspaper.'

He put the paper to one side and offered to go and buy her coffee.

'That can wait, Jamie,' said Isabel. 'I've been reading the newspaper too.'

He glanced at the paper. 'And?'

'The *Evening News*,' she went on. 'In the library.'

'What an odd thing to do,' he said. 'Unless . . .' He paused. Isabel had that look about her which told him she was on to something. He could always tell when she was about to embark on some temporary obsession. It was a look in her eyes, perhaps, a look of determination, a look that said *I shall not rest until I get to the bottom of this*.

For a moment Isabel appeared embarrassed. 'Yes,' she said quietly. 'I suppose that I am on to something.' She held up a hand. 'I know, I know: you don't have to tell me again.'

Jamie sighed. 'I wasn't going to lecture you. I know that that's no use – you'll go right ahead, no matter what I say. All I would say is this: Be careful. One of these days you're going to get involved in something which gets seriously out of hand. You will, you know. You really will.'

'I understand that perfectly well,' said Isabel. 'And I'm grateful to you for saying it. I do listen to you, you know.'

Jamie took a sip of his coffee. He wiped a small trace of milk from his upper lip. 'It doesn't always seem like that to me.'

'But I do!' protested Isabel. 'I listened to you over that business with Minty Auchterlonie. I listened to you very seriously.'

'You were lucky there,' said Jamie. 'You could have got seriously out of your depth. But let's not talk about the past. What are you getting involved in now?'

Over the next few minutes Isabel told him about her chance meeting with Ian and about their conversation at the Scottish Arts Club. Jamie was interested – she could tell that – although he, like Isabel herself, seemed incredulous when she mentioned cellular memory.

'There's a rational explanation for these things,' he said when she had finished talking. 'There always is. And I just don't see how anything other than brain cells could store memory. I just don't. And that's on the strength of my school biology course. It's that basic.'

'But that's exactly the problem,' retorted Isabel. 'We're all stuck with the same tried and trusted ideas. If we refused to entertain the possibility of something radically different, then we'd never make any progress – ever. We'd still be thinking that the sun revolved round the earth.'

Jamie affected surprise. 'Isabel, don't start challenging *that* now!'

Isabel accepted his scepticism good-naturedly. 'I should point out that I'm completely agnostic on all this,' she said. 'All I'm doing is trying to keep an open mind.'

'And where does this take you?' asked Jamie. 'So what if the cells in the transplanted heart or whatever think they remember a face. So what?'

Isabel looked about her, for no reason other than that she felt a slight twinge of fear. That was in itself irrational, but she felt it.

'The face that he remembers could be the face of the driver who killed the donor,' she said. 'It could have been imprinted in memory – whatever sort of memory – after he had been knocked down and the driver came and looked down at him.'

Jamie's lip curled. 'Really, Isabel!'

'Yes,' she said quickly. 'Really. And if it is the face of the driver, then we may have a description of the person responsible for the death.'

Jamie thought for a moment. It was now obvious to him what Isabel had been doing in the library. 'You've found a report of the accident?' he asked. 'You know who the donor was?'

'I think so,' said Isabel. 'We know that the donor was a young man. That's as much as Ian knows. So I put two and two together and concluded that a sudden, violent death on the day on which they called Ian in for his transplant would probably supply the identity of the donor. And it has. There's nothing brilliant in that. It's all pretty obvious.'

But was it? It crossed her mind that she was assuming too much, and too readily. There might have been other incidents, other young men who could have been donors, but no, Edinburgh was not a very large place. It would be unlikely that two young men had died a sudden death that night. Her assumption, she decided, was reasonable.

Rather against his better judgement, Jamie felt himself being drawn in. He could not resist Isabel, he had decided. There was something about her that fascinated him: the intellectual curiosity, the style, the verve. And she was an attractive woman too. If she had been a bit younger – quite a bit younger – then he could have imagined that she would have been every bit as exciting as Cat. Damn Cat!

'So?' he said. 'So who is he? And what do we do?'

We do, he thought. I should have said *you* do, but once again, I've played straight into Isabel's hands. I'm trapped. In nets of golden wires.

Isabel was oblivious of Jamie's struggle with himself. She had invited him to meet her to discuss what she had found out; she had not asked him to join her in her inquiry. Of course, if he wished to do so, then that would be very help-ful; but she had not asked him.

'Well,' she began, 'we now know who that unfortunate young man was and where he lived. We know that the police appealed for information.'

'And that's it,' said Jamie. 'We . . . you don't know whether they ever found the driver.'

Isabel conceded that this remained unknown. But now, at least, they had a description of the person who might have been responsible.

'But what do you do with that?' asked Jamie. 'Go to the police? What would you tell them? That somebody else is having visions of a face and here's a drawing?' He laughed. 'You can imagine the reception you'd get.'

Isabel thought about this. She had not imagined going to the police – just yet. Jamie was right in thinking that it would be difficult to convince them to take her seriously and that they would be unlikely to pursue the matter further; unless, of course, the push came from the family of the victim. If they could be persuaded to do something about it, then the police could hardly refuse a request from them at least to consider Ian's story.

Her thoughts were interrupted by Jamie. 'Why are you doing this, Isabel?' he asked mildly. 'What's the point?'

She looked at him. It was her duty, was it not? If this was really information about who was responsible for the hit-and-run incident, then surely she had a duty to do something about it – any citizen would have that duty simply because he or she was a citizen. And there was more to it than that. By listening to Ian's story, she felt that she had been drawn into a moral relationship with him and his situation. Isabel had firm views on moral proximity and the obligations it created. We cannot choose the situations in which we become involved in this life; we are caught up in them whether we like it or not. If one encounters the need of another, because of who one happens to be, or where one happens to find oneself, and one is in a position to help, then one should do so. It was as simple as that.

She shrugged. 'The point is that I have to do this,' she said. 'I can't walk away from it. That driver needs to be called to account. And Ian needs to know why he's seeing that face. In each case, the solution lies in the uncovering of the truth.'

Jamie looked at his watch. He had another pupil – this time one who came to his flat in Saxe-Coburg Street on the other side of town, and he would have to leave. But he still wanted to find out what the next step was. Isabel may have been incorrigible in his view – and she was – but he still found everything that she did very interesting.

'What now?'

'I go and see the family,' said Isabel.

'And tell them that you know who might have been responsible for their son's death?'

'Probably,' said Isabel. 'Although I shall have to be careful about that. One never knows.'

'I've said it before,' warned Jamie. 'Just be careful. You can't go charging into people's grief, you know.'

Jamie said that and then stood up. He had not intended to offend Isabel, but he had. She looked down at the table, which was of darkened pine board, with no cloth. It had been a refectory table somewhere, in a school perhaps, and was worn with age. She stared at it.

Jamie reached out and put a hand on her shoulder, lightly. 'I'm sorry,' he said. 'I didn't mean it to come out like that.'

She said nothing. Jamie had made her sound like one of those people who intruded on the sorrow of others; those reporters from the gutter press who hounded the bereaved so that they could get a story or a photograph. It was not like that with her. She did not want to see these people out of curiosity; she did not want to see them at all. Did Jamie not understand that she was acting out of duty? That there were times when you just had to do that? The easiest thing to do would be to forget all about this; to tell Ian that she had been interested in his story but that she could do nothing about these visions of his. But that would be to ignore the fact that the family of the young man who had been killed might have a very strong desire to find out who was responsible for the incident. What might they say to her if they knew that she knew something and had not brought it to their attention?

Jamie sat down again. 'Look,' he said. 'I have to go. And I'm sorry that I said that. I'll phone you soon. And I'll help you do whatever it is that you want to do. Is that all right?'

'Yes. But you don't have to.'

'I know I don't, Isabel. But you seem . . . Well, let's just leave it. We're friends, aren't we? You help your friends. That's just the way it is. Sometimes I wish you were . . . a bit different, but you aren't.' He stood up again, picking up his bassoon case as he did. 'And I actually rather like you the way you are, you know?'

Isabel looked up at him. 'Thank you,' she said. 'You've been a very good friend to me.'

He left, turning round and waving to her as he went out of the front door. She returned his wave and then, after treating herself to a Danish pastry and a quick cup of coffee, she left too. Outside, at the end of George IV Bridge, where the road sloped down to the Grassmarket, a small group of tourists stood about the statue of the small Scottish terrier, Greyfriars Bobby. Isabel walked past them slowly and heard the guide intone: 'This statue commemorates the loyalty of a dog who sat by his master's grave in the Greyfriars Kirkyard for fourteen years. He never left his post.'

She saw the expression on the face of one of the members of the group as he heard this. She saw him lean forward, shaking his head in disbelief. But such loyalty did exist, and not just amongst dogs. People stuck by others for years and years, in the face of all the odds, and it should be relief, not disbelief, that one felt on witnessing it. Jamie was loyal, she thought. There he was remaining devoted to Cat, even when there was no hope. It was touching, in a way – rather like the story of Greyfriars Bobby. Perhaps there should be a statue of Jamie somewhere in Bruntsfield. *This young man stood outside his former girlfriend's delicatessen for fourteen years*, the inscription might state. Isabel smiled at the ridiculous idea. One should not smile about such things, she thought, but what was the alternative? To be miserable?

13

She had not intended to visit the house in Nile Grove until a few days later, but after an evening of thinking about it, she decided that she would go the next morning. It would be difficult to explain over the phone what she had in mind. That would be difficult enough to do face-to-face, but still easier, she thought.

Nile Grove was a Victorian terrace, built in honey-coloured stone that had turned light grey with the passage of time. It was an attractive street, a number of the houses having ornamentation on their façades. Small, well-kept gardens separated the fronts of the houses from the street, and on many of the houses creepers, ivy or clematis, climbed up beside the high sash windows. It was an expensive street; a quiet place to live; a street untroubled by commerce or passers-by. It was not, thought Isabel, a street through which one would imagine a reckless motorist careering; nor one which would host the tragedy of Rory Macleod's death.

Isabel found the house and opened the small painted iron-work gate that led to the front path. A few moments later she was standing outside the front door. There was a bell pull – one of the old-fashioned ones – connected to a wire that caused a tinkling sound somewhere deep inside the house, just audible from without. Isabel pulled this and then waited. She had no idea if anybody was in, and after a minute or so she felt inclined to walk back up the path and give up – with some relief – the idea of seeing the Macleod family. But then the door was suddenly opened and a woman stood before her.

Isabel looked at the woman. This was the Rose Macleod who had been mentioned in the *Evening News*. She was a bit older than Isabel – perhaps very late forties – and was wearing a rather shapeless shift in light blue. The face was an alert, intelligent one, a face that was immediately striking and which once would have been described as beautiful. While much of the beauty, in the conventional sense, might have been lost, there remained a quality of peacefulness and calm. This was the face of a musician, perhaps; a violinist, Isabel guessed.

'Yes? What can I do for you?' Rose Macleod's voice was very much as Isabel had imagined it would be: quiet, with the slight burr of south Edinburgh.

'Mrs Macleod?' Isabel asked.

Rose Macleod nodded, and smiled uncertainly at her visitor.

'My name is Isabel Dalhousie,' said Isabel. 'I live round the corner – or farther down, actually. In Merchiston.' She paused. 'I suppose I'm a sort of neighbour.'

Rose Macleod smiled. 'I see.' She hesitated for a moment. Then, 'Would you care to come in?'

Isabel followed her into the hall and through a door that led into a downstairs living room. It was a comfortable room, on the street side of the house, with bookshelves up one wall. It was typical, Isabel thought, of the rooms one would find in any of the houses along Nile Grove: a room which spoke to the solid, educated taste of the neighbourhood. Above the ornate Edwardian fireplace, with its *fin de siècle* painted tiles, was a painting of a young man's face in the style of Stephen Mangan – flat, almost one-dimensional, slightly haunting. A pair of Chinese bowls, *famille rose*, stood on the mantelpiece.

Isabel was pleased that Rose Macleod had invited her in. It seemed trusting, these days, to ask a stranger in, but it was still done in Edinburgh, or parts of Edinburgh at least. She took a seat on a small tub chair near the fireplace.

'I'm sorry to descend on you like this,' Isabel began. 'We haven't met, of course, but I know about . . . about your son. I'm so sorry.'

Rose inclined her head slightly. 'Thank you. That was some months ago, as you know, but . . . but it still seems very recent.'

'Do you have other children?' asked Isabel.

Rose nodded. 'We had three sons. Rory was the oldest. The other two are away at university. One in Glasgow. One in Aberdeen. Both studying engineering.' She paused, appraising Isabel with piercing blue eyes. 'I lost my husband some years ago. He was an engineer too.'

There was silence. Isabel had clasped her hands together and felt the bony outline of her knuckles. Rose looked at her expectantly.

'The reason why I came to see you,' Isabel began, 'is to do with the accident. I was wondering whether the police had made any progress. I saw something in the *Evening News* – something in which they called for witnesses. Did anybody turn up?'

Rose looked away. 'No,' she said. 'Not a squeak. Nothing. The police have said now that although the case remains technically open, it's very unlikely that they will get anything further to go on.' She reached out and took a coaster from a table beside her chair and fiddled with it. 'What they're effectively saying is that we shouldn't expect them ever to come up with an answer as to what happened. That's more or less it.'

'That must be difficult for you,' said Isabel. 'Not knowing.'

Rose put the coaster down on the table. 'Of course it is. It leaves things up in the air – unresolved.' She paused and looked at Isabel again. 'But, may I ask, why have you come to see me about this? Do you know something, Mrs . . . Mrs Dalhousie?'

'Miss,' said Isabel. 'No, I don't know anything definite, I'm afraid, but I might have some information which could have a bearing on the incident. It's just possible.'

The effect of this on Rose was immediate. Suddenly she was tense, and she leant forward in her chair. 'Please tell me what it is,' she said quietly. 'Even if you think that it's unimportant. Please tell me.'

Isabel was about to begin. She had worked out what she

was going to say, which would effectively be the story of her meeting with Ian and the story that he had told her. She was not going to say much about the other case – the case which Ian had told her about – but would be prepared to say something about that if Rose appeared unduly sceptical.

She started to speak. 'I met a man completely by chance . . .'

Outside the room there was the sound of a door opening. Rose raised a hand to stop Isabel.

'Graeme,' she said. 'My partner. Could you hold on a moment? I'd like him to hear what you have to say.'

She rose from the chair and opened the living-room door, which she had closed behind her when they had entered the room. Isabel heard her say something to somebody outside and then a man entered. He was a tall man, about the same age as Rose. Isabel looked at him. She saw the high brow, with the scar, and the eyes, which were hooded, markedly so. And she knew, immediately and with utter certainty, that this was the man whose face had appeared to Ian.

She took the hand which was proffered to her and shook it. The act of introduction, the formality of the handshake, at least gave her some time to think, and her mind raced through the possibilities. She could hardly go ahead and say what she had proposed saying now that Graeme had come in. She could hardly sit there and give a description of the man on the other side of the room. Nor could she suddenly claim that she had forgotten what she was going to say.

For some inexplicable reason, Grace came to her mind, and Isabel knew what she would say. As Rose explained to Graeme that Isabel had come with some information, she

135

refined her story. She would keep Ian out of this now, and would claim the vision herself.

'I know you'll think this rather ridiculous,' she said. 'People often do. I'm a medium, you see.'

She saw Graeme glance at Rose. He does think it's ridiculous, thought Isabel. Good. But Rose declined his look of complicity. 'I don't think that,' she said softly. 'The police have often used mediums. I've read about it. They can be quite useful.'

Graeme pursed his lips. He clearly did not think so. But was he anxious? Isabel wondered. If he was the hit-and-run driver, would he be anxious about some eccentric medium coming up with something which might just throw suspicion upon him? And why, she asked, would he have left Rory in the street if he had knocked him down inadvertently? The answer occurred to her immediately. If he had been driving under the influence of alcohol at the time, then running somebody over could lead to a ten-year jail sentence. Everybody knew that. Of course one would panic in such circumstances.

'Please tell us,' Rose said imploringly. 'Please tell us what you've seen.'

Isabel studied her hands. 'I saw a man driving a car down a road,' she said. 'And then I saw a young man walk out in front of the car and get knocked down. The man stopped the car and got out. I saw him bending over the young man. I saw that the man in the car was shortish, slightly chubby in fact, and had fair hair. That's what I saw.'

Isabel looked up from the study of her hands. She saw that Graeme, who had been standing when she began to talk, was

now sitting down. He seemed to have relaxed, and was looking at Rose with a smile on his lips.

'You don't believe me, Mr . . .'

'Forbes,' he supplied. 'No, please don't be offended. I just
don't see how these things can work. I'm sorry. No disre-
spect intended to your . . . your calling.'

'That's fair enough,' said Isabel, rising to her feet. 'I
wouldn't wish to impose my vision on those who do not
want to receive it. That's not the way we work. Please forgive me.'

Rose was quick to get to her feet too. She took a step
forward and reached out for Isabel's hand.

'I appreciate your having come to see us,' she said. 'I really
do. And I can pass on what you've said to the police. I promise you that.'

Isabel now wanted nothing more than to leave. Graeme's
arrival had disturbed her greatly, and the subterfuge to which
she had then resorted had hardly improved the situation.
It was a serious matter to deceive a bereaved mother in this
way, she felt, even if she had not had much alternative in the
circumstances.

'Please don't feel that you have to go right away,' said
Rose. 'I haven't offered you anything yet. What about a cup
of tea? Or coffee?'

'You're very kind,' said Isabel. 'But I've taken up enough
of your time already. I don't think I should have come in the
first place.'

'Of course you should have come,' Rose said quickly. 'I'm
glad you did, you know. I'm really glad you did.' She
stopped, and then, releasing Isabel's hand, she asked, through

137

tears, 'Did you see . . . did you see my son's face in this dream of yours? Did he come to you?'

Isabel took a deep breath. She had intervened in the life of this woman without being asked. And now she had compounded the potential harm by leading her to believe that she had seen her son. What had been intended as a quick response to an unexpected development – a story designed not to be taken seriously – had touched this woman in an unexpectedly profound way.

'I'm sorry,' she said. 'I didn't really see his face. He didn't speak to me. I'm sorry.'

Graeme had now got up from his chair and had placed a protective arm round Rose's shoulder. He glared at Isabel.

'Please leave this house,' he said, the anger rising in his voice. 'Please leave now.'

Isabel went that afternoon to Jamie's flat in Saxe-Coburg Street. She had returned home after her visit to the house in Nile Grove, but had been unable to settle. Grace had sensed that something was wrong, and had asked if she was all right. Isabel would have liked to have spoken to Grace, but could not. What prevented her was embarrassment over the ridiculous claim that she had made, the claim that she was a medium. She came out of that rather badly, she thought, even if it had been a lie dreamt up to deal with a totally unexpected situation. So she reassured Grace that nothing was amiss – another lie, although a very common one – and decided instead to see Jamie as soon as possible – that afternoon, in fact.

It was one of Jamie's afternoons for teaching in his flat.

Isabel knew that he did not like to be disturbed while teaching but this was an extraordinary situation that called for extraordinary action. So she crossed town on foot, walking down Dundas Street and stopping briefly at the galleries to pass the time before Jamie might be expected to be on his last pupil. There was nothing to interest her in the gallery windows, and nothing inside either; she was too uneasy to appreciate art.

On Henderson Row, groups of boys were coming out of the Edinburgh Academy, clad in their grey tweed blazers, engaged in the earnest conversation which boys seem to have in groups. In the distance, somewhere within the school buildings, the Academy Pipe Band was practising and she stopped for a moment to listen to the drifting sound of the bagpipes. 'Dark Island', she thought; like so many Scottish tunes a haunting melody, redolent of loss and separation. Scotland had produced such fine laments, such fine accounts of sorrow and longing, whereas Ireland had been so much jauntier . . .

She continued walking, the sound of the pipes gradually becoming fainter and fainter. Saxe-Coburg Street was just round the corner from the Academy; indeed the windows at the back of Jamie's flat gave a view down into the school's grounds and into the large skylights of the art department. One could stand there, if one wanted, and watch the senior boys painting in their life class, or the younger ones throwing clay, making the shapeless pots which would be taken back to admiring parents and consigned after a decent interval to a cupboard. She did not ring the bell at the bottom of the mutual stair, but walked up the several flights of stone stairway to Jamie's front door. She paused there and listened. There was silence, and then a murmur of voices and the sound of a scale being played on a bassoon, hesitantly at first and then with greater speed. She looked at her watch. She had thought he might be finished by now, but she had misjudged. She decided to knock anyway, loudly, so that Jamie might hear her in the back room that he used as his studio.

He came to the door, clutching a music manuscript book. 'Isabel!'

He was surprised to see her but not discouraging.

'I'm still teaching,' he said, his voice lowered. 'Come in and wait in the kitchen. I'll be another' – he took her wrist, gently, and glanced at her watch – 'another ten minutes. That's all.'

'I wouldn't have disturbed you,' she said as she entered the hall. 'It's just that . . .'

'Don't worry,' he said, pointing in the direction of his studio. 'Later.'

Isabel saw a boy in an Academy jacket sitting in a chair near the piano, holding a bassoon. The boy was craning his neck to see who had arrived. Isabel gave a wave and the boy, embarrassed, nodded his head. She went through to the kitchen and sat down at Jamie's pine table. There was a copy of *Woodwind* magazine on the tabletop and she paged her way idly through it. There was an article on contrabass instruments and the illustrations caught her eye. A man stood beside a contrabass saxophone, one hand supporting it, the other pointing to it in a triumphant gesture. It was as if he had captured a rare specimen, which the instrument appeared to be, according to the article. It had been made by a factory in Italy which was still prepared to make such large instruments, in return for – she was shocked by the price. But what a beautiful piece of construction with all its gleaming keys and rods and great leather hole pads, like inverted saucers.

Jamie stood in front of her, the boy by his side.

'That's a real stunner, isn't it?' he said to the boy.

Isabel looked up. The magazine was laid flat on the table and the boy was looking at the picture of the contrabass saxophone.

'Would you like one of those, John?' asked Jamie.

The boy smiled. 'How do you lift it?'

'They come with stands,' said Jamie. 'I know somebody who has an ordinary bass saxophone, which is slightly smaller. He has a stand for it. A stand with wheels.' He paused. 'This is Isabel Dalhousie, John. Isabel is a friend of mine. She's quite a good pianist, you know, although she's too modest to say much about that.'

Isabel rose to her feet and shook the boy's hand. He was at the easily embarrassed stage and he blushed. It must be very hard, she thought, to be so in between; not a man yet, but not a little boy either. Just something in between, and struggling with bassoon lessons.

The boy left, nodding politely to Isabel. Jamie saw him out of the front door and then returned to the kitchen.

'Well,' he said. 'That's the last adolescent for the day.'

'He seems nice enough,' said Isabel.

'I suppose he is,' said Jamie. 'But he's lazy. He doesn't practise. He says he does, but he doesn't.'

'Ambitious parents?' asked Isabel.

'Pushy mother,' said Jamie. 'Edinburgh is full of pushy

141

mothers. And most of them send their sons to learn bassoon with me.' He smiled. 'All my bills are paid by pushy mothers. I thrive on maternal push.'

He moved over to the end of the kitchen and filled a kettle with water.

'Something's happened, hasn't it?' He looked at her, almost dolefully. 'Come on. Tell me.'

Jamie was good at detecting Isabel's moods; he could read her, she had always thought that. And it was a slightly alarming thought, because if he could read her as well as she imagined he could, then would he have had some inkling of her feelings for him – those feelings, as she called them – which she had now got quite under control and which were not a problem any longer? She was not sure if she would want him to have known; we do not always wish for those for whom we long to know that we long for them, especially if the longing is impossible, or inappropriate. It was so easy, for instance, for a middle-aged man to fall for a young woman because of her beauty, or her litheness, or some such quality, and in most cases the response from the young woman would be one of horror, or rejection; to be loved by the unlovable was not something that most people could cope with. And so feelings should be concealed, as she had concealed her feelings from Jamie – or so she hoped.

'I went to see them,' she said simply. 'I went to see those people. Rose Macleod. The mother.'

Jamie sat down at the table. He folded his arms. 'And?'

'I went to the house in Nile Grove,' Isabel said. 'I spoke to the mother, who invited me in. She was a rather nice woman. An interesting face.'

'And?'

'And I was just about to tell her about Ian's vision of the man with the high brow and the hooded eyes when somebody arrived.'

Jamie urged her to continue. He hasn't guessed yet, thought Isabel.

'It was her partner, her bidie-in,' she went on. 'He came into the room and I looked up and saw that he was the man whom Ian had seen. Yes. A high brow and hooded eyes. Scarred. Exactly the man I had imagined from Ian's description.'

For a moment Jamie said nothing. He unfolded his arms, and then he looked down at the table before lifting his gaze again to fix Isabel with a stare.

'Oh no,' he said quietly. And then, even more quietly, 'Isabel.'

'Yes,' said Isabel. 'I was stopped in my tracks, as you might imagine. So I made up some ridiculous story about being a medium and having seen the accident in my mind. It was terrible, melodramatic stuff. Ghastly. But I couldn't think of anything else to say.'

Jamie thought for a moment. 'That was quite clever of you,' he said. 'I'm not sure that I would have been so quick on my feet.'

'I felt pretty bad,' said Isabel. 'That poor woman. It's a pretty awful thing to do – to lie to somebody in her grief and claim to have seen the person she's lost.'

'You didn't set out to do that,' said Jamie. 'It's not as if you're some charlatan exploiting bereaved people. I wouldn't think any more about that.'

Isabel looked up. 'Really?'

'Yes,' said Jamie, rising to his feet to make the tea. 'Really. Your trouble, Isabel, is that you agonise too much. You worry about everything. You need to be a bit more robust. Lay off the guilt for a while.'

She made a helpless gesture. 'It's not that easy,' she said.

'Easier than you think,' said Jamie. 'Look at me. I don't worry about what I do all the time. You don't see me plagued by guilt.'

'That may be because you haven't done anything you feel guilty about,' countered Isabel. 'Tabula rasa – a blank leaf.'

'You'd be surprised,' said Jamie. He hesitated for a moment and then he said, 'I had an affair with a married woman. Remember that? You yourself took a dim view of it.'

'That was because—' Isabel stopped herself. She had already hinted that she was jealous of Jamie's company; she should not spell it out.

'And then I did something else,' said Jamie. 'A long time ago. When I was about sixteen.'

Isabel raised a hand. 'I don't want to hear about it, Jamie,' she said.

'All right. Let's get back to this visit of yours. What a mess.'

'Yes,' she said. 'What do I do now? If Ian's theory is correct, then the hit-and-run driver is the mother's partner. And I suppose it's a theory that isn't all that improbable. Let's imagine that he had been driving back from a party, or from the pub, and he's had too much to drink. He's almost home when Rory steps out from behind a parked car and he knocks him over. He's sober enough to realise that if the police are called – and they would of course turn up if an ambulance were summoned – he will be tested and found to be under the influence. Every driver these days knows that that means prison if you kill somebody in such a state – and a long sentence too. So he panics and drives round the corner or wherever it is that he parks. He checks the paint-work – no obvious marks. So then he goes home and pretends it never happened.'

Jamie listened carefully. 'That sounds perfectly credible,' he said once Isabel had finished. 'So what now?'

'I just don't know,' said Isabel. 'It's not very straightfor-ward, is it?'

Jamie shrugged. 'Isn't it? Let's say Ian's description means anything, then all you've done is find out in pretty quick time that the person the police should be questioning is this man the mother's living with. You just have to pass the infor-mation on to the police. And that will be that. You can drop out of it.'

Isabel did not agree. 'But what if he's innocent? What if Ian's story means nothing? Imagine the impact of my inter-vention on their marriage, or their relationship, or whatever it is they have.'

'It's one of your nice moral dilemmas, isn't it?' said Jamie, smiling. 'You write about them a lot in your editorials in that *Review* of yours, don't you? Well, here's one for you in real life. Very real life. I'm sorry, Isabel. You solve it. I'm a musician, not a philosopher.'

14

Sceptical me, thought Isabel. But one has to be, because if one were not sceptical about things like this, then one would end up believing all sorts of untenable things. The list of traps for the gullible was a long one, and seemed to grow by the day: remote healing, auras, spoon-bending, extrasensory perception. Of course there was telepathy, which seemed to be something of an exception to these New Age enthusiasms; it had been around for so long that it had almost become respectable. So many people claimed to have had telepathic experiences – level-headed, rational people too – that there might be something in it. And yet had not Edinburgh University's professor of para-psychology done exhaustive tests on telepathic communication and come up with – nothing? And if groups of volunteers, hundreds of them, could sit for hours in his laboratories and

try to guess what card somebody in the next room was looking at, and never get above the level of chance in their
replies, then how could people insist that it was anything
more than coincidence that they thought of somebody the
moment before that person telephoned? Chance; pure
chance. But chance was a dull explanation because it denied
the possibility of the paranormal, and people were often disappointed by dull explanations. Mystery and the unknown
were far more exciting because they suggested that our world
was not quite as prosaic as we feared it might bc. Yct we had
to abjure those temptations because they lead to a world of
darkness and fear.

And yet here I am, thought Isabel, walking through
Charlotte Square with Grace, bound for the spiritualist
meeting rooms on Queensferry Road. It was part of her
effort to be open-minded, she told herself; there had, after
all, been people in Europe who had laughed at the idea of
America before America was discovered by Europe. And
there werc people in Europe who still laughed at the idea of
America; people who condescended to the New World.
This infuriated her, because of the ignorance that lay behind
such attitudes – on both sides. There were people in New
York, or, more to the point, in places like Houston, who
thought Europe – and the rest of the world – quaint and
unsanitary. And there were people in places like Paris who
thought all Americans were geographically challenged xeno-
phobes. Such narrow prejudices.

Mind you, there were at least some people in Houston
who would probably find it difficult to locate Paris, or anywhere else for that matter, on a map, and who might be less

than well informed about the concerns of French culture. That was indeed possible. She glanced at Grace as they walked round the south side of the square. Grace had left school at seventeen. But she had had, before that, the benefit of a traditional Scottish education, with its emphasis on learning grammar and mathematics, and geography. Would she know where Houston was? It would be interesting to know just what degree of Houston-awareness there was amongst people in general, and where Grace fitted into that. But could she ask her, directly? That would sound rude: one did not say to somebody out of the blue, Where's Houston? (Unless, of course, one was actively looking for it at the time.)

These were her thoughts when a heavily built man in a lightweight jacket, accompanied by a woman in a beige trouser suit, stepped up to them. The man extracted a folded map from the pocket of his jacket. Isabel noticed the fairness of his skin and the sun spots on the brow below the hairline.

'Excuse me?' he said. 'We're looking for the National Gallery and I think . . .'

Isabel smiled at him. 'You're not far away,' she said. 'You can reach it if you walk along Princes Street, which is just down there.'

She took the map from him and showed him where they were. Then she looked up. She had an ear for accents. 'Texas?' she asked. 'Louisiana?'

His smile was warm. 'Houston,' he said.

Isabel returned the map to him and wished them a successful trip. She and Grace began to cross the road.

'Houston, Grace,' said Isabel conversationally.

'I've never been there,' said Grace. 'I went to Detroit once to see an aunt of mine who went to live out there.'

Isabel could not resist the temptation. 'Some distance apart, aren't they?' she said. 'Such a big country. Houston and Detroit.'

'Depends on how you travel,' said Grace.

Isabel did not give up. 'I sometimes get Houston mixed up,' she said. 'All these places. I get a bit confused.'

'Look at a map,' replied Grace helpfully. 'It'll show you where Houston is.'

Isabel was silent as they walked down the narrow lane that led past West Register House to Queensferry Road. It had been an extraordinary coincidence that she should have thought of Houston, of all places, at precisely the moment that the visitor from Houston was about to ask directions. And it was unnerving, too, that this had all taken place in the context of thoughts about telepathy, and, to add to the strangeness of the situation, while she was on her way, as Grace's guest, to a séance at the spiritualist meeting rooms, where they would presumably love to hear about such a thing.

They reached Queensferry Road and Grace pointed to a building on the corner. 'That's the place,' she said. 'On the third floor there.'

Isabel looked at the building on the corner of the road. It formed the end of an elegant terrace of grey stone, classical and restrained as all buildings were in the great sweep of the Georgian New Town. On the ground floor there were shop windows: a jeweller, with a display of silver, and a newsagent displaying the *Scotsman*'s blue thistle motif. It could have been any office building; nothing indicated that it was anything different.

They crossed Queensferry Road and entered through the blue door. A stone staircase led from a small entrance hall up to the floors above. The stairs themselves were worn, indented where feet had trodden on the stone for over two hundred years, gradually wearing it down.

'We're at the top,' said Grace. 'We've had trouble with this building, by the way. Lead pipes – everything had to be replaced.'

Isabel sympathised. It was all very well living in an aged city, but the pleasure came with a large bill attached to it in the form of maintenance costs. And even the spiritualists would have to bear the burden of those; no help could come from the other side.

They made their way up to the top of the stairs. As they ascended, a man came down, a man in a brown felt hat. He nodded to Grace as he passed them on the stairs and she returned the greeting.

'He lived all his life with his mother,' Grace whispered, once the man was out of earshot. 'She crossed over a few months ago and now he's trying to get information from her about some bank accounts. He doesn't know where the bank accounts were kept.' She shook her head. 'That's not what this is meant to be about. We're not meant to get that sort of information. People on the other side are above all that. They give us messages about how to live our lives – useful things like that.'

Isabel was about to say that she thought that it would be very useful to know where bank accounts were, but stopped herself. She said instead, 'He must be lonely.'

'He is,' said Grace.

They came to an open door on the top landing and went into the hall beyond. It had been an ordinary flat, Isabel thought – a house with the ordinary family rooms, not built as a place of pilgrimage or seeking, but now just that to the handful of people she could see seated in the meeting room beyond.

Grace pointed through another doorway which gave off the hall. 'The library,' she said. 'One of the best collections of books on the subject in the whole country.'

Isabel glanced at the wall of books. These were books about those things that could not be seen or touched, but in that respect they were probably no different from books about pure mathematics. She made an appreciative but non-committal sound.

Grace now led the way into the meeting room, a large room with, at one end, a fireplace in front of which a platform and podium stood. Beside the podium was an easy chair and a table with an arrangement of flowers. A rather angular-looking woman, of about Isabel's age, was sitting in the easy chair, her hands resting on her lap. She was gazing up at the ceiling, although as Grace and Isabel entered, her glance rested briefly, appraisingly, upon them. In the body of the room, rows of chairs had been set out in ranks. Grace pointed to seats near the back.

'The best place to see what's going on,' she said.

Once seated, Isabel looked about her, discreetly. There was always a certain awkwardness, she felt, in the witnessing of the religious – or spiritual – rituals of others. It was rather like being an outsider at a family party, a Protestant in St

Peter's Basilica, a Gentile at the Wailing Wall. One might sense the mystery, and understand its value for others, but one could not share it. Each of us is born into our own mysteries, thought Isabel, gazing at the flowers and then at the impassive face of the medium, but the mystery of another might just take us in and embrace us. And then what a sense of homecoming, of belonging!

A man entered the room and took a seat immediately behind them. He leant forward and whispered something to Grace, who smiled and said something in reply that Isabel did not hear. Isabel noticed his coat, which he had not taken off and which was an expensive one. She saw his regular profile and his head of thick hair. He looked to all intents and purposes like . . . like what? she wondered. An accountant or bank manager? Somebody with a certain assurance about him.

She noticed that the medium had transferred her gaze from the ceiling and was looking at the man seated behind them. It was not a stare, but a gaze which moved on to somebody else, and then came back to him.

A man in a dark suit walked up the aisle between the rows of chairs and mounted the platform. He nodded to the medium and turned to face the thirty or so people who were now seated in the room. 'My friends,' he began, 'you are welcome. Whether you are a stranger or a member of this body, you are welcome.' Isabel listened closely. The accent was Hebridean, she thought; a lilting voice from the islands. She noticed his suit, which was one of those black ill-fitting suits that Scottish crofters wore on Sundays, and she remembered, suddenly, how once as a young woman she had been on the island of Skye – was it with John Liamor? yes, it was – and they had driven past a croft house, low and white-painted, surrounded by fields and with a line of hills in the distance, and had seen a suit like that, freshly washed, hanging out to dry on the clothesline before the house. And the wind had been in the arms and legs of the suit and had given it life.

A few announcements were made and then the man introduced the medium. He did not give a surname; she was just Anna. And then he stepped down from the podium and sat down in the front row.

The medium stood up. She looked at the people in the room and smiled. Her hands were clasped loosely in front of her, and now she opened them in a gesture of supplication. She closed her eyes, her head lifted up. 'Let us each dwell on our thoughts,' she said. 'Let us open our hearts to the world of spirit.'

They sat in silence for ten minutes, or more. Eventually the medium spoke again.

'I have somebody here,' she said, so quietly that Isabel had to strain to hear the words. 'I have somebody here. There is a child coming through.'

Isabel saw a woman in front of her stiffen, and she knew from this the nature of her loss. Such pain.

The medium opened her eyes. 'Yes, there is a child coming through and she is saying something to me . . .'

The woman in the row in front leant forward and the medium's gaze fell upon her.

'It is you, my dear, isn't it?' said the medium. 'It is for you, isn't it?'

The woman nodded silently. Another woman seated near her reached out and touched her gently on the shoulder.

The medium took a step forward. 'My dear, there is a little girl who says that she is with you and watching over you. She says that her love will always be with you and around you . . . around you every moment until you join her. She says you are to be brave. Yes, that's what she says. She says that you are to be brave. Which you are, she says. She says that you have always been brave.'

'It's a little boy she lost,' whispered Grace. 'But sometimes they can't see very well into the other side. It's easy to get little boys and little girls mixed up.'

'Now,' said the medium, 'I pass to another person in spirit who is coming to me. Yes, this person is saying very clearly to me that there is somebody in this room who has not forgiven him for what he did. That is what he is saying. This person says that he is very sorry for what he did and begs this other person on this side to forgive him. It is not too late to forgive, even now.'

She looked out over the rows of seats. A woman at the end of the second row had risen to her feet. 'This message might be for me,' she said, her voice uneven. 'I think that it might be for me.'

The medium turned to face her. 'I think it is, my dear. Yes, I think it is for you.' She paused. 'And do you have that forgiveness in your heart? Can I tell this person in spirit that he has your forgiveness? Can I tell him that?'

The woman who had been standing up suddenly sank back into her seat. She put her hands up to her face and covered her eyes. She was sobbing. A woman behind her reached forward to comfort her.

The medium said nothing. When the woman's sobbing had subsided, she sat down again and looked up at the ceiling, and did so for a good fifteen minutes. She rose to her feet and looked about the room, her gaze alighting on the man behind Grace.

'I have somebody coming through for you,' she said. 'I have somebody here. Yes. This is your wife. She is here. She is with me. She is with you. Can you sense her presence?'

Isabel did not like to turn and stare, but did so anyway, discreetly. The man's eyes were fixed on the medium; he was listening intently. In response to her question he nodded.

'Good,' said the medium. 'She is coming through very strongly now. She says that she is still with you. She . . .' The medium hesitated, and frowned. 'She is concerned for you. She is concerned that there is one who is trying to get to know you better. She is concerned that this person is not the right person for you. That is what she says.'

The relaying of this message had its effect on the room, and there were whispers. One or two people turned round and looked in the direction of the man to whom it was directed. Others looked firmly ahead at the medium. Isabel glanced at Grace, who was looking down at the floor and who seemed hunched up, as if hoping for the moment of embarrassment around her to pass.

There was little more after that. The world of spirit, momentarily goaded into action by the medium, must have been exhausted, and after a few minutes the medium declared that she had finished her communication with the

155

other side. Now it was time for tea, and they all withdrew to a cheerfully furnished room next to the library. There were plates of biscuits and cups of strong, warm tea.

'Very interesting,' whispered Isabel. 'Thank you, Grace.'

Grace nodded. She seemed preoccupied, though, and did not say anything as she helped Isabel to a cup of tea and a biscuit. Isabel looked about her. She saw the medium standing at the side of the room. She was sipping at a cup of tea and talking to the man who had introduced her, the man in the black suit. But as she talked, Isabel saw her eyes move about the room, as if seeking somebody out. And they fixed on the man who had been seated behind her, the man who had received the message from his wife. Isabel looked at the medium's expression, and at her eyes in particular. It was very clear to her, as it would be clear, she thought, to any woman. She had seen enough.

15

'What's it like?' Ian asked. 'I know it may sound like a rather simple question, naïve perhaps, but what's it like – being a philosopher?'

Isabel looked out of the window. It was mid-morning and they were sitting in her study, the tang of freshly brewed coffee in the air. Outside, on the corners of her lawn, the weeds had begun to make their presence increasingly obvious. She needed several hours, she thought, several hours which she would never find, for digging and raking. *One must cultivate one's garden*, said Voltaire; and there, he said, is happiness to be found rather than in philosophising. She thought for a moment of the juxtaposition of philosophy and the everyday: zen and the art of motorcycle maintenance had been an inspired combination for its moment, but there might be others, as novel and surprising. 'Voltaire and the control of weeds,' she muttered.

'Voltaire and . . . ?' asked Ian.

'Just musing,' said Isabel. 'But in answer to your question: It's much the same as being anything else. You carry your profession with you, I suppose, in much the same way as a doctor or, I should imagine, a psychologist does. You see the world in a particular way, don't you? As a psychologist?'

Ian followed her gaze out into the garden. 'To an extent,' he said, but sounded doubtful. 'Being a philosopher, though, must be rather different from being anything else. You must *think* about everything. You must spend your time pondering over what things mean. A somewhat higher realm than the rest of us inhabit.'

Isabel drew herself away from the lawn. She had been thinking about weeds. But weeds, and what to do about them, were very much a part of everyday life, and everyday life was exactly what philosophy was about. We were rooted in it, inevitably, and how we reacted to it – our customs, our observances – was the very stuff of moral philosophy. Hume had called them, these little conventions, *a kind of lesser morality*, and in her view he had been right.

'It's much more mundane and everyday than you would imagine,' she began. And then she stopped. One could easily simplify too much and discussions about social convention could give him the wrong idea. How you drank your coffee was *not* what it was about, but the fact that you drank coffee *together* was of tremendous significance. But she could not say that, because that statement could be made only after a great deal of earlier ground had been covered and understood.

158

Ian nodded. 'I see. Well, that's a little bit disappointing. I imagined that you spent all your time pacing about trying to work out the nature of reality – wondering whether the world outside is real enough to take a walk in. That sort of thing.'

Isabel laughed. 'Sorry to disabuse you of such amusing notions. No. But I must admit that my calling – if I can call it that – sometimes makes life a little difficult for me.'

This interested him. 'In what way?'

'Well, it's mostly a question of duty,' Isabel said. She sighed, thinking of her demons; moral obligation was the real problem. This was the cross she bore, the rack on which she was obliged to lie – even the metaphors were uncomfortable.

'I find myself thinking very carefully about what I should do in any given situation,' she went on. 'And it can get a little bit burdensome for me. In fact, sometimes I feel rather like those unfortunate people with OCD – you know, obsessive-compulsive disorder; of course you know that, you're a clinical psychologist – but I sometimes think I'm like those people who have to check ten times that they've turned the oven off or who have to wash their hands again and again to get rid of germs. I think I can understand how they feel.'

'Now you're on familiar ground,' he said. 'I had quite a few patients with OCD. One woman I knew had a thing about doorhandles. She had to cover the doorhandle with a handkerchief before she could open it. Tricky, sometimes. And public washrooms were a real agony for her. She had to use her foot to flush. She lifted a foot and pushed the lever down by stepping on it.'

Isabel thought for a moment. 'Very wise,' she said with a smile. 'Imagine what results you'd get if you took a swab from one of those handles and cultured it. Imagine.'

'Maybe,' said Ian. 'But we need to be exposed to germs, don't we? All this hygiene and refined foods – what's the result? Allergies galore. Everyone will eventually have asthma.' He paused. 'But back to philosophy. Those papers over there – are they submissions for that journal of yours?'

Isabel glanced at the pile of manuscripts and suppressed a shudder. Guilt, she thought, can sometimes be measured in physical quantities. A heavy drinker might measure his guilt in gallons or litres; a glutton in inches round the waist; and the editor of a journal in terms of the height of the stack of manuscripts awaiting her attention. This was almost eighteen inches of guilt.

'I should be reading those,' she said. 'And I will. But, as Saint Augustine said about chastity, not just yet.'

'You don't want to read them?' Ian asked.

'I do and I don't,' said Isabel. 'I don't want to read them in one sense, but in another sense I want to read them and get them finished.' She looked again at the pile. 'Most of those are for a special issue we're bringing out. It's on friendship.'

Ian looked puzzled. 'What has philosophy got to do with that?' he asked.

'A great deal,' Isabel replied. 'It's one of the great topics. What is the nature of friendship? How are we to treat our friends? Can we prefer our friends to others who are not our friends?'

'Of course we can,' said Ian. 'Isn't that why they're our friends in the first place?'

Isabel shook her head. She arose from her chair and went to stand by the window, looking out on the lawn, but averting her gaze from the weeds. Weeds had a closer relationship with guilt than did grass.

'There are some philosophers who say that we shouldn't do that at all,' she said. 'They say that we have a moral duty to treat others equally. We shouldn't discriminate among people who need our help. We should allocate such help as we can give absolutely even-handedly.'

'But that's inhuman!' Ian protested.

'I think so,' said Isabel. 'But it's not all that easy to make a sound case for preferring the claims of your friends. I think one can do it, but you're up against some powerful counter-arguments.'

'Do philosophers tend to have many friends?' asked Ian. 'If that's the way they think . . .'

'It depends on the extent to which they possess the virtues that make friendship thrive,' Isabel answered. 'A virtuous person will have friends in the true sense. A person whose character is afflicted with vices won't.'

She turned away from the window and faced Ian. 'We can return to this topic, if you like, Ian, but I'm afraid this is not why I invited you for coffee today. It's something else altogether—'

'I can guess,' he interrupted. 'You've been thinking about what I said to you.'

'Yes. I have. And I've been acting on it, too.'

He looked at her anxiously. 'I hadn't intended to draw you in,' he began. 'I didn't imagine that—'

'Of course you didn't,' she interjected. 'But you may recall that I said something about obligation earlier on. One of the consequences of being a philosopher is that you get involved. You ask yourself whether you need to do something and so often the answer comes up yes, you do.' She paused for a moment. It occurred to her that she should be careful not to make Ian feel stressed. Presumably he had to avoid stress, and shock, too. 'I've traced the family of your donor. It wasn't hard. You could have done it, if you thought about it.'

'I didn't have the courage,' he said. 'I wanted to thank them but . . .'

'And I've found your man,' Isabel continued. 'The man with the high forehead and the hooded eyes. I've found him for you.'

He was silent; sitting there in his chair, staring at Isabel, completely taken aback, quite silent. Eventually he cleared his throat. 'Well, I'm not sure if I was looking forward to that. But I suppose . . . Well, I suppose that if I don't do something about this, I'm not really going to give myself much of a chance, am I? I told you earlier on that I thought this thing would kill me – this sadness, this dread, whatever we call it. I think it'll prevent the new heart from . . . from taking, so to speak.' He looked at her, and she saw the anguish in his eyes. 'Maybe it's best to know,' he said. 'Do you think so?'

'Maybe,' said Isabel. 'But remember, there are some things which we would probably prefer not to know once we've found them out. This may be one of them.'

He looked confused. 'I don't see how—'

Isabel raised a hand to stop him. 'You see, the difficulty is that this man – the man who looks so like the man of your . . . your imaginings – lives with the mother of the young man who was the donor.'

He frowned slightly, taking in the information. 'How did he die?' he asked. 'Did you find out?'

'A hit-and-run accident,' she said. 'Still unsolved. It was very close to the house. He was knocked over and he died shortly thereafter in hospital. He was unconscious when they found him, which meant that he was unable to say anything about what happened. But . . .'

'But,' he said, 'but he could have been conscious immediately after being knocked over, and the driver could have bent over him and looked at him?'

'Exactly,' said Isabel.

For a few minutes nothing further was said by either of them. Isabel turned away again and looked out into the garden, oblivious now of the weeds, thinking only of the dilemma which she had created for herself and from which there seemed no easy, painless escape. Unless she handed it over to Ian, though he had done nothing to bring the situation about in the first place – other than to tell her about what had happened.

Ian's voice broke the silence. 'Does she know?' he asked.

'Know what?' Isabel had not told him that she had been unable to speak about his vision. 'I didn't tell her about you,' she said. 'I couldn't. He was there.'

'No,' said Ian. 'That's not what I meant. What I meant was, does the mother of the donor know that this man could have been the hit-and-run driver?'

The question surprised Isabel. She had not thought about that, but it was an obvious possibility. She had assumed that she did not, but what if she did? That put a very different complexion on the matter.

'If she knows, then she'd be sheltering the person who killed her son,' she said. 'Would any mother do that, do you think?'

Ian thought for a moment before giving his answer. 'Yes,' he said. 'Many would. These domestic killings that occur from time to time – the woman often shelters the man. A violent partner harms one of the children. The woman stays silent. Perhaps out of fear, perhaps out of helplessness. Perhaps out of misplaced loyalty. It's not uncommon.'

Isabel thought back to her conversation with Rose Macleod. She remembered her expression of eagerness when Isabel had revealed that she might have some information on the incident. That had not been feigned, she thought. Nor was she mistaken about the man's anxiety, shown in the tension of his body language when she had broached the subject – a tension which had visibly dissipated when she had come up with a description of the driver which so clearly excluded him.

'I'm sure that she doesn't know,' she said. 'I really think she doesn't.'

'Very well,' Ian said. 'She doesn't know. Now what?'

Isabel laughed. 'Precisely. Now what?'

'We can go to the police,' Ian said quietly. 'We can just hand the thing over.'

'Which will lead to nothing happening,' said Isabel. 'The police aren't going to go and accuse him of being the driver on the basis of what they will probably call a dream.'

She saw that he agreed with this, and she continued, 'So

the issue now is whether we have a duty to go and inform that woman that the man with whom she lives was possibly the hit-and-run driver who killed her son. Just possibly, note. The whole argument is based, after all, on the pretty shaky premise that your vision has anything to do with anything. A very shaky premise.

'But let's say that we believe it may be relevant information. Let's say that the mother takes the same view and believes it, even if it can't be proved. What we will have succeeded in doing then will be to have introduced an awful, corrosive doubt into her life. We might effectively destroy her relationship with that man. And so she will have lost not only her son, but her man as well.'

When Ian spoke, his tone was resigned. He sounded tired. 'In which case we keep quiet.'

'We can't,' said Isabel. She did not explain why she said this, as she had noticed Ian's weariness and she was concerned not to tire him. It was to do with formal justice, and the duty that one has to the community at large not to allow people like drunken drivers – if he had been drunk – to go unpunished if they cause death on the road. That was profoundly important, and outweighed any consideration of the emotional happiness of one unfortunate woman. It was a hard decision, but one which Isabel now seemed to be seeing her way to reaching. But even as she reached it, she thought how much easier it would be to walk away from this, to say that the business of others was no business of hers. That, of course, required one to believe that we are all strangers to one another – which was just not true, in Isabel's view, indeed it was as alien to her as it had been to John

Donne when he wrote those echoing, haunting words about islands and community. *If a clod be washed away by the sea, Europe is the less*, he had said. Yes. It is.

But even if she had reached the view that considerations of community and moral duty obliged them to act, she still had no idea what form this action should take. It was a curious, slightly disconcerting state to be in: to know that one should act, but not knowing how. It was rather like being in a phoney war, before the bombs and bullets are exchanged.

In Cat's delicatessen, to which Isabel now made her way, Eddie was creating a small stack of tubs of Patum Peperium, an anchovy paste, on the counter, alongside a display of socially responsible chocolate bars. It was a quiet spell and there was only one customer, a well-dressed man looking at oatcakes and having inordinate difficulty in choosing between two brands. Eddie, watching him, caught Cat's eye and shrugged. Cat smiled and crossed the floor to offer him advice.

'That brand on the left has less salt than the one on the right,' she offered. 'Otherwise I think they taste very much the same.'

The man turned round and looked at her anxiously. 'What I'm really looking for,' he said, 'is a triangular oatcake. That's the shape that oatcakes should be, you know. Triangular, but with one side a bit rounded. Oatcake shaped.'

Cat picked up a box of oatcakes and inspected it. 'These are round,' she said. 'And those other ones are round, too. I'm sorry. We only seem to have round oatcakes.'

'They still make them, though,' said the man, fingering

the cuffs of his expensive cashmere jacket. 'You could get them, couldn't you?'

'Yes,' said Cat. 'We could get hold of triangular oatcakes. Nobody has particularly asked . . .'

The man sighed. 'You may think it's ridiculous,' he said. 'But it's just that there are so few things in this world which are authentic. Local. Little things – like the shape of oatcakes – are very important. It's nice to have these familiar things about one. There are so many people who want to make things the same. They want to take our Scottish things away from us.'

The poignancy of his words struck Cat. It was true, she thought – a small country like Scotland had to make an effort to keep control of its everyday life. And she could see how it could be upsetting, if one felt at all vulnerable, to see familiar Scottish things taken away from you.

'They've taken away so many of our banks,' said the man. 'Look what happened to our banks. They've taken our Scottish regiments. They want to take away everything that's distinctive.'

Cat smiled. 'But they've given us back our Parliament,' she said. 'We've got that, haven't we?'

The man thought. 'Maybe,' he said. 'But what can it do? Legislate for triangular oatcakes?'

He laughed, and Cat laughed too, with relief. She had been thinking him a crank, but cranks never laughed at themselves.

'I'll try to get hold of some triangular oatcakes,' she said. 'Can you give me a week or two? I'll ask our suppliers.'

He thanked her and left the shop, and Cat went back to

167

the counter. Eddie, having finished creating his carefully balanced stack of Patum Peperium, turned round. He saw Isabel outside, at the door, and called Cat.

'Isabel's here,' he said. 'Outside. Coming in.'

Cat greeted her aunt. 'I've just had a wonderful conversation about oatcakes and cultural identity,' she said. 'You would have loved it.'

Isabel nodded vaguely. She did not want to talk about oatcakes; she wanted to sit quietly with a cup of coffee and one of Cat's Continental newspapers – *Le Monde*, perhaps. It never seemed to matter quite so much if foreign newspapers were out of date; yesterday's *Scotsman* rapidly began to seem stale, but a newspaper in a foreign language remained engaging. *Le Monde* had been taken by somebody, but there was a three-day-old copy of *Corriere della Sera* which she appropriated and took with her to a table.

'Do you mind, Cat?' she said. 'Sometimes one wants to talk. Sometimes one wants to think or' – she flourished the paper in the air – 'or read this.'

Cat understood, and busied herself with a task in the back office while Eddie prepared a cup of coffee for Isabel. Once that was ready he took it across to her table and placed it before her. Isabel looked up from her paper and smiled encouragingly at Eddie. Her week of running the delicatessen had cemented the friendship between them, but it was a friendship that relied more on smiles and gestures than on the exchange of ideas and confidences. At the end of her time there, Isabel had felt that she now knew him rather better, although he had told her nothing about himself. Where did Eddie live? She had asked him outright, and he had simply said on the south side, which was half the city, more or less, and gave nothing away. Did he live by himself, or did he stay at home? At home, he answered, but had not volunteered anything about who else was there. Isabel had left it at that; one had to respect the privacy of people. Some people did not like others to know about their domestic circumstances – out of shame, Isabel assumed. For a young man of Eddie's age to be living at home was not all that unusual, but he may have thought that perhaps it reflected badly on him never to have left. I live at home, thought Isabel, suddenly. I live in the house to which I was taken from the Simpson Memorial Maternity Pavilion by my sainted American mother. I haven't gone very far.

She would find out more about Eddie in future, she felt. And then she might be able to do something for him. If he wanted to take a course somewhere, Telford College perhaps, then she could pay for it – if he would accept. She already supported two students at the University of Edinburgh through her private charitable trust. Not that they knew, of course; they thought it came from Simon Macintosh, her lawyer, which it did in so far as he administered it, but the real purse from which it was drawn was Isabel's.

She thanked Eddie for the coffee and he beamed at her. 'Did that Italian phone you yet?' he asked.

Isabel looked at him blankly. 'Italian?'

'Tomasso. He was in here earlier today. He asked Cat for your telephone number.'

Isabel glanced down at her coffee. 'No,' she said. 'He hasn't phoned.'

She felt strangely agitated. She had offered to show him round the city – that was all – but the prospect of his getting in touch with her had an unexpected effect on her.

Eddie bent forward. 'Cat's giving him no encouragement,' he whispered. 'I don't think that she thinks much of him.'

Isabel raised an eyebrow. 'Maybe she doesn't want him to feel that there's more to it than friendship,' she said.

'I feel sorry for him,' said Eddie. 'To come over all the way from Italy to see her and then this.'

Isabel smiled. 'I suspect that he can look after himself,' she said. 'He doesn't strike me as being the vulnerable type.'

Eddie nodded. 'Maybe,' he said.

He moved away. It was the longest conversation that Isabel had ever had with him, and she was surprised by the fact that Eddie had picked up on Cat's attitude towards Tomasso. She had assumed that he would be indifferent to such matters, but now she realised that this might be a serious underestimation of the young man's powers of observation. And of his inner life too, she thought. We ignore quiet people, the shy observers, the bystanders; we forget that they are watching.

She returned to her perusal of the *Corriere della Sera*, but it was difficult for her to concentrate. She thought of Tomasso, and of when she might expect his call. She wondered what he would want to do in Edinburgh. There were museums and galleries, of course; all the usual sites of Scottish history, but she was not sure whether that would be what he wanted. Perhaps he would want to go out to dinner somewhere; she could arrange that. Cat would not come, presumably, and it would just be the two of them. What would Tomasso eat? He would not be a vegetarian, she thought: Italians were not vegetarians. They drank, they womanised, they sang; oh, blissful race of heroes!

She looked at the paper and struggled with a review of a book about suppressed photographs of Mussolini. Il Duce, apparently, took a strong interest in his appearance in photographs – well, she thought, he was an *Italian* dictator, and if Italian dictators aren't stylish, then which dictators would be? The paper showed a few samples. Mussolini on a horse, looking ridiculous, like a sack of potatoes, or spaghetti perhaps. Mussolini with a group of nuns flocking around him like excited sparrows. (He did not like to be in the same photograph as nuns or clerics of any sort; and why was that? Isabel asked herself. Guilt, of course.) Mussolini dressed as an aviator, with white jacket and white flying helmet, in an open cockpit aeroplane – he pretended to be able to fly while the plane was actually controlled by a real pilot, crouching on the floor. And when he entered the lion cage at Rome Zoo, a splendid show of public bravado, the lions had been drugged; they would have had no appetite that day for a stout dictator! She smiled as she read the review. What a distance now stood between those days and these; ancient history to so many people, but just one generation, really, and did not Italy still come up with flashy, vain politicians who were often on the wrong side of the law? And yet how could one not love Italy and the Italians; they were so very human, built such gorgeous cities, and made such good, loyal friends. If one had to choose a nationality, in the anteroom of birth, would it not be tempting to choose to be an Italian? Isabel thought it would be, although the options might all be taken up before it was one's turn and the grim news would be given: We're sorry, but you're going to have to be something else. What, she wondered, would be the most difficult identity to bear? Probably that of being something in the wrong place – one of those obscure minorities in some distant republic where all hands, and hearts, were turned against one.

So absorbed was Isabel in these ruminations that she did not notice the other tables in the delicatessen filling up. When she lowered the paper and reached for her cup of coffee, now cold from neglect, she saw that a number of people had entered the shop. Cat was at the counter attending to customers, and Eddie was hunched over the coffee machine in the background. Isabel looked at the new arrivals and immediately froze. Two tables away, near the large basket of baguettes, were Rose Macleod and her partner, Graeme. They had both been served coffee by Eddie and were talking to one another. Graeme had in his hand a list which he showed to Rose, who nodded.

Isabel did not want to see them. Her embarrassment over her encounter with them was still fresh in her mind and she did not imagine that they would particularly want to see her. She quickly looked down again at her paper. If she sat there, absorbed in the news from Italy, they might not notice and they would eventually go away. But what if Cat came over to speak to her, or Eddie topped up her coffee? That would draw attention to her.

She tried to concentrate on the newspaper, but could not. After reading the same sentence three times, the meaning jumbled in her mind, she sneaked a glance at the other table, and looked directly into Rose's stare. Now she could not very well look away, and so she began to force a smile of recognition. The other woman was clearly shocked by the encounter; she smiled too, hesitantly, raised a hand in a gesture of greeting, and then dropped it again as if uncertain that it had been the right thing to do.

Isabel lowered her eyes to the paper again. She felt calmer; they had met, greeted one another after a fashion, and that would be that – they could go their separate ways. She thought, though, that if she had had the courage she would have walked across to the couple's table and told Rose that she had misled her. Then she might have made a confession as to why she had come to see her in the first place. She could have given them the full facts, related Ian's extraordinary experiences, and left it up to them to decide what to do about them. And if there were any remaining public duty, she could have encouraged Ian to contact the police and tell them too. And that would have been the end of the whole affair. But she did not do this, and thus remained enmeshed in a situation which was causing her growing moral discomfort.

She looked again at the couple. Graeme was leaning forward and saying something to Rose, something urgent and angry. Rose was listening, but shaking her head. Graeme's manner seemed to become more animated. She saw him lay a finger on the tabletop and move it up and down in a fussy, insistent way, as if emphasising a point. Then he turned and looked in Isabel's direction, and she saw a look of pure malevolence directed at her. Meeting his gaze was like being assaulted physically – a tidal wave of dislike and contempt, moving across the room and crushing her.

He stood up, reached for his coat, and walked away from the table. Rose watched him leave. She almost got to her feet, but then sank back into her chair. Once he was out of the door, she reached for her cup of coffee, picked it up, and made her way over to Isabel's table.

'Do you mind?' Rose asked. 'Do you mind my joining you?' She put down her cup alongside the *Corriere della Sera*. 'You do remember me, don't you? Rose Macleod. You came to my house.'

Isabel indicated the empty chair. 'Please sit down. Of course I remember you. I wanted to say how sorry . . .'

Rose cut her off. 'Please,' she said. 'I'm the one who should be sorry about what happened. Graeme was very short with you when you came to the house. He shouldn't have said what he did. I was very cross with him.'

Isabel had not expected this. 'He had every right to be angry with me,' she said. 'I barged into your house like that and told you something that, well, was just not true.'

Rose frowned. Isabel noticed the high cheekbones and the delicacy of her features. She was an even more attractive woman than she had appeared to be when Isabel had seen her first. There was a particular delicacy in her face, a sorrow perhaps. The sorrowing face is, in a way, a calm face. There is no complexity and change: just one constant emotion.

'Not true?' Rose asked.

Isabel sighed. 'I'm not a medium,' she said. 'That was utter nonsense. I had intended to say something quite different to you, and then I panicked and made up that ridiculous story.' She paused. She could see that her disclosure was not being well received.

'Then why did you say . . .' Rose could not continue. Her disappointment was written on her face.

Isabel reached a decision. The whole ridiculous situation needed to be resolved. She had to get back to truth and rationality and put an end to this absurd dalliance with the paranormal. 'I'm going to have to tell you a rather odd story,' she said. 'I don't come out of it very well, I'm afraid, but I suppose I might say in my defence that I was well intentioned.'

Rose looked at her. Her disappointment now seemed to be turning to distrust. 'I'm not sure,' she began. She made as if to get up, but Isabel put out a hand to stop her.

'Please listen,' she said. 'I know it might sound unlikely to you, but please hear me out.'

Rose sat back. 'All right,' she said coldly. 'Tell me whatever it is that you want to say.'

'It began right there,' Isabel said, pointing to a nearby table. 'I was looking after this place while my niece was away. I found myself talking to a man who came in for his lunch. He told me that he had recently been given a heart transplant.' She paused, waiting to see whether the mention of the heart transplant had any effect on Rose. But Rose remained impassive.

'I met him on another occasion,' she said. 'He's a perfectly rational man. Very level-headed and sane – a clinical psychologist, in fact. He spoke to me about the effects of the operation, and one of these was a rather unexpected one.'

Rose, who had been listening courteously, now shrugged. 'I don't know what this has got to do with my son. Frankly, I don't see where this is going.'

Isabel looked at her in surprise. 'But your son was the donor,' she said. 'This man I spoke to has his heart.'

The effect of this on Rose was immediate. 'I think that you've made some fundamental mistake,' she said. 'I don't know why you think this has anything to do with us. Why do you say that my son was the donor? What on earth are you talking about?'

For a moment Isabel was too confused to say anything. Then, with Rose looking at her in slightly irritated puzzlement, she continued, 'Your son was the heart donor. They transplanted his heart into Ian. They took it over to Glasgow.'

'My son was not a donor of anything,' said Rose hotly. 'I think that you've got things rather badly mixed up, Miss . . . Dalhousie, was it?'

In her confusion, all that Isabel could manage was a lame 'Are you sure?'

'Of course I'm sure,' said Rose, her irritation coming to the surface. 'If my son had been a donor, they would have asked us, wouldn't they? Nobody told us anything about all this. Nobody . . .' She struggled with the words that followed. 'Nobody took his heart.'

For a few minutes neither of them said anything. Rose looked at Isabel reproachfully, and Isabel looked down at the table.

'I've obviously made a very bad mistake,' she said after a while, her voice tentative and uneven. 'I shouldn't have leapt to conclusions. I really do apologise to you for causing you this obvious distress. I had . . . I had no idea.'

Rose sighed. 'There's no real harm done,' she said. But she

did not intend to leave it at that. 'I'm sorry, but you're going to have to set your friend right on this. We have nothing to do with his operation — nothing. This doesn't concern us at all.'

Isabel nodded miserably. 'I feel very bad about this,' she said. 'I barged in without checking to see what sort of ground I was standing on.'

'Let's just forget all about it,' said Rose. 'There's been a bit of confusion — that's all.'

There was nothing more for them to say to each other. Mutely, Rose got up, nodded to Isabel, and then walked out of the delicatessen. She did not turn round; she did not bother to look. And Isabel, folding up her paper, took her cup back to the counter.

'What was that about?' asked Cat, nodding in the direction of the door. 'Who was that woman?'

'It was all about a misunderstanding,' said Isabel. 'And it was also about me. It was about my tendency to get the wrong end of things. To make assumptions. To interfere. That's what that was about.'

'Aren't you being a bit hard on yourself?' Cat said. She was used to Isabel's self-critical assessments and her frequent moral debates with herself — and with anybody else within earshot. But the self-abasement in her aunt's voice was more profound than usual.

'That's my trouble,' said Isabel. 'I'm not hard enough on myself. I have to stop this ridiculous assumption that just because somebody speaks to me I am bound to take up a cause. Well, I've had enough of that. I'm going to stop.'

'Will you?' asked Cat. 'Do you really think you will?'

177

Isabel hesitated before answering, but only for a short while. Then she said, 'No. No, I don't. But I'll try.'

Cat burst out laughing, and Eddie, who had caught the conversation, looked up and met Isabel's eye.

'You're very nice as you are,' he muttered. 'Don't change.'

But Isabel did not hear what he said.

16

Grace had taken the call from Tomasso, and when Isabel returned home she found the note on her desk. It was written on one of the cards on which Grace liked to scribble her messages – cards which Isabel used to log in manuscripts. She resented Grace's use of these cards for this purpose – a scrap of paper would have sufficed – but she had decided not to tackle her housekeeper about it. Grace was sensitive, and even a modest suggestion could easily be interpreted as criticism.

A very interesting man telephoned, wrote Grace. *Tom some-body. Foreign. He'll call again at three. I never get calls like that. But be careful.*

Grace was still in the house, working upstairs, and when she heard Isabel come in she made her way downstairs and popped her head round the door of Isabel's study.

'You saw that message?'

Isabel nodded. 'Thank you. He's called Tomasso. And he's Italian.'

Grace smiled. 'I liked the sound of his voice,' she said.

'Yes, it's very . . .' Isabel thought for a moment. 'Well, I suppose there's only one word for it. Sexy.'

'Good luck,' said Grace.

Isabel smiled. 'Well,' she said, hesitantly. 'Maybe. I don't know.'

Grace opened the door fully and came into the room. 'Don't be defeatist. I don't see any reason why you shouldn't find somebody. You're a very attractive woman. You're kind. Men like you. Yes, they do. They love talking to you. I've seen it.'

'They may like talking to me,' said Isabel. 'But that's about it. They're frightened of me, I suspect. Men don't like women who think too much. They want to do the thinking.'

Grace thought about this for a moment. 'I'm not sure if you're right about that,' she said. 'Some men may be like that, but by no means all. Look at Jamie. Yes, look at him. He worships the ground you walk upon. I can tell that from a mile away.' She paused, and then added, 'Pity that he's still just a boy.'

Isabel moved over to the window and looked out into the garden. She felt slightly embarrassed by the direction in which the conversation was going. She could discuss men in general, but she could not discuss Jamie. That was too raw, too dangerous. 'And what about you, Grace? What about the men in your life?'

She had never before spoken to Grace like that, and she was not sure what her housekeeper's reaction would be. She looked round and saw that Grace had not taken offence at the question. She decided to be more specific. 'You told me the other day that you had met somebody at the spiritualist meetings. Remember?'

Grace picked up a pencil from the desk and examined its tip nonchalantly. 'Did I? Well, perhaps I did.'

'Yes,' said Isabel. 'You told me about him and then I think I saw him when I went there with you. That man sitting behind us – that good-looking man – the one who had lost his wife. That was him, wasn't it?'

The pencil became more interesting to Grace. 'Could be.'

'Ah!' said Isabel. 'Well, I must say that I thought him rather nice. And he obviously liked you. I could tell.'

'He's easy to talk to,' said Grace. 'He's one of those men who listens to what you have to say. I always like that. A gentleman.'

'Yes,' agreed Isabel. 'A gentleman. Now that's a useful word, isn't it? And yet everybody's too embarrassed to use it these days, for some reason. Is it considered snobbish, do you think? Is that it?'

Grace put the pencil back on the desk. 'Maybe,' she said. 'I wouldn't think that, though. You get all sorts of gentlemen. It doesn't matter where they're from or who they are. They're just gentlemen. You can trust them.'

Isabel thought, And then you get men like John Liamor. And you know, or you should know, that he's not a gentleman. She had known that, of course, and had ignored it because one of the effects of those who are not gentlemen is that one's judgement is overcome. You don't care. But she did not want to think about him now because she realised that time was doing its healing and he seemed to have become more and more distant. And she liked the feeling of forgetting, of the slow conversion into the state of his being just another person, somebody whom she could think about, if he came to mind, without feeling a pang of loss and of longing.

She looked at Grace. If this conversation went too far, then Grace would simply remember that she had something to do and would go off and do it, leaving the exchange in midair. This sometimes happened when she had argued herself into a corner over some point and could not retract; the ironing would suddenly call, or something would be remembered upstairs. But now she was showing no signs of ending their conversation, and so Isabel continued.

'Of course, you may not be the only one to like him,' Isabel said. She tried to make the observation a casual one, but there was an edge to her voice, which Grace noticed. She looked up sharply.

'Why do you say that?'

Isabel swallowed hard. How would one put this? 'I thought that the medium showed an interest,' she said. 'She certainly kept her eyes on him. Over tea afterwards . . .'

'She often looks at people,' said Grace defensively. 'That's the way they communicate. They have to establish a rapport with the people there so that the other side can get in touch.'

Isabel thought for a moment. Grace was showing loyalty to the medium, which she should have expected. 'But — and please correct me if I'm wrong — wasn't that message she gave about somebody's wife being concerned that somebody else was trying to get to know him better – wasn't that directed at your friend? Didn't you see his reaction?'

Grace pursed her lips. 'I wasn't watching very closely,' she said.

'Well, I was,' said Isabel. 'And I could tell that he thought the message was for him. It was as if somebody had hit him over the head with a rolled-up newspaper.'

Grace sniffed. 'I don't know. Some of these messages are rather general. That could have been for anybody there. Most of the men who go to these meetings have lost their wives, you know. That man isn't the only one.'

Isabel stared at Grace. Her housekeeper had many merits, she thought. She was direct in her manner, she was utterly truthful, and she had no time for hypocrisy. But when she chose to deny the obvious, she could do so with a tenacity that was infinitely frustrating.

'Grace,' she said. 'I didn't want to spell it out, but you force me to do so. I thought the medium had eyes just for that man. She was devouring him. Now then, imagine that you are a medium and you notice that the man you're after is getting a bit too friendly with another woman. What do you do? Suddenly you discover that the wife is coming through from the other side and, lo and behold, she tells him that the opposition is bad for him. And since he believes it's his wife talking, he takes the warning seriously. End of romance for . . . well, sorry to put it this way, but, end of possible romance for you.'

While Isabel was talking, Grace had fixed her with an unblinking stare. Now, picking up the pencil again, she twirled it gently between her fingers. Then she laughed.

'But what if the wife has got it right? What if I'm not good for him? What then?'

Isabel thought quickly. Her analysis, which she was sure was true, was based on the assumption that the medium was inventing the message. It was inconceivable to her that there was any communication with the dead wife, and so she had to think this. But if, like Grace, one thought that the message could be genuine, then quite another conclusion might be reached.

'If you believe that,' she said, 'then I suppose you might keep away from each other.'

'Exactly,' said Grace.

Isabel was puzzled. Most women did not abandon a man to another woman without at least some attempt at a fight. And yet Grace seemed to be prepared to hand victory to the medium. 'I'm surprised that you're giving up so easily,' she said. 'In my view, that woman is resorting to a cheap trick. And you're letting her get away with it.'

'I may not agree,' said Grace. 'So there we are.' She looked at her watch and turned away. The conversation had come to an end. 'There's work to be done,' she said. 'What about you? Is the *Review* up to date?'

Isabel rose to her feet. 'It never is,' she said. 'It's a Sisyphean labour for me. I push a rock up a hill and then it rolls down again.'

'Everybody's job is like that,' said Grace. 'I wash things and they become dirty and need washing again. You publish one set of articles and another sack of them comes in. Even the Queen's job is like that. She opens one bridge and they build another. She signs one law and they pass another.' She sighed, as if weighed down by the thought of the royal burden.

'Our lot is labour,' said Isabel.

Grace, who had picked up a piece of paper from the floor, nodded. '*Consider the lilies of the field*,' she said, '*they neither . . .*'

'*Toil nor spin*,' supplied Isabel.

'That's right,' Grace went on, completing the quotation. '*And even Solomon in all his glory was not arrayed like one of these.*'

'Solomon,' mused Isabel. 'What do you think his glory was like? Gold trappings and all that sort of thing?'

Grace examined the piece of paper she had retrieved from the floor. It was a page detached from a manuscript – something about sorrow and loss. It would never be reunited with its fellow pages, she thought, as she placed it on the desk. 'I suppose so. Heavy robes with lots of gold. Very hot for that part of the world. Most uncomfortable. Have you seen the paintings of Mary, Queen of Scots? How hot and uncomfortable they must have been in those dresses. And they had no deodorants, you know.'

'But everybody was in the same boat,' said Isabel. 'I think they didn't notice.' She paused, remembering her trip to Russia in the dying days of Communism, when there was nothing to be seen in the shops but echoing emptiness. She had travelled in the Moscow underground at the height of the rush hour, and the shortage of soap and the nonexistence of deodorant had made itself evident. She had noticed, but did the Russians?

'There was a very old man who lived near my uncle in

Kelso,' Grace said. 'I remember him as a child, when I went down there to stay with my uncle and aunt. He used to sit outside his front door, staring out onto the fields. They said that he was past his ninety-eighth birthday and that he hadn't washed since the hot-water system in his cottage broke down twenty years before. He claimed that this explained his longevity.'

'Nonsense,' said Isabel, but she immediately thought, Was it really nonsense? There were friendly bacteria, were there not? Colonies of tiny beings who lived on us in perfect harmony with their hosts and were ready to deal with the real invaders, the unfriendly infections, when they arrived; and yet at every bath we depleted their ranks, washing away their cities, their dynasties, their cultures. So she retracted, and said, 'Well, perhaps not.' But Grace had already left the room.

Tomasso's telephone call, when it came later that afternoon, was an invitation to dinner. He apologised for giving her such short notice – he explained that he had tried to contact her earlier – but would she be free that evening? Isabel had a friend who would never accept, as a firm rule, an invitation to do anything that day, as this would suggest that her diary was empty. That was pride, which could deprive one of so much fun; Isabel had no such compunction, and accepted immediately.

He chose the restaurant, a fish restaurant in Leith, the city's port. It was in a small stone building that had been a fisherman's house in simpler days, with a view across a cobbled street to a shipping basin. It had the air of a French bistro, with its plain-board floor, its gingham tablecloths, and the day's specials written in coloured chalk on a large blackboard. Tomasso looked around quickly and gave Isabel an apologetic look. 'They recommended it at the hotel,' he whispered. 'I hope that it is all right.' As he leant towards her to whisper, she caught a whiff of cologne, that expensive, spicy smell that she associated with the turn-down scratch-and-sniff pages of the glossy magazines.

Isabel assumed that he was used to something smarter; he looked so elegant, in his tailored jacket and his expensive shoes with their tasteful buckles. 'It's very good,' she said. 'Everyone knows this place.'

Her comment seemed to reassure him, and he relaxed. He looked around again. 'It's difficult when you're away from home,' he said. 'If we were in Bologna, or Milan even, I'd know where to take you. When you're abroad you are so vulnerable.'

'It's hard to see you as vulnerable,' she said, and immediately she regretted this, as he gave her a curious look.

'But you don't know me,' he said. 'How can you tell?'

Isabel looked at him, noticing what she had not noticed earlier on – the silk tie, the collar of his shirt, which was hard-shiny white, as if it had been starched; the perfectly groomed hair, dark auburn plastered back so scrupulously, not a strand out of place. He had that look about him, the look which Isabel described as *classic dancing instructor*, a look which normally she would have dismissed, or written off as the outward sign of an inward vanity, but which now, for some unfathomable reason, pleased her. And she realised that as they had entered the restaurant, she had felt a thrill of pride to be seen with this man; she wanted others to see her with him. And that, she realised, was what people felt when in the company of the beautiful, and why they sought that company; beauty, glamour, sexual appeal rub off on those around the blessed object.

They were shown to their table, beside the window. She sat down; she had not looked at the other diners, and now did. A woman two tables away who was looking at her discreetly, and at Tomasso, turned away briefly so as not to be seen staring, and now looked back. Isabel recognised her, but could not work out why. They smiled at one another.

Tomasso looked at the other table. 'Your friends?'

'Friends I don't really know,' said Isabel. 'That is what this city is like. It's not very big.'

'I like it,' said Tomasso. 'I feel as if I'm in Siena, or somewhere like that. But more exciting – for me, at least. Scotland is very exciting.'

'It has its moments,' said Isabel. The waiter had arrived and handed her a menu. He was a young man, a student perhaps, with regular features and a wide grin. He smiled at her and then at Tomasso. Tomasso looked up at him, and for a moment Isabel imagined that she saw something, a look, a moment of understanding, pass between them. Or had she? She watched Tomasso's eyes. He had glanced at the open menu placed in his hands, and now he looked back at the waiter.

Tomasso asked her whether she could recommend anything, but Isabel did not hear him. She was studying the menu and thinking about what she had seen, if she had seen anything. Tomasso repeated his question. 'Is there anything you can recommend? I don't know, you see, these Scottish dishes . . .'

Isabel looked up from her menu. 'I can recommend honesty,' she said. 'And kindness. Both of those. I can recommend both of those.'

The effect of this on the waiter was to make him start. He had his notebook in his hand, and he clutched it to his chest in his surprise. And Tomasso's head gave a small jolt, as if a string had been pulled.

Then the waiter laughed, immediately putting a hand up to his mouth. 'Not on the menu tonight,' he said. 'Not really . . .' He trailed off.

Isabel smiled. 'I'm sorry,' she said. 'I was feeling flippant. I don't know why I said that.'

Tomasso seemed confused. He turned to the waiter and asked him about one of the options, and was told about it. Isabel studied her menu. She was not sure what had prompted her curious comment. Perhaps it was the incongruity of the situation – that she was dining with the man who had been pursuing her niece, although he was her own age; who was so slick and elegant, and who had given the young male waiter what had struck her as an appreciative look. Yet none of that justified rudeness or a weak attempt to be funny.

She looked up from the menu and made a suggestion as to what they might have. The waiter, still eyeing her in a bemused way, agreed with her choice, and Tomasso nodded his assent. A bottle of chilled white wine, which Tomasso had chosen, was produced and their glasses filled.

The earlier awkwardness soon passed. Tomasso spoke about his day in Edinburgh and about his plans to drive up to Glencoe.

'Will Cat be going with you?' she asked. She knew the answer, but asked nonetheless.

He looked into his glass, and she realised that there was an issue of pride; he was the rejected suitor – rejected gently, and with humour, no doubt, but rejected. 'She will not,' he said. 'She has the business to look after. She cannot leave that.' He sipped the wine. Then, his face brightening, as if an idea had just occurred, he said, 'Perhaps you would care to accompany me? The Bugatti has two seats. It is not the most comfortable of cars, but it is very beautiful.'

Isabel tried not to let her uncertainty show. 'Glencoe?'

'And beyond,' said Tomasso, describing a wide movement with a hand. 'We could drive across that island – the large one – Skye? And then . . . and then there is so much more. There is so much of Scotland.'

'But how long would we need to be away?' asked Isabel.

Tomasso shrugged. 'A week? Ten days? If you could not manage that, we could make it less. Five days?'

She did not answer immediately. The last time that somebody had invited her to go away like this was when John Liamor had suggested Ireland, and they had caught the ferry to Cork. And that was in another life, she thought, or almost, and now here she was, in this restaurant in Edinburgh with this man whom she hardly knew, being asked to go away.

She picked up her wineglass. 'We barely know one another,' she said.

'Which makes it more of an adventure,' he said quickly. 'But if you think . . .'

'No,' she said. 'I don't think that. It's just that to drop everything and go off . . .'

He reached out and touched her wrist, briefly, and then withdrew his hand. 'But that is what makes it so exciting.'

Isabel took a deep breath. 'Let me think about it,' she said. 'I need to think.'

Her answer seemed to satisfy him. He sat back in his chair and smiled at her. 'Please do,' he said. 'I am in no hurry to leave Edinburgh. It is very – how should I put it? – very congenial. Does that sound right to you?'

Isabel nodded. 'It's close enough.' She moved her fork and knife slightly so that they were parallel with each other; a small detail, perhaps, but that was what zero tolerance was all about. One started with the cutlery.

Tomasso was staring at her, as if waiting for her to say something. Well, she decided, I can ask.

'You're in no hurry to get back to Italy,' she said. 'May I ask: What do you actually do? Do you have a job to get back to, or . . .'

The *or* hung ambiguously in the air, but he did not seem to mind. 'We have a family company,' he said. 'There are many people who work in it. They do not need me all the time.'

'And what does this company do?' She was prepared for evasion, but somehow, face-to-face with him, what he, or the company, did seemed less important; *a handsome face/absolves disgrace*, the words came to her unbidden, and original, too, she thought.

'We make shoes,' said Tomasso. 'Mostly shoes for ladies.'

191

'Where?' Isabel asked. She asked the question, and knew it was abrupt, even rude.

Tomasso did not appear to mind the examination. 'We have two factories. One in the south,' he said. 'And another in Milan. The designs all come from Milan.'

'Ah yes,' said Isabel. 'Cat told me about the shoes. I remember now.'

Tomasso nodded. 'She met many members of my family at the wedding. That is where I met her. At one of the parties.'

'And that is when you decided that you would come to see her in Scotland?'

His right hand moved to his left cuff, which he fingered. She noticed the manicured nails. There were no men in Scotland with manicured nails.

'That is when I decided to come to Scotland,' he said. 'I have one or two things to do here. Family things. But I also hoped to get to know Cat better. I did not think that she would be so busy.'

'Perhaps she considers you too old for her,' said Isabel, and she thought, *family things*. What did he mean by family things? Mafia things?

He did not react immediately. He looked down at the plate to his side, and dabbed at an imaginary crumb with a forefinger. Then: 'In Italy, you know, it is not at all unusual for a man in his early forties – which is what I am – to marry a girl in her early twenties. That is normal, in fact.' He looked at her evenly, holding her gaze.

'That's interesting,' said Isabel. 'It's not normal here. Maybe because we consider that equality is important in relationships. The woman in those circumstances will never be the equal of the man.'

He drew back slightly at her comment, feigning surprise. 'Equality? Who wants equality?'

'I do, for one,' said Isabel.

'Do you really?' he asked. 'Are you sure about that? Don't you find equality a little bit . . . well, dull?'

Isabel thought for a moment. Yes, he was right. Equality was dull, and goodness was dull, too, if one reflected on it; and Nietzsche, of course, would have agreed. Peace was dull; conflict and violence were exciting. And this man, sitting on the other side of the table from her, was far from dull.

'Yes,' she said. 'It is a bit dull. But then I'd probably prefer dullness to unfairness. I'd rather live in a society that was fair to its citizens than one in which there was great injustice. I'd rather live in Sweden than . . .' She had to think. What had happened to all the truly dreadful countries? Where were they? The usual whipping boys, exhausted by criticism, had caved in. But there were still places, were there not, where there were gross disparities of wealth and power. Paraguay? She had no idea. They had been saddled with a picture-book dictator, but had he not been deposed? Were there still vast latifundia there? And what about those Arab countries where sheikhs and princes viewed the public treasuries as their private purses? There was plenty of injustice that nobody talked about very much. There was slavery still; debt bondage; enforced prostitution; trafficking in children. It was all there, but the voices that spoke about it were so hard to hear amongst all the trivia and noise and the profound loss of moral seriousness.

'Than where?' he pressed. 'Than Italy?'

'Of course not. I would love to live in Italy.'

He held his hands apart, in a gesture of welcome. 'Why not come? Why not move to the hills above Florence, like all those other British ladies?'

Perhaps he had intended the remark to be a compliment, or perhaps it had meant nothing very much. But he had said *other British ladies*, and that put her into the category of artistic spinsters and eccentrics who haunted places like Fiesole; not a glamorous set, but faded, chintzy, dreamy exponents of Botticelli and Tuscan cookery; maiden aunts, actual or in the making. He had invited her to travel to the Highlands in his Bugatti, and she had almost accepted; but this, she thought, is how he sees me. I would be company; a guide; somebody to read the map and explain the massacre of Glencoe. And I, my head momentarily turned, had thought that I could possibly be of romantic or even sexual interest to this man.

The waiter arrived with the first course. He placed the plate in front of her, scallops on a bed of shredded red and green peppers. As she looked at her plate, she teetered on the edge of self-pity, and then pulled back. Why should I agonise? she asked herself. Why should I always weigh the rights and wrongs of things? What if I just *acted*? What if I became, for a short time, the huntress and showed him that I was not what he imagined? What if I made a conquest?

She looked up. The waiter had a pepper mill in his hand and was offering her pepper. This always irritated her; that the proprietors of restaurants should not trust their pepper mills to the hands of their guests. But it was not the waiter's fault, and she dismissed the thought.

She looked across the table. 'I'd like to think about your offer of that trip,' she said. 'Next week perhaps?'

She studied his reaction, watching for any sign. But he gave little away – little beyond the slightest twitch of a smile at the sides of his mouth and a brief change in the light in his eyes, a flicker, a change in reflection, brought about, no doubt, by a trick of light, a movement of the head.

17

Jamie did not like playing for the ballet. From where he sat in the orchestra pit, just beneath the overhang of the stage, he found the sound of the dancers' feet disconcerting. This is what it would be like to live, he thought, on the first floor, with noisy neighbours on the second. But it was work, and well-paid work at that, and he thought it better than listening to his pupils. That afternoon, on the day after Isabel's dinner with Tomasso, he had played for the Scottish Ballet in a matinée performance, and had agreed to meet Isabel in the Festival Theatre café after the show.

She had to talk to him, she explained. And he had begun to ask, 'About . . .' and then had stopped, because he knew what it was about, without having to ask. 'Tell me when we meet,' he said, and added, as an afterthought, 'You haven't done anything unwise, have you, Isabel?'

Isabel realised that the answer to that was yes, but did not say so. She had virtually agreed to go off to the Highlands with an almost complete stranger (not that she intended to tell Jamie about that – just yet); she had impersonated a medium; she had reduced Graeme, on first meeting, to a state of tight-lipped enmity; all of which, she thought, was unwise. And while her sense of moral obligation lay behind two of these bad decisions, behind the other one lay nothing but a sudden urge to show bravado. And yet that very act, the reckless flirtation with Tomasso (a flirtation on her side, now, if not yet on his), was the one unwise thing of the three that she did not regret. Indeed, the mere thought of it was pleasurable: a shameless, erotic challenge, a delectable fantasy. My Italian lover, she would be able to say; and then, with regret: Yes, I used him, I confess I did. Of course, she would never be able to utter that to anybody, although she might think it in private, and find comfort in the thought. *My Italian lover* – how many women would love to be able to say that to themselves, when confronted with the humdrum, the brute limitations of their lives: *Yes, I know, I know – but I have had an Italian lover.*

In the café at the Festival Theatre, Isabel looked out through the glass wall to the Royal College of Surgeons on the other side of the road. A small cluster of men and women was emerging from the gate at the side of the college, examinees poring over a piece of paper. One of the men jabbed at the paper with a finger, making some remark to the others. There was a shaking of heads and Isabel felt a pang of sympathy – what had the poor man suggested? Removing the wrong organ? These were doctors who came

197

from their hospital posts all over the world to attempt the fellowship examinations, and only a small number passed. She had heard a surgeon friend comment on it: seven – out of sixty hopefuls, sometimes – invited to join the Fellows in some inner sanctum, the rest politely dispersed. The doctor who had gestured to the paper looked down at the ground; a woman beside him put her hand on his shoulder to comfort him. There would be a melancholy homecoming.

Jamie slipped into the chair beside her; she turned and he was there, smiling in the way she found so appealing. 'Arvo Pärt,' he said.

'Very slow,' she said. 'Silences. Repetitive pätterns.'

He laughed. 'Exactly. But I enjoy it, you know. This ballet we've just done uses a piece he wrote called *Psalom*. Gorgeous ärchitecture.'

'So you're feeling in a good mood?'

He scratched his head and looked out onto the street. 'I think so,' he said. 'Yes, in fact I am in a good mood. Are you going to spoil it for me? Has something happened?'

'Let's go for a walk,' said Isabel. 'I feel a bit cooped up. We could talk while we're walking. Do you mind?'

Jamie left his bassoon with a young woman at the ticket desk and joined Isabel on the pavement outside the theatre. They crossed the road and made their way down Nicolson Street to South Bridge. They passed Thin's Bookshop, as Isabel still called it, and turned down Infirmary Street. The Old College of the university towered above and behind them, a great quadrangle of grey stone. Above the dome, a gleaming statue of a naked youth, torch in hand, caught the late afternoon sun, gold against the high background of cloud. Isabel tended to look up when she walked round Edinburgh because that was where the forgotten delights were – the carved stone thistles, the Scottish gargoyles straddling roof gables, the all but obliterated signs of the nineteenth century: PENS, INKS, LOANS – a palimpsest of the life and commerce of the town.

Jamie was talking about the Arvo Pärt and about his next engagement, a concert with the Scottish Chamber Orchestra. Isabel listened. She had her own topics which she wanted to raise with him, but Jamie was still exhilarated by the performance and she was content to let him talk. At the end of Infirmary Street the road dipped down sharply to the Cowgate, a cobbled slide for incautious cars and pedestrians. They branched off behind the morgue, heading for the stone steps that descended beside a shabby tenement block. There was broken glass on the steps and the large abandoned buckle of a belt.

'Things happen in this city,' said Jamie, glancing at the buckle.

'They do,' said Isabel. 'You turn a corner, take a few steps, and you're in a different world.' She pointed behind her to the statue on the high dome of the university. 'He's carrying a lighted torch for a reason.'

Jamie glanced behind him and for a moment his expression clouded over. He looked at Isabel. Then he stared at the wall of the tenement beside them, a place of poverty and hardship still, and at the steps worn down by the feet of centuries.

'This is all very different from the Pärt,' he said. 'Music always is. You can exist for a while in a world of music and then you walk out into the street and the street reminds you that this is what is real.' He stared at her for a moment, in a silence of friends. 'What's happened, Isabel?'

She took his arm gently. She did not touch Jamie very often, although she wanted to, but now she took his arm and they went down the remaining steps together. She explained to him about the meeting with Rose in the delicatessen, and Rose's disclosure that her son had not been the donor. He listened attentively as they walked down to Holyrood Road. Then, when she finished, they stood still. They were standing opposite the offices of the *Scotsman*, facing the large glass building with its backdrop of crags and hill.

'I don't know what you're worrying about,' said Jamie. 'This character, Ian, has simply been hallucinating, or whatever you call it. It just so happens that the hallucination took a form which fitted that woman's partner. That's what we call coincidence, isn't it?'

'And so what do I do?' asked Isabel.

Jamie leant forward and tapped Isabel's wrist with a forefinger. 'You do absolutely nothing. Nothing. You've done what you can for that man and you've come up against a dead end. You don't want to go chasing after the real donor . . .'

She stopped him. 'The real donor?'

Jamie shrugged. 'Well, he got the heart from somebody. You jumped to conclusions too quickly. There must have been another sudden death involving a young man. You saw the one that happened to be in the *Evening News*. But not everybody who dies ends up in the *Evening News* or the

Scotsman. Some deaths are unreported. Some people don't put notices in the paper.'

She said nothing. He looked at her, waiting for her to speak, but she did not. She was staring at the *Scotsman* building, watching a man in a black overcoat make his way out of the revolving door and down the steps to a taxi that was waiting for him at the kerb.

'I could ask him,' she muttered.

'Who?'

Isabel pointed. 'Him. Over there. I know him. Angus Spens. He's a journalist on the *Scotsman*. He can find anything out. Anything. All we need from him is a name. That's all.'

'But why would he do this for you?'

'It's complicated,' said Isabel. 'We used to share a bath together.' She laughed. 'When we were five. My mother and his mother were very close. We saw a lot of each other.'

Jamie frowned. 'What's the point? Do you really think it likely that this other donor, whoever he is, was done in by a person with, whatever it is, a high forehead? Really, Isabel! Really!'

'I have to see this thing through,' she said. Because you have to finish what you start, she thought, and I have started this. I have tossed a stone into a loch. But there was more to it than that. For Ian, the finding of an explanation for what was happening to him was a matter of life and death. He had told her that he felt his recovery depended on the resolution of these strange experiences, and she was sure that he meant it. People sometimes knew when they were going to die. They might not be able to explain it, but they knew.

And she remembered standing in a gallery once, the Phillips, looking at an early painting by Modigliani. The artist had painted a road that led off towards the horizon, green fields on either side, hills in the distance, but that stopped short, before it reached any destination. And that, she had been told by the person beside her, was because the artist knew that his life was going to be a short one. He knew.

She turned away from Jamie, watching the taxi which had picked up Angus Spens speed off up the road. From the mist of early years she could still summon the memory of sitting in a vast white tub with a little boy at the other end, splashing water in her face and laughing, and her mother standing beside her and reaching down for her; her mother, whose face she saw sometimes at night, in her dreams, as if she had never gone away, and who was still there, as we often think of the dead, in the background, like a cloud of love, against which weather we conduct our lives.

Isabel and Jamie walked back up Holyrood Road, mostly in silence; he was thinking, she suspected, of Pärt again, and she had Angus Spens to think of now, and of how she would approach him. Just before the Cowgate they said their goodbyes, and Jamie made his way up a narrow alley that led back up to Infirmary Street. She watched him for a few moments; he turned round, waved, and then went on. Isabel continued along the Cowgate, a street which ran under South Bridge and George IV Bridge – a sunken level of the old part of the city. On either side high stone buildings, darkened by ancient smoke, riddled with passages and closes, climbed up to the light above. It was a curious street, Isabel felt, the dark heart of the Old Town, a street in which the inhabitants, troglodytes all, did not seem to show their faces and doorways were barred; a street of echoes.

She reached the point at which the Cowgate opened out into the Grassmarket. Crossing the road, she began to make her way up Candlemaker Row. Following this route, she could pass Greyfriars Kirkyard, head across the Meadows and be home within half an hour. She looked up again; to her right was the wall of the kirkyard, a high grey-stone wall behind which lay the bones of religious heroes, the Covenanters who had signed their names in blood to protect Scottish religious freedom. They had died for their pains. That anybody should believe so strongly, thought Isabel, so strongly as to die for a vision of what was right; but people did, all the time, people who had a sufficiency of courage. And do I have such a measure of courage? she asked herself. Or any courage at all? She thought that she did not; people who thought about courage, as she did, often were not courageous themselves.

Candlemaker Row was largely deserted, apart from a couple of boys from George Heriot's School round the corner. The schoolboys, their white shirts hanging out, stood back against the wall to let Isabel pass, and then giggled. Isabel smiled, and looked back for a moment because one of the boys had had an impish face and it amused her, an *echt* small boy in an age in which children had suddenly and absurdly become *young adults*. And that is when she saw him, on the other side of the street, some distance behind her, but walking in the same direction as she was. She turned away immediately and walked on, her head lowered. She did not want to see Graeme again; she did not want to catch his eye and feel the force of his hostility.

She reached the top of Candlemaker Row and continued round the corner to Forrest Road. There were people about now, people and traffic. A bus lumbered past; a man with a scruffy black dog on a lead stood in front of a shop window; two teenaged girls in short skirts walked towards Isabel; a male student, his jeans slipping down, barely suspended, deliberately exposing his boxer shorts, walked with his arm around his girlfriend, while her hand sought out the sanctuary of his rear pocket in a casual intimacy that she did not bother to conceal. Isabel only wanted to establish a distance between herself and Graeme. He would have to turn at the top of Candlemaker Row, and he could be heading for George IV Bridge. But he did not. When she glanced back again, he was there a few yards behind her, not looking at her, but so close now that he would soon draw level with her and could not fail to see her.

She increased her pace, glancing back quickly. He was nearer now, and she saw that he was looking at her. She turned her head away; she was on Sandy Bell's corner, the signs – WHISKIES, ALES, and MUSIC NIGHTLY – immediately beside her. She hesitated for a moment, and then turned in, pushing open the swing door and entering the wood-panelled *howff* with its long, polished-mahogany bar and its array of whisky bottles on shelves. To her relief she saw that the room was quite full, even now, just after five o'clock; later it would be packed, exuberant with music, filled with the sound of fiddles, whistles, singing. She

204

approached the bar, pleased to find herself beside a woman, rather than a man. Isabel did not frequent bars, but this, now, was where she wanted to be, with people, in safety. She was convinced that Graeme had been following her, even if this was an absurd thought; people did not follow others in daylight on the streets of Edinburgh, or at least not on *these* streets.

The woman beside her looked at the new arrival and nodded. Isabel smiled, noticing the lines around the woman's mouth, the small lines that advertised her status as a smoker. The other woman was, she thought, somewhere in her thirties, but was ageing quickly – from alcohol, cares, smoking.

The barman raised an eyebrow expectantly, and for a moment she was tongue-tied. All those years ago she had gone into pubs with John Liamor, who drank Guinness, and what had she had? She looked ahead of her at the rows of bottles, and remembered the whisky nosing she had attended when Charlie Maclean had used those peculiar terms of his. She had forgotten which whisky was which but now she saw a name she recognised, which she thought he had spoken of, and she pointed to it. The barman nodded and reached for the bottle.

The woman beside her touched her glass, which was almost empty. Isabel was pleased to respond.

'May I?' she asked, gesturing towards the barman.

The woman's face lit up. 'Thank you, hen.' Isabel liked the characteristically Scottish term of affection. *Hen*. It was warm and old-fashioned.

'I've had a day and a half,' said the woman. 'I've been on since ten this morning. Nonstop.'

Isabel raised her glass to her new companion. 'What do you do?'

'Taxi,' said the woman. 'My man and me. Both of us. Taxis.'

Isabel was about to say something about this, how difficult it must be with the traffic, but then she saw him further along the bar, taking a glass of beer from the barman. The woman beside her followed her gaze.

'Recognise somebody?'

Isabel felt hollow. Graeme must have come in immediately behind her, followed her. Or could it be a coincidence? Had he been heading for Sandy Bell's at just the time that she happened to be walking up Candlemaker Row? She did not know what to think.

She lowered herself onto a bar stool beside the other woman. Now she could not see him any more, nor he her, she imagined.

The taxi driver glanced down the bar again. 'You're upset about something, hen,' she said, her voice lowered. 'Are you all right?' Then she added, 'Men. Always men. The cause of all our troubles. Men.'

In spite of her shock, Isabel was able to smile. The woman's remark cheered her with its assumption of solidarity. We are strong together. Women were not alone in the face of bullies. As long as they could call one another *hen* and stand together.

Isabel noticed that the woman had placed a small phone on the bar, next to her glass, and the sight of it gave her an idea. She had her pocket diary in her bag, and in it were the telephone numbers she had been using recently, noted down in the pages at the end.

'Could I ask you a favour? I need to make a telephone call.'

The woman willingly slid the phone along the bar. Isabel picked it up and dialled. Her fingers fumbled, and she dialled again. He answered. He could come, if she insisted. Was it important? Yes, he would be there in however long it took to call a taxi and to make the short trip to Sandy Bell's.

'Please hurry,' said Isabel, her voice barely more than a whisper.

As Isabel waited, she exchanged a few words with the woman beside her.

'You're frightened of somebody, aren't you? That fellow down there?'

Isabel could not bring herself to say that she was frightened of anybody. Her world – her normal world – did not involve fear of others, but she knew that many people lived in fear. We forget.

'I think he followed me in.'

The woman grimaced. 'Oh, that sort. Pathetic, isn't it? They're just pathetic.' She sipped at her drink. 'Do you want me to have a wee word with him? I get those types in the taxi. I know how to deal with them.'

Isabel declined the offer.

The other woman seemed taken aback. 'Are you sure?'

'I'm sure. I don't want a confrontation.'

'Don't let them get away with it.' The advice was given with feeling. 'Just don't.'

For a while they sat together in silence, Isabel grateful for the company but engrossed in her own thoughts. And then Ian arrived, unobtrusively; suddenly he was beside her, a hand on her shoulder. This was the signal for the other woman to push her empty glass away and get up from her bar stool. 'Remember, hen,' she whispered. 'Remember. Take nae nonsense. Stand up for yoursel'.'

Ian sat down on the vacated stool. He was dressed less formally than he had been when Isabel had seen him on previous occasions. His sweater and moleskin trousers were in keeping with the clothes of the drinkers in the bar. He looked relaxed.

'This is a bit of a surprise,' he began, looking about the room. 'I used to come here years ago, you know. Hamish Henderson often sat over there. I heard him sing "Farewell to Sicily". It made quite an impression on me.'

'I heard it, too,' said Isabel. 'Not here. At the School of Scottish Studies once. He sang while standing on a chair, as I recall.'

Ian smiled at the thought. 'That great, shuffling figure. The teeth all over the place . . . You know, we took them for granted then, didn't we? We had all those people amongst us, those poets, those Scots *makars* – Norman MacCaig, Sydney Goodsir Smith, Hamish himself. And you could see them in the street. There they were.' He looked at her. 'Do you remember "The lament for the makars", Isabel?'

Isabel remembered: warm afternoons during the summer term at school, sitting on the grass with Miss Crichton, who taught them English and who loved the early Scottish poets.

'I have that entire poem in my head,' Ian said. 'It's such a striking idea – just to list all the poets, all the poets who have gone before. And then Dunbar says that he's probably next! *The good Sir Hew of Eglintoun, /Ettrick, Heriot, and Wintoun, /He has tane out of this cuntrie:–/Timor Mortis conturbat me.*'

He caught the eye of the barman and pointed to a whisky. 'Taken out of the country, Isabel. Such clear good language. *I am taken out of the country. I am taken from you.* I was almost taken out of the country, Isabel, until that young man, whoever he was, and those surgeons came to my rescue.'

The barman passed him a small glass of whisky and he raised it, giving the Gaelic toast. 'Slainte.'

Isabel raised her own glass in acknowledgement.

Ian looked at her enquiringly. 'Why have you asked me here, Isabel? Not to discuss poetry.'

She lifted her glass and looked into the whisky, which she was not enjoying. It was too strong for her.

'That man I told you about,' she began. 'Graeme. The man I found.'

His expression changed; he now became tense. 'You've decided on something?'

Isabel lowered her voice. 'He's here. Right here. But I've found out something. He's got nothing to do with the person who donated for you. Nothing!'

He did not look round immediately, but stared ahead, at the bottles of whisky on the shelf. Then, very slowly, he turned his head and looked towards the back of the bar.

'Where?' he muttered. 'I can't see anybody . . .' He

stopped, and Isabel saw his bottom lip drop slightly. His right hand, resting on the bar, was suddenly clenched.

Graeme was sitting on a bench at the back. He had a newspaper unfolded on his lap. In front of him, on a small table, was a half-empty glass of beer.

'Is that him?' Isabel asked. 'Is that the man you keep seeing?'

Ian's eyes were fixed on the figure at the other end of the bar. Now he turned back to face Isabel. 'I don't know what to think,' he said. 'I feel very strange.'

'But it's him?' Isabel pressed.

Ian looked over his shoulder again. As he did so, Graeme turned his head, and Isabel saw his glance come in her direction. She stared back at him, and they looked at one another, across the room, for almost a minute. Then he turned back to his paper.

Ian suddenly reached for Isabel's arm. He clutched at her, and she felt his grip through the material of her sleeve. 'I'm not feeling well,' he said. 'I'm going to have to go. I'm sorry . . . I'm feeling very odd.'

Isabel experienced a moment of sudden alarm. His face looked drawn, pale; he had slumped slightly on his stool, his right arm slipping off the bar. She imagined the heart within him, the alien organ, sensing the adrenalin from the shock that he had experienced on seeing the face of his imaginings. It was folly to have invited him here, and for what reason? That he should confront this man, who had nothing to do with him anyway, since his partner's son had not been the donor?

She put her arm round him, half to support him, half to comfort him.

'Shall I call somebody? A doctor?'

He opened his mouth to speak, but said nothing. It seemed to Isabel that he was gasping for air, and she looked about wildly. The barman, from behind the bar, leant forward in concern. 'Sir? Sir?'

Ian looked up. 'I'm all right,' he said. 'I'm all right.'

'Let me take you to a doctor,' said Isabel. 'You don't look all right. You really don't.'

'It sometimes happens like this,' he said. 'It's nothing to do with the heart. It's the drugs, I think. My system is at sixes and sevens with itself. I suddenly feel weak.'

Isabel said nothing. She still had her arm about him and now he stood up, gently pushing her aside.

'That looks like him,' he said. 'It's very odd, isn't it? That's the face I've been seeing. Now, there he is. Sitting over there.'

'I'm not sure that I should have asked you to come,' said Isabel. 'You see, I thought that he had followed me in here. It occurred to me that at least we should establish whether it was him.'

Ian shrugged. 'It's him. But I don't want to speak to him.' He made a helpless gesture. 'And what would I say to him, anyway? You tell me that he's got nothing to do with what happened. So where does that leave us?'

They left the bar together, not looking back at Graeme. Isabel asked him whether he would mind walking with her round the corner to the taxi rank outside the high Gothic edifice of George Heriot's School. He agreed, and they walked off slowly. He still seemed slightly breathless, and she walked at the pace he set.

211

'I'm worried about you,' she said. 'I shouldn't have done this.' And as she got into the taxi, she said, through the open window, 'Ian, would you like me to do nothing more? To keep out of the whole thing?'

He shook his head. 'No,' he said. 'I wouldn't want that.'

Very well. But there was another thing that had puzzled her. 'Your wife, Ian? What does she think of my involvement in this? I'm sorry, but I can't help wondering what she thinks about your seeing me, rushing out to meet me in a bar, for example.'

He looked away. 'I haven't told her. I haven't told her about anything.'

'Is that wise?'

'Probably not. But don't we often lie to people we love, or not tell them things, precisely because we love them?'

Isabel looked into his eyes for a moment. Yes. He was right. She closed the window. He walked to the next taxi on the rank and opened the door, and then both taxis moved out into the traffic. Isabel sat back in her seat. Before the taxi turned, to make its way along Lauriston Place, she looked back to the end of Forrest Road, half expecting to see Graeme appear, coming round the corner. But she did not see him and she upbraided herself for her overactive imagination. He had no reason to follow her. He was an entirely innocent man who was simply annoyed with her for upsetting his partner. She should keep out of his way – as she had been trying to do. She could imagine how he felt about her. She imagined his saying to a friend: *There's a silly woman, a so-called medium, who has upset Rose. There are people like that, you know: they can't let the dead lie down.*

Isabel settled herself back in the taxi seat. The key question in her mind was this: When their eyes had met in Sandy Bell's, when Graeme had turned his head and seen her, had he looked surprised?

18

Grace brought the morning mail through to Isabel's study. There were many more letters than usual, prompting a grimace from Grace as she laid the towering pile of envelopes and packages on the desk.

Isabel gasped. If she were not there, how quickly would the mail pile up, gradually filling room after room, until the house itself was full. 'What would happen if I went away, Grace? What if I went off to . . .' She did not continue. She was planning to go away, or almost planning to go away, with an Italian, no less, in a Bugatti. But she could hardly say that to Grace – just yet.

'Twenty-five letters today,' said Grace. 'I counted them. Ten manuscripts – ten! Four parcels that look like books, one of them extremely heavy. And eleven letters, of which three are bills, in my opinion.'

Isabel thanked her. It had become something of a ritual in recent months for Grace to attend the opening of the mail and for Isabel to hand on to her those items that could be placed straight in the recycling pile. Some were placed in the pile unsullied; others were torn up by Grace according to a system of her own devising. She never tore up anything from the Conservatives, but the other parties were torn up or spared according to her view of their current performance.

Isabel opened a letter with a neatly typed envelope. 'My friend, Julian,' she said. She read the brief letter, laughing aloud at its conclusion.

'I believe he's serious,' she said, passing the letter to Grace. 'An offer of a paper on the ethics of the buffet bar.'

Grace read the letter and passed it back to Isabel. 'Of course it's theft,' she said. 'Helping oneself to bread rolls like that. Surely he can see that.'

'Julian Baggini is a subtle man,' said Isabel. 'And his question is a serious one. Is it ethical to take extra bread rolls from the hotel buffet? And use them for your picnic lunch?'

'Really,' Grace snorted. 'Is that what your readers want to read about?'

Isabel thought for a moment. 'We could do a special issue on the ethics of food,' she mused. 'We could use Julian's paper there.'

'The ethics of food?'

Isabel picked up her paper-knife and stroked the edge. 'Food is a more complex subject than one might think, you know. There is every reason why a philosopher should think about food.'

'One of them being hunger,' retorted Grace.

Isabel conceded the point. 'Philosophers are no different from anybody else. Philosophers have their needs.' She looked at the letter again. 'Buffet bars. Yes. I can just imagine the problems.'

'Theft,' repeated Grace. 'You shouldn't take what's not yours. Is there anything more you can say about it?'

Isabel put her hands behind her head and looked up at the ceiling. Grace was in some matters, though not in others, a reductionist, a consummate wielder of Occam's razor; which was a good thing, in a way.

'But it's not always clear what's yours and what isn't yours,' Isabel countered. 'You may think that you're entitled to that extra bread roll, but what if you're not? What if the hotel intends that you should take only one?'

'Then you've taken something that you think is yours, but which isn't,' said Grace. 'And that isn't theft – at least it's not theft in my book.'

Isabel contemplated this for a moment. Two people go to a party, she thought, both with similar-looking umbrellas. One person leaves the party early. He takes an umbrella which he thinks is his, but he discovers when he gets home that it is the wrong one. That, she imagined, was not theft, in the moral sense at least, and surely it would not be theft in the legal sense. Somewhere in the back of her mind she remembered a discussion with a lawyer about that, a sharp-nosed advocate who spoke in a deliberate, pedantic way but who had a mind like . . . well, Occam's razor. He had said something about how the law allowed a defence of error, as long as one's error was reasonable; which in itself seemed reasonable enough.

'The law uses tests of reasonableness,' he had said, and he had proceeded to give her examples which had stuck in her mind.

'Take causation,' he went on. 'You're responsible for those consequences of your acts which a reasonable person would foresee. You aren't responsible for anything outside that. So let me tell you about a real case. *A* had assaulted *B* and *B* was lying on the ground, bleeding from a head wound. Along came *C*, who had attended a first-aid course. He had been taught about tourniquets and so he applied a tourniquet.'

'To the neck?'

'Unfortunately, yes. And the question was whether *A* was responsible for *B*'s death – which of course was by asphyxiation rather than loss of blood. What do you do about an unreasonable rescuer?'

Isabel had managed to keep a straight face, but only just. This was, after all, a tragedy. 'And was he?' she asked.

The lawyer frowned. 'Sorry,' he replied. 'I can't for the life of me remember the outcome. But here's another one. *A* has a fight with *B*, who pushes him out of the window. *A* doesn't fall very far as he's wearing braces, or suspenders, as the Americans rather more accurately call them. These get caught on the balcony and he ends up suspended. A crowd gathers down below and a rescuer appears on the balcony. "Get him down," the crowd shouts. Whereupon the helpful rescuer cuts the elastic.'

'That's very sad,' said Isabel. 'Poor man.'

The lawyer had remembered the outcome of that case, and had told her. But now Isabel had forgotten what he said it was. She looked at Grace.

'But do you think that the person who takes the extra roll thinks that he's entitled to it?' she asked.

'He may,' said Grace. 'If I leave something on a table and say *Help yourself*, then surely you're entitled to do just that.'

'But what if I took everything?' objected Isabel. 'What if I brought my suitcase down and filled it with food? Enough for a week?'

'That would be selfish,' said Grace.

Isabel nodded her agreement. 'Very selfish,' she said. 'And is selfishness wrong, or is it something which the virtuous person should merely avoid?' She thought for a moment. 'Perhaps the solution is that the invitation to help yourself is subject to an implied limitation. What it means is *Help yourself to what you need*.'

'For breakfast,' added Grace. 'Help yourself to what you need *for breakfast*.'

'Exactly,' said Isabel. 'I'm not sure how far we can get with the ethics of the buffet bar, but there are some rather interesting problems there. Shall I write to Julian or would you like to do that?'

Grace laughed. 'You, I think. Nobody would listen to me.'

'They would listen to you,' Isabel said.

Grace shuffled through the letters. 'I don't think so. And why should they? I'm just the cleaning lady to them.'

'You're not,' said Isabel stoutly. 'You're the housekeeper. And there's a distinction.'

'They wouldn't think so,' said Grace.

'There have been some very talented, very famous housekeepers,' said Isabel.

Grace's interest was aroused. 'Oh yes? Such as?'

Isabel looked at the ceiling for inspiration. 'Oh well,' she said. And then she said 'Well' again. She had made the comment without thinking, and now, when she put her mind to it, she could not come up with any. Who were the mute, unsung heroines? There must have been many, but now she could think only of the woman who had put Carlyle's manuscript in the fire. She was a maid, was she not, or was she a housekeeper? Was there a distinction? She thought about it briefly and then decided that she was getting nowhere with anything and the pile of mail was effectively as high as it had been before she had started to think about buffet bars, and bread rolls, and housekeepers.

She looked at the next letter, but put it down again before opening it. Her mind had returned to the possible special issue on the ethics of food. There would have to be a paper on the moral issues raised by chocolate; the more she thought of it, the richer became the philosophical dimensions of chocolate. It brought *akrasia*, weakness of the will, into sharp focus. If we know that chocolate is bad for us (and *in some respects* chocolate is bad for us, in the sense that it makes us put on weight), then how is it that we end up eating too much of it? That suggests that our will is weak. But if we eat chocolate, then it must be that we think that it is in our best interests to do so; our will moves us to do what we know we will like. So our will is not weak – it is actually quite strong, and prompts us to do that which we *really* want to do (to eat chocolate). Chocolate was not simple.

She worked solidly that day until three in the afternoon, when she telephoned Angus Spens at the *Scotsman* offices.

Angus was not there to take her call, but he called back fifteen minutes later, when Isabel was in the kitchen, making herself a cup of tea.

'I saw you the other day,' she said. 'You were getting into a taxi outside your office. You looked terribly smart, Angus, in your black coat. Very smart.'

'I was off to interview another Stuart pretender,' he said. 'We get these people turning up from time to time, claiming to be descendants of Bonnie Prince Charlie or his dad. They're a pretty motley crew, as you can imagine.'

'Cranks?' asked Isabel.

'Some of them,' said Angus. 'The problem, as you no doubt know, is that Prince Charlie had no legitimate offspring. And his brother, who was a cardinal, enjoyed a very happy bachelor existence. He died full of years, but not exactly surrounded by descendants. So that was the end of the direct Stuart line. You learnt that in school, didn't you? I certainly did.'

'But not everybody wants to believe it?'

There was silence for a moment. Then Angus sighed. 'One of the problems of being in the newspaper business is that you get contacted by an awful lot of people who think the world is otherwise than we are told it is. They really believe that. And these Stuart people are a little bit like that. Some of them are perfectly reasonable people who really believe that they have a claim – and back it up with books on the subject. But others are fantasists, although every so often one comes along who appears to have a rather better claim. This one was an Italian and had been bombarding the Lord Lyon for ages with his papers. They took the view that he

220

was at least who he said he was, and that there were interesting lines to explore, whatever they meant by that.'

'And?'

'And he turned out to be a most agreeable person to interview,' said Angus. 'Very modest. Very charming. And you know what else? He bore a striking resemblance to James the sixth. It could have been old Jamie Sext himself sitting there. It was the bone structure, not the colouring. Just something about the cheekbones and the eyes. I was astonished.'

'There's a good few generations in between,' said Isabel.

'Yes, but family looks go down the ages. Anyway, there he was, brimming with Jacobite enthusiasm. I wondered whether he imagined that the clans would rise again if the Lord Lyon pronounced in his favour.'

'Well it was all rather romantic,' said Isabel.

'And Jamie Sext was an interesting monarch. An intellectual. Probably bisexual, or, should one put it, he ruled both ways?'

'You're very amusing, Angus,' said Isabel drily. Then she laughed. 'Wouldn't you like to have had dinner with him?'

Angus would not. 'It would have been highly dangerous to have dinner with any Scottish king,' he said. 'That is, until recently, if you can call the Hanoverians Scottish. No, I don't think dinner would have been a good idea. Look at Darnley and what happened to Rizzio.'

Isabel was not prepared to let this go. Rizzio, the Italian secretary of Mary, Queen of Scots, had been murdered in Edinburgh before the Queen's very eyes by a group of armed men. Mary's husband, Lord Darnley, was said to have been one of the murderers, acting out of jealousy. But Isabel felt that there was inadequate proof of this.

'Where exactly is your evidence, Angus?' she challenged. 'You can't go round defaming people like that. You do Darnley a great injustice.'

Angus laughed. 'How can you speak like that? This all happened in – when was it? – fifteen sixty-something. Can you do an injustice to somebody who hasn't been with us for over four hundred years? Hardly.'

Again Isabel felt that she had to protest. As it happened, she was interested in the philosophical issue of whether you can harm the dead. There was more than one view on that . . . but perhaps this was not the time.

'I think that we shall have to come back to Lord Darnley some other time,' she said. 'And in particular, I should like to discuss with you the precise circumstances of his own death, or murder, as it undoubtedly was. I have views on that, you know.'

Isabel heard a sigh from the other end of the line. 'Well, well, Isabel! So you might be able to solve that little issue. Now that would be a very good story. Can the *Scotsman* have the exclusive?'

'That depends on your attitude,' she said. 'But look, Angus, I didn't telephone you to discuss Scottish history. I want to call in a favour.'

Angus sounded surprised. 'I thought you owed me . . . Remember . . .'

'Let's not count too scrupulously,' Isabel said hurriedly. 'Just a small favour. A name, that's all.'

She told him what she wanted, and he listened quietly.

She thought it would be easy, she said, and that surely he had his contacts in the health service or the hospital. Did he not have favours of his own to call in?

'As it happens I do,' he said. 'There's a certain doctor who had very sympathetic coverage from us when he appeared before the General Medical Council on a complaint. I felt genuinely sorry for him and thought he was in the right. Some of the other papers went for him in a big way. He was very grateful to me.'

'Ask him,' said Isabel.

'All right, but I won't press him if he's at all unwilling.'

They agreed that he would call her back if he heard anything, or even if he did not hear anything. Then they rang off, and Isabel turned to her cup of tea. She liked to mix Earl Grey with Darjeeling. Earl Grey by itself she found too scented; Darjeeling took the edge off that. Flowers and smoke, she thought, and wondered for a moment about what Mary, Queen of Scots drank. She made a mental note to ask her friend Rosalind Marshall about that; she knew everything about Scottish queens and wrote books about them, in her house in Morningside. Poor Mary – she had spent so much time locked up in castles, poor woman, working away at her elaborate French needlework and writing those rather poignant letters of hers. Drinking chocolate had reached Spain by then, but had probably not reached the Scottish court. And tea did not arrive until the beginning of the seventeenth century, she believed. So it must have been some sort of herbal infusion, then, although she thought they did not drink infusions for pleasure; there was French wine for that. Smoke and flowers, flavours of exile, and of a

Scotland whose echoes one might just detect, now and then, in the lilt of a voice, in an old Scots word, in a shadow across the face, in a trick of the light.

Angus did phone, as he said he would, but much more quickly than Isabel had imagined. She had finished her second cup of tea and was about to take the cup to the sink when the telephone rang.

'Here's your name,' he said. 'Macleod. Is that what you were after?'

She stood quite still. In her left hand, the empty teacup tilted, allowing a few last drops to fall to the floor.

'Isabel?'

She had been thinking; over her second cup of tea she had been thinking about something else he had said, and now she wanted another name from him. 'Thank you. But before you go, Angus, that Italian you interviewed – what was he called?'

'One of those very long, aristocratic Italian names,' he said. 'But I simply addressed him as Tomasso.'

19

Isabel left the house and walked briskly along Merchiston Crescent to Bruntsfield. It was now shortly before seven, a good three hours after she had taken the telephone call from Angus with its two pieces of surprising information. And yet, three hours later, she could think of nothing else and wanted to talk to somebody. She had debated with herself as to whether she should contact Jamie, and had eventually decided to do so even if she had some misgivings. If she was looking for advice from him, then she had already had his opinion, which he had volunteered the day before on their walk to Holyrood. He had made it clear that there was nothing further that she could, or should, do. But that was before she had received the news from Angus. Now everything was different. Rose had deliberately concealed from her the fact that her son had been the donor. And that suggested, Isabel concluded, that she had something more significant to hide. The most likely explanation was that Rose knew about Graeme's involvement in the death of her son and had decided to protect him. And if that were true, then Isabel felt that she should have no compunction in passing on the information she had, such as it was. There would be no danger in those circumstances of destroying the relationship between the two of them on a mere suspicion.

It was a relief to her to know this. She could do what she had to do, and then start minding her own business once again. But taking the decision to do something was not quite so easy if one had to take it without discussing it with anybody. And the only person she could really discuss it with was Jamie. Nobody else knew about this, except for Ian, of course, and after the scare in Sandy Bell's, when he seemed to be buckling under stress, she was unwilling to expose him to more anxiety.

So it would have to be Jamie, and fortunately he had been free for dinner.

She had been candid over the telephone. 'It's an invitation with a price tag,' she had explained. 'I want to ask you something. I won't talk too much about it. But I do want to ask your advice.'

'About . . .'

'Yes,' she had interjected. 'About that.'

She had expected him to sigh, or even to groan, and she was taken aback by his upbeat reply. 'That's fine,' he said. 'In fact, I wanted to talk to you about that too.'

She did not conceal her astonishment. 'You did?'

'Yes. But we can talk about it over dinner. That's my doorbell. Adolescent number three. He's the one who tries to play the bassoon with chewing gum in his mouth. Would you believe it?'

Isabel suddenly thought of Tomasso and of the disclosure made by Angus Spens. 'I would believe absolutely anything,' she said. 'Anything.'

She walked into town, making her way across the Meadows against the stream of students coming from the direction of the university. The students walked in twos and threes, engaged in animated conversation, and she thought for a moment of how she herself had done precisely the same thing, walking with her classmates, talking about the same issues, and with the same intensity, as these young people. They thought, of course, that the only people who were interesting, who really counted, were those who were twenty, or thereabouts. She had thought that too. And now? Did people of Isabel's age, in their early forties, think that the world was composed of people in their early forties? She believed not. And the difference was this, she mused: those who are twenty don't know what it is like to be forty, whereas those who are forty know what it is like to be twenty. It was a bit like discussing a foreign country with somebody who has never been there. They are prepared to listen, but it's not quite real for them. We are all interested to hear what Argentina is like, but it's difficult to *feel* for it unless one has actually been there.

The problem with being me, thought Isabel, as she walked along George IV Bridge, is that I keep thinking about the problem of being me. Her thoughts went off in all sorts of

227

directions, exploring, probing, even fantasising. She suspected that most other people did not think like this at all. In fact, she had often wondered what other people thought about as they walked through the streets of Edinburgh. Did they think about the sort of things that she thought about – about what one should do, about what one should allow oneself to think? She was sure that they did not. And when she had asked Cat what she thought about when she walked every morning from her flat to the delicatessen, she had simply replied, 'Cheese.'

Isabel had been taken aback. 'All the time? Does cheese give you enough to think about?'

Cat had thought for a moment before answering. 'Well, not just cheese, I suppose. I think about things in the delicatessen. Olives, too, I suppose. Salami sometimes.'

'In other words,' said Isabel, 'you think about your work.'

Cat shrugged. 'I suppose I do. But sometimes my mind just wanders. I think about my friends. I think about what I should wear. I even think about men sometimes.'

'Who doesn't?' said Isabel.

Cat had raised an eyebrow. 'Do you?'

'I am just like anybody else,' said Isabel. 'Although sometimes, I suppose, I think about . . .'

Cat had laughed. 'I suppose if one wrote down all one's thoughts through the day it would make very odd reading.'

'It would,' said Isabel. 'And one of the reasons why it would make such odd reading is that language would be inadequate to describe our thoughts. We don't think in words all the time. We don't engage in one long soliloquy. We don't mentally say things like: "I must go into town

228

today." We don't use those actual words, but we may still make a decision to go into town. Mental acts and mental states don't require language.'

'So a person who never learnt a language could think in the same way as we do?' Cat sounded doubtful. How could one know one was going into town unless one had the word for *going* and the word for *town*?

'Yes,' said Isabel. 'A person like that would have mental pictures. He would have feelings. He would have memories of what has happened to him and knowledge of what may happen in the future. The only difference is that he would find difficulty in communicating these, or recording them for that matter.'

And she thought of Brother Fox, who had no language, other than a howl or yelp, but who knew about danger and fear, and who presumably had very precise memories of the layout of the walled gardens which composed his territory. She had looked into the eyes of Brother Fox on a number of occasions when they had surprised one another, and she had seen recognition in those eyes, and an understanding that he should be cautious of her, but not terrified. So there were memories in that mind, and at least some mute processes of thought, unfathomable to us. *What is it like to be Brother Fox?* Only Brother Fox knew the answer to that, and he was not in a position to reveal it.

Isabel had reserved a table near the front window of the Café St Honoré. From where they sat they could look up the short, steep section of cobbled road that led to Thistle Street. It was a small restaurant and well suited for a conversational dinner, although the proximity of tables to one another could be a problem if what one had to say was private. Isabel had heard, without consciously trying, snippets of choice gossip here such as the terms of a cohabitation agreement between a fashionable doctor and his much younger girlfriend – she was to receive a half-interest in the house and there was to be an independent bank account. And all of this came from his lawyer, who was talking to his own girlfriend, who was urging him on for further details. Isabel had looked away, but could hardly stuff her fingers into her ears. And then she had turned round and stared in reproach at the lawyer, whom she recognised, but was greeted with a cheerful wave rather than a look of contrition.

Jamie examined the menu while Isabel discreetly looked at the other diners. Her friends, Peter and Susie Stevenson, out for dinner with another couple, nodded and smiled. At the nearest table, sitting by himself, the heir to a famous Scottish house, weighed down by history and ghosts, turned the pages of a book he had brought with him. Isabel glanced at him and felt a pang of sympathy: each in his separate loneliness, she thought. And I, the lucky one, able to come to this place with this handsome young man, and it does not matter in the slightest if they look at me and think, *There is a woman out for dinner with her younger boyfriend.* But then the thought occurred to her: they might not think that at all, but think, instead, *Cradle snatch.*

That was a disturbing thought, and a melancholy one. She consciously put it out of her mind and looked across the menu at Jamie. He had been in a good mood when she had entered the restaurant and found him already at the table. He had risen to his feet, smiled, and leant across to plant a quick kiss on her cheek – which had excited her, and made her blush, even if it was only a social kiss.

Jamie smiled back at her. 'I've had some good news,' he said. 'I've been looking forward to telling you.'

She laid down the menu. Asparagus and red snapper could wait. 'A recording contract?' she teased. 'Your own disc?'

'Almost as good,' he said. 'Oh yes, almost as good as that.'

She felt a sudden sense of dread. He had found a new girl-friend, would get married, and that would be the end for her. Yes, that was what had happened. This was a last supper. She glanced at the man at his single table, with his book; that would be her lot from now on, sitting at a single table with a copy of Daniel Dennett's *Consciousness Explained* open in front of her among the salt cellars and butter dishes, and the olive oil, of course.

'I don't think I told you,' he said, 'that I was having an audition yesterday. In fact, I'm pretty sure I didn't tell you. I wouldn't want to have to say to you that I didn't get in. I suppose it's a question of pride.'

Isabel's anxiety was replaced by relief. Auditions were no threat. Unless . . .

'The London Symphony,' he said.

For a moment she said nothing. The London Symphony was in London.

'Well!' she exclaimed with a Herculean effort of fellow feeling. 'That's very good.' Was 'very good' too faint praise? She decided that it was – if she were to conceal her sudden, overwhelming despair. 'That's wonderful!'

Jamie sat back in his seat. He was beaming with pleasure. 'It was the most intimidating experience of my life. I went down just for the day, and they heard me at noon. There were about ten other players hanging around. One of them showed me his new CD, complete with his picture on the back. I almost gave up there and then.'

'What an ordeal.' She could not manage an exclamation mark. She was too dispirited.

'It was. Until I started to play.' He threw up his hands. 'Something came upon me – I don't know what it was. But I could hardly believe the sound of my own playing.'

Isabel looked down at the table, at the knives and forks. I have to expect this, she said to herself; it was inevitable that I would lose him, quite inevitable. And when one lost a friend, what was the right thing to do? To mourn the loss, or to take pleasure in the memories of the friendship? Of course it was the latter – she was well aware of that – but it was difficult, in the Café St Honoré, to behave correctly when one's heart was a cold stone within one.

Jamie continued with his story. 'They told us that they would not reach a decision that day, but they called me anyway, just as I was getting on the train to come home. And they said that they had chosen me.'

'No surprise that,' said Isabel. 'Of course you've always been a very fine player, Jamie. I've always known that.'

He seemed embarrassed by the praise, and waved it aside. 'Anyway, we can talk about that later on. What about you?'

'Working,' said Isabel. 'At the job I'm meant to do, and . . .'

Jamie cast his eyes up in a gesture of mock impatience. 'And at what you're not meant to be doing, too, no doubt.'

'I know,' said Isabel. 'I know what you're going to say.' And she thought of what it would be like when Jamie had gone and they could not have these discussions. Could she get involved in what she called her *issues* if she had nobody to sound them out with, nobody to advise her? For that is what the loss of Jamie would mean to her.

Jamie reached for the glass of water that the waiter had brought him. 'But I'm not going to say it,' he said. 'Instead I'm going to give you a piece of information which I hope will –'

Isabel reached out and touched him on the arm. 'Before you do, let me tell you something. I know you feel that I should disengage from this issue. I know you think I've followed totally the wrong path. I know that. But I heard today from that journalist we saw. Remember him?'

'The one you shared a bath with?'

'The very one. We were extremely small then, let me remind you. And the bath, as I recall, was quite large. Anyway, he found out from some medical contact the name of the donor. And it's Macleod.'

She lowered her voice to impart this information, although nobody was in a position to hear, except possibly the man immersed in his book. But he did not know who Isabel was, although she knew exactly who he was, and he would never have eavesdropped.

She had expected her announcement to have a marked effect on Jamie, but his reaction was mild. In fact, he smiled and nodded his agreement. 'Just so,' he said.

Isabel leant forward. 'Macleod,' she repeated. 'Macleod. And that means that that woman lied to me. And it also means that Graeme, her man, could be the man whom Ian sees – if he really sees anybody, but let's just imagine for the moment that he does.'

Again Jamie received this with equanimity. 'Yes,' he acknowledged. 'Macleod.'

Isabel felt her irritation grow. 'You don't seem to be in the least bit surprised,' she muttered, picking up the menu to examine it again. 'I won't burden you with this. I suggest that we change the subject.'

Jamie made a calming gesture. 'Sorry, but you see, I'm not surprised. And the reason is . . . Well, I know that it's Macleod. But it's not the Macleod you think it is.'

Isabel stared at him in incomprehension. 'You're losing me,' she said.

Jamie took another sip of his water. 'The other day after you left me, I decided to drop into the library on George IV Bridge,' he said. 'Like you, I went through the *Evening News* for the week that you talked about. And I found what I'm afraid you missed, Isabel. Not that I'm trying to rub it in . . .'

'You found something else about the accident?'

Jamie shook his head. 'No. It had nothing to do with that accident. It was an entirely unrelated death – of a young man. Tucked away in the death notices, on exactly the same day.'

Yes, thought Isabel. It had been an obvious mistake on her part. She should have checked to see whether there was any other young man who died that day in the Edinburgh area.

But she had not, and yet . . . She reminded herself that Angus had confirmed that the name of the donor was Macleod. So she was right; even if there had been another young man who had died that day, Rose's son had been the donor.

'But we know that the donor was called Macleod,' she said defensively. 'That rather suggests that my initial assumption was correct.'

'So was the other young man,' said Jamie simply. 'Two Macleods.'

She stared at him open-mouthed. 'Both . . .'

'Remember those stories about Hebridean islands where everybody's called Macleod?' Jamie said lightly. 'Well Edinburgh's not quite like that, but there are lots of Macleods, you know. And it just so happens that two Macleods unfortunately died on that day. The other Macleod, Gavin, lived just outside town, in West Linton. The death notice gave the name of his mother, Jean, and a younger brother and sister. No father was mentioned. But I looked up J. Macleod in the phone book and there's a J. Macleod in West Linton. So that's your answer.'

He finished speaking and sat back in his seat again. Then he spread his hands, palms outward, in a gesture of finality, as if to say that the case was closed. He tilted his head quizzically. 'Are you going to leave it at that? Aren't you going to have to accept that coincidences happen? And that some things are just inexplicable, or just meaningless – such as visions of faces by people who have had heart surgery? Can't you just accept that?'

Isabel made an immediate decision. 'No,' she said. 'I might

in due course, but not just yet. I'd like to know a little bit more. How did your Macleod die?'

'The death notice said that he died peacefully, at the age of twenty-two,' Jamie said, '"after a bravely borne illness" – those were the exact words. So no accident. Nothing like that.' He paused. 'Which makes your man with the high forehead a bit superfluous, doesn't it?'

Isabel realised that she had much to think about, but for the moment she would say nothing more about it to Jamie, who would simply advise her to keep out of matters that did not concern her. He was clearly pleased with his findings, which made Isabel look a bit hasty. Well, he could enjoy his moment of triumph; she did not begrudge him that, but she had a duty to Ian to see things through, and she would.

She dodged his question. If Graeme was the man with the high forehead, then it was difficult to see where he fitted in. But he could not be the man. Graeme's resemblance to the man whom Ian saw was purely coincidental, one of those highly unlikely chances that simply materialised to remind us that chance still existed. And Graeme's irritation with her was purely an irritation based on his belief that she was inter-fering in things that did not concern her. And who could blame him? No, Graeme was irrelevant now.

'Well, you've given me something to think about,' she said. 'Thank you. And now, perhaps we can catch the waiter's eye and order. There are other things to talk about. The London Symphony, for instance.'

Jamie beamed with pleasure. 'The London Symphony!' he said. 'Good, isn't it?'

Isabel tried to smile. Perhaps I've managed a down-turned

smile, she thought, one of those smiles where the lips go down at the side. A rueful smile; full of rue, of sorrow.

'Where will you live in London?' she enquired. 'Not that it'll mean much to me. My geography of London is pretty shaky. North of the river? South of the river? And don't some people actually live *on* the river? Londoners and New Yorkers and people like that are so resourceful. They live in all sorts of caves and corners. Look at the Queen; she lives at the *back* of a palace . . .'

Jamie cut her short. 'Some people live in houseboats,' he said. 'I know somebody who has one. Pretty damp way to live. No, I'm not going to live in London.'

'You'll commute?' asked Isabel. 'What about concerts finishing late? Don't the trains stop? And what happens if you try to talk to your fellow commuters? If the silence gets too much for you? Do you realise that people die of boredom in London suburbs? It's the second biggest cause of death amongst the English in general. Sheer boredom . . .'

'I'm not going, Isabel,' said Jamie. 'Sorry, I should have told you right at the beginning. I'm not going to take the job.'

It took her a moment to react to what he had said. Her first feeling was one of joy, that she was not going to lose him after all. It was simple joy.

'I'm so glad,' she said. And then, correcting herself, she said quickly, 'But why? Why go for the audition if you didn't want the job?'

Jamie explained that he had wanted the job, and that he had spent half the rail journey back thinking about when he would move and where he would live and so on. But the other half, from York onwards, was spent making up his mind to decline the offer.

'By the time I reached Edinburgh, my mind was made up,' he said. 'I decided to stay.'

There was a tone of finality in his voice. Isabel hesitated for a moment; the simplest thing to do would be to say that she thought this was a good idea and leave it at that. But she was curious as to why he should have changed his mind. And then it came to her. Cat. He would not leave Edinburgh as long as he entertained a hope that Cat might change her mind about him.

'It's Cat,' she said quietly. 'It is her, isn't it?'

Jamie met her eyes, but then looked away in embarrass-ment. 'Maybe. Maybe . . .' He trailed off. Then, 'Yes,' he said. 'It is. When I faced up to it, as I did on the train, that was what I decided. I don't want to leave her, Isabel. I just don't.'

From the heights of the elation she had experienced when Jamie had announced that he would not go to London after all, Isabel now descended to the depths of doubt. Once again the problem lay in the fact that she was a philosopher and that she thought about duty and obligation. From the selfish point of view she should say nothing; but Isabel was not self-ish. And so she felt compelled to say to Jamie that he should not turn down something that was important to him in the hope, the vain hope, she had to say, that Cat would come back to him.

'She won't come back to you, Jamie,' she said softly. 'You can't spend your life hoping for something that is never going to happen.'

Every word of her advice went against the grain of what she herself wanted. She wanted him to stay; she wanted things to remain as they were; she wanted him for herself. But in spite of this, she knew that she had to say the opposite of what she wanted.

She could tell that her words were having their effect, as he remained silent, staring at her, his eyes wide. His eyes had in them a light which seemed to dim now, to change its quality. What is beauty, she thought, but the promise of happiness, as Stendhal said it was? But it was more than that. It was a glimpse of what life might be if there were no disharmony, no loss, no death. She wanted to reach out, to touch his cheek and say, *Jamie, my beautiful Jamie*, but she could not, of course. She could neither say what she wanted to say, nor do what she wanted to do. Such is the lot of the philosopher, and most of the rest of us, too, if we are honest with ourselves.

When Jamie spoke, he spoke quietly. 'Just keep out of it, Isabel,' he said, between clenched teeth. 'Just mind your own business.'

She drew back, shocked by his intensity. 'I'm sorry,' she said. 'I was only trying . . .'

'Please shut up,' said Jamie, his voice raised. 'Just shut up.'

His words cut into her, hung in the air. She looked anxiously in the direction of the neighbouring table. There was no sign of anything having been heard, but he must have heard, the man with the book.

Then Jamie pushed his chair back, noisily, and stood up. 'I'm sorry,' he said. 'I just don't feel in the mood for dinner tonight.'

239

She could not believe it. 'You're going?'

'Yes. Sorry.'

She sat alone at the table, frozen in her embarrassment. The waiter came to the table swiftly and discreetly pushed Jamie's chair back against the table. His manner was sympathetic. And then, crossing quietly from the other side of the restaurant, Peter Stevenson was at her side, bending down to whisper to her.

'Come over and join us,' he said. 'We can't let you have dinner by yourself.'

Isabel looked up at him in gratitude. 'I think the evening's rather ruined for me,' she said.

'Surely there was no need for your friend to walk out like that,' said Peter.

'It's my fault,' said Isabel. 'I said something that I shouldn't. I touched the very rawest of nerves. I shouldn't have done it.'

Peter placed a hand on her shoulder. 'We all say things,' he said. 'Phone him tomorrow and patch up. It'll look different then.'

'I don't know,' said Isabel. She decided that some explanation was necessary. At the beginning of the evening she had rather relished the thought that people might imagine that she was with a younger lover; now she was not so sure whether that was what she would want people to believe.

'He and I are only friends,' she said to Peter. 'I wouldn't want you to think that there was anything more to it than that.'

Peter smiled. 'How disappointing! Susie and I have just been admiring your choice in men.' He looked at her mischievously. 'We were also hoping that this might mean you were spending less time fussing about ethical issues, and more time enjoying yourself.'

'I don't seem to be terribly good at enjoying myself,' said Isabel. 'But thanks for the advice.' She hesitated; yes, he was right – she should enjoy herself. And for that, well, there was Tomasso. She could think about him, and their planned trip away together; that moment of – what was it? – irresponsibility? No, she would look upon it as a moment of perfectly rational decision.

Peter nodded in the direction of his table. 'Come along,' he said. 'Join us. That's Hugh and Pippa Lockhart at our table. They met playing together in the Really Terrible Orchestra with us. She's less terrible at the trumpet than he is – in fact, she's quite good. You'll like them. Come on.'

She rose to her feet. The remains of the evening could be salvaged, a small scrap of dignity recovered. She had had misunderstandings with Jamie before, and she would apologise to him tomorrow. And then she reminded herself who she was. She was the editor of the *Review of Applied Ethics*. She was not a love-struck girl abandoned by a petulant boyfriend. These were restorative thoughts, and her mood lifted. She had done her duty and given him the advice that she was morally obliged to give him, so she had nothing to reproach herself for there. And, besides all this, she had the overwhelmingly good news that he would not be leaving Edinburgh. It was as if a weather warning had been lifted. There had been a mistake: winter was cancelled and we would move straight to spring.

So she crossed the restaurant to join Peter and Susie, oblivious to the furtive, pitying glances from those who had witnessed the sudden departure of Jamie. She held her head high; she had no need of pity. She might apologise to Jamie tomorrow, but she had no reason to apologise to these people. Edinburgh was a nosy town. People should mind their own business.

20

She liked the road out to West Linton, and always had. It snaked round the side of the Pentland Hills, past old farmsteads and fields of grazing sheep, past steep hillsides of heather and scars of scree, past Nine Mile Burn and Carlops; and all the while, to the south-east, the misty Lammermuirs, blue and distant, crouched against the horizon. It was a drive that was too short for her, for the thoughts that she wanted to think on such a road, and she would gladly, if ridiculously, have doubled back and turned round and done it all over again so that she could prolong the pleasure. But she had a mission, a meeting with Jean Macleod, whom she had phoned and asked to see. She had said, I need to talk to you about your son, the son you lost, and the woman at the other end of the line had caught her breath and been silent for a moment before she said that Isabel could come and see her.

The village of West Linton clung to the side of a hill. The Edinburgh road followed a high contour, with the village itself hugging the hillside down to the low ground below. On either side of the Edinburgh road there were Victorian villas, houses with wide gardens and conservatories and names that one might see in any small town in Scotland, names redolent of a douce Scotland of golf and romanticism. It was not Isabel's world; she was urban, not small town, but she knew it to be the Scottish hinterland, ignored by the cities, condescended to by the urbanites, but still there. It was a Scotland of quiet manners and reserved friendliness, a Scotland in which nothing much happened, where lives were lived unadventurously, and sometimes narrowly, to the grave. The lives of such people could be read in the local kirkyard, their loyalty and their persistence etched into granite: *Thomas Anderson, Farmer of East Mains, Beloved Husband of fifty-two years of* . . . and so on. These were people with a place, wed to the very ground in which they would eventually be placed. The urban dead were reduced to ashes, disposed of, leaving no markers, and then forgotten; memory here was longer and gave the illusion that we counted for more. It was a simple matter of identity, thought Isabel. If people do not know who we are, then naturally we are the less to them. Here, in this village, everybody would know who the other was, which made that crucial difference.

She branched off the main road and slowly wound her way down into the village. On either side of the narrow main street, small stone buildings rose – houses, shops, a pocket-sized hotel. There was a bookshop run by somebody she knew, and she would call in there afterwards, but for now she had to find the Wester Dalgowan Cottage, to which Jean Macleod had given her careful directions.

It was just off the road that led towards Peebles and Moffat – a small house constructed from the grey stone of the valley, at the end of a short section of potholed, unpaved track. Behind it the open fields stretched away to the south; in front of it a small patch of untended garden, suffocated by thriving rhododendrons, gave the house privacy from the road. An old Land-Rover, painted in British racing green, was parked beside the house.

The front door opened as Isabel approached it and Jean Macleod stepped out to greet her visitor. They shook hands, awkwardly, and Isabel noticed that Jean's skin was rough and dry. The hands of a farmer, she thought.

'You found your way,' said Jean. 'People often drive right past us and end up on the Moffat road.'

'I know the village a bit,' said Isabel. 'I occasionally come out to see Derek Watson at his bookshop. I like this place.'

'It's changing,' said Jean. 'But we're happy enough. We used to be quite an important little town, you know. When they drove the cattle down to the Borders. Then we went to sleep for a century or so.'

Jean ushered her into the front room of the cottage, a small sitting room furnished simply but comfortably. There was a table at one side piled with papers and journals. Isabel noticed a copy of the *Veterinary Journal* and drew her conclusions.

Jean noticed her glance. 'Yes,' she said. 'I'm a vet. I help out in a practice near Penicuik. It's small animal work. I used to do a lot of horses, but nowadays . . .' She left the sentence unfinished. She looked out of the window, out towards the fields on the other side of the road.

Isabel had learnt from her visit to the other Macleod. She would be direct now.

'I'm very sorry about your son,' she said. 'I don't know you and I didn't know him. But I'm sorry.'

Jean nodded. 'Thank you.' She looked at Isabel, waiting for her to continue. But then she said, 'I take it that you're one of the bipolar support group. Have you got a child affected by it?'

The question made clear the nature of the illness to which the newspaper notice had referred.

'No,' said Isabel. 'I haven't. I know what that's all about, but I haven't.'

Jean looked puzzled. 'Then, forgive my asking, but why have you come to see me?'

Isabel held her gaze. 'I've come because chance brought me into contact with somebody who has had a heart trans-plant.'

Jean's reaction to Isabel's words made it clear that Jamie's assumption had been correct. For a brief while she said nothing, but seemed to grasp for words. Then she moved over to the window and stood quite still, looking away from Isabel, gripping the windowsill with both hands. When she spoke her voice was low, and Isabel had to strain to hear what she said.

'We asked for privacy,' she said. 'We very specifically did

not want to meet whoever it was. We did not want to pro-long the whole agony of it.'

Suddenly she spun round, her eyes showing her anger. 'I said yes, they could use the heart. But that was it. I didn't want my other son to know. I didn't want my daughter to know. It seemed to me that it would just make it all the more difficult for them. Another thing to come to terms with – that somebody else had a bit of their brother. That a bit of their brother was still alive.'

Isabel was silent. It was not for her, she thought, to tell others how to deal with this most intimate of tragedies. One could debate the matter at great length in the bio-ethical literature, but those who wrote of honesty and disclosure and the nobility of gift might not have lost a brother.

Jean sat down again, staring at her hands. 'So, what do you want of me?' she asked.

Isabel waited a moment before she answered, but when Jean looked up again she spoke. Then she told her of her conversations with Ian and of Ian's anguish. 'I know it sounds fanciful,' she said. 'You're a scientist, after all. You know that tissue is tissue and that memory, conscious-ness, is something else altogether. I know this just doesn't make any sense. But that man, that man whose life your son saved, is experiencing what he claims to be experi-encing.'

Isabel was going to say a bit more, but Jean had raised a hand to stop her. 'It's his father,' she said flatly. 'That descrip-tion is of my husband. Or it sounds like him.'

It was a repetition, Isabel thought, of what had happened

before. She found it hard to believe. Coincidence piled upon coincidence. Names. Faces. All coincidence.

Jean had risen to her feet and opened the drawer in the table behind her. 'My husband will be my ex-husband, I suppose, in a few months. When the lawyers get a move on.' She paused, riffling through papers. Then she extracted a small coloured photograph of the sort used for passport applications and passed it to Isabel. 'That's him.'

Isabel took the photograph and looked at it. A pleasant-looking, open-faced man stared at the camera. There was a high forehead, and the eyes were slightly hooded. She looked for a scar, but could not see one; there was not enough resolution in the picture. She handed back the photograph and Jean tossed it into the drawer.

'I don't know why I should keep that,' she said. 'There's a lot of his stuff in the house. I'll get round to clearing things out one of these days, I suppose.'

She closed the drawer and turned to face Isabel again. 'You don't know what happened, do you? Has anybody told you?'

'All I know is what I've told you,' said Isabel. 'I know nothing about you, or your son. Nothing.'

Jean sighed. 'My son had not seen his father for months – almost a year, in fact. When Euan – that's my husband – left us, both of my sons refused to have anything more to do with him. They were angry. I thought they would come round, but they did not. And so when my Gavin died – and it was the depressive illness that killed him, of course, he was in a very deep depression when he took his own life – he had not seen or talked to his father for a long time. He died in a state of estrangement. And Euan, you know, did not come to the memorial service. He did not attend his own son's service.' She spoke slowly, but in a controlled way, looking at Isabel as she talked. 'I assume that he felt massively guilty, and I suppose I feel sorry for him. But there we are. It's done. It's over. He has to live with his feelings now.'

She looked helplessly at Isabel. 'He can't bring himself to approach me for help. So that's it. He still lives in the village, you know. So we have to try to avoid seeing each other. He drives out the other way, although it's longer for him to get to his practice – he's a vet, too. He can't face the children.'

Isabel felt that there was not much that she could say. She wondered, though, what Jean felt about Ian's claims. She had shown no real reaction to them and Isabel assumed that she discounted them.

'I hope that you don't mind my coming here with this story,' she said. 'I feel very awkward about it. But I felt I had to come.'

Jean shrugged. 'Don't worry about it. As for the story itself, well, people are always imagining these things, aren't they? I'm afraid that I'm a complete rationalist on all this. I've got no time for mumbo-jumbo.' She smiled at Isabel; the no-nonsense veterinarian, the believer in science. 'I'm afraid, Miss Dalhousie,' she went on, 'that I have never believed in any form of personal immortality. The end of consciousness is the end of us. And as for souls, well, the thing that strikes me is that if we have them, then so must animals. And if we survive death, then why should they not do so? So heaven, or whatever you want to call it, will be an awfully crowded place, with all those cats and dogs and cattle and so on. Does it make sense to you? It doesn't to me.'

249

There were things which Isabel might normally have said to this. We were not the same as other animals, she thought: their consciousness was very different from ours. But at the same time she did not believe, as Descartes had asserted, that dogs were machines. If the concept of a soul had any meaning, then there was some sort of canine soul there, and it was a loving one, was it not? And if there was any survival of consciousness, then she did not imagine that it would be attached to a bodily form; in which case if there were any place in which this survival was located, it could well be full of doggy souls as well as human souls. But on all of this she had an open mind. We strove for God – or many people did – and did it really matter what form we gave to that concept of God? In her mind it was a striving for the good. And what was wrong with striving for good in a way which made sense to the individual? Grace paid her visits to the spiritualist meetings; priests and bishops celebrated their rites at an altar; people bathed in the Ganges, travelled to Mecca. It was all the same urge, surely, and an urge that seemed an ineradicable part of our very humanity. We needed holy places, as Auden pointed out in his poem to water: *Wishing, I thought, the least of men their/Figures of splendour, their holy places.* As always, such a generous sentiment expressed in a few beautiful words.

She looked at Jean. She had survived the death of her son without the comfort of religious belief. And to do that, and not to have surrendered to despair, she must be a strong woman, who believes in something, in either just getting by in this life or continuing in the face of emptiness and lack of hope. Isabel glanced at Jean's hands, those hands rendered rough, no doubt, from the soap that she had to use constantly in her work; and she reminded herself that this woman brought relief from suffering every single working day and that she must do that for a reason other than the need to live. So there was purpose there, even if she did not acknowledge it, or talk about it.

There was something else that Isabel wanted to ask her, and she asked it as she rose to her feet to take her leave. Did her husband know that his son's heart had been transplanted? No, said Jean. She had told him of the death by telephone and their conversation had been short. He did not know.

On the way back she stopped at the bookshop in the village. Derek Watson greeted her warmly and led her into his kitchen behind the second-hand section. On the table a musical score was spread out, an arrangement in progress, with pencil markings and notes. He put on the kettle and fetched a battered biscuit tin.

Isabel looked at her friend. 'You must forgive me, Derek,' she said. 'I have come to see you, and yet I do not feel like talking. I have just been to see Jean Macleod.'

Derek stopped where he was, halfway between a cupboard and the table. He winced. 'That poor woman. Her son used to come in here regularly,' he said. 'He was interested in books about the Highlands. I used to look out for things for him and he would pore over them out there in the shop. And then I used to see him staring out of the window, across the street there, at his father's house. Sitting there staring.'

Isabel said nothing. 'Could you just talk to me, Derek, and let me sit here and listen? Talk to me about your composers, if you like.' He had written several biographies of composers.

'If you insist,' he said. 'I know how you feel, by the way. Sometimes I just like to listen.'

Isabel sat and listened. Derek was working on a defence of the work of Giacomo Meyerbeer.

'It's shocking,' he said. 'In the nineteenth century there was Meyerbeer, widely revered as one of the great figures of grand opera. Then suddenly – bang! – he fell from grace. And I'm very sorry to say that Wagner must take some of the blame for that, with his anti-Semitic views. Such an injustice. Meyerbeer was a compassionate man, a man of universalist outlook. A good man. And he was dropped. When did you last hear one of his operas? Well, there you are.'

Isabel sipped her tea. Should she be doing more to rescue the reputation of Giacomo Meyerbeer? No, her plate was full enough as it was. She would leave Meyerbeer to Derek.

'And then,' Derek continued, 'I'm working on a symphonic poem. That's it over there on the table. It's all about Saint Mungo, for whom I have a great deal of time. His grandfather, as you know, was King Lot of Orkney, but they had that peculiar pimple-shaped hill down near Haddington. When Lot discovered that his daughter had been taken advantage of by one Prince Owain – in a pigsty, mark you – he had her, poor girl, thrown off the hill. She survived, only to be put in a boat and let loose in the Forth. Not very kind. We treat single mothers so much better these days, don't you think?'

He refilled Isabel's teacup. 'She drifted over the Forth and landed near Culross. There she was rescued by Saint Serf, no

less, and she gave birth to Saint Mungo. So out of unkind-
ness and a lack of charity can come something good at the
end of the day.' He paused. 'I propose to capture that in a
symphonic poem. Or, rather, I shall try to.'

Isabel smiled. Listening to Derek had made her feel better.
There were countless injustices and difficulties in this world,
but small points of light too, where the darkness was held
back.

21

The note from Jamie was short and to the point. *I shall not be surprised*, he wrote, *if you do not wish to see me again. If I were you, I wouldn't. So all I can say is this: I should not have walked out of the St Honoré like that. It was childish and silly. I'm very sorry.*

'Dear Jamie,' she wrote in reply. 'If there is anybody with any apologising to do, it is me. I had intended to telephone you and tell you how sorry I am but I didn't get round to it in the excitement of . . . Oh, there I go. You won't approve of what I've done, but I have to tell you nonetheless. I went out to West Linton and spoke to the mother. It wasn't easy. But now I know, and I think that I am slowly coming to a full *and rational* explanation of what has happened. I am very pleased about that, even if you don't approve of what you think of as my meddling. (I am not a meddler, Jamie, I am an

254

intromitter. Yes, that's an old Scots law term which I rather like. It describes somebody who gets involved. A person who gets involved without good excuse is called a *vitious intromitter.* Isn't that a wonderful term? I, though, am *not* a *vitious intromitter.*)

'But an apology is due from me and you are getting it. Your feelings for Cat are your affair and I have no business passing comment on them. I shall not do that again. So please forgive me for telling you what to do when you hadn't asked for my advice in the first place.

'There is one further thing. I am *very* pleased that you have decided not to go to London. London is all very well, in its place, which is four hundred miles or so south of Edinburgh. Londoners are perfectly agreeable people – very cheerful, in spite of everything – but I'm sure that you are so much more appreciated in Edinburgh than you would be in London. I, for one, appreciate you, and I know that Grace does too, and then there are all those pupils of yours whose musicianship would take a dive were you to absent yourself. In short, we have all had a narrow escape.

'Does that all sound selfish? Yes, it does to me. It sounds to me as if I am giving you all sorts of reasons to stay in Edinburgh while really only thinking of myself and how much I would miss your company if you were to go. So you must discount my advice on that score and do exactly as you wish, should a future opportunity arise. And I must do the same. Although I have no desire to go anywhere, except for Western Australia, and the city of Mobile in Alabama, and Havana, and Buenos Aires, and . . .'

She finished the letter, addressed it, and placed it on the

hall table. When she left to go home in the afternoon, Grace would pick up the mail and deposit it in the postbox at the top of the road. Jamie would get her apology tomorrow and she would arrange to see him the day afterwards. She could ask him to bring some music and they would go into the music room and she would play the piano while he sang and it became dark outside. The editor of the *Review of Applied Ethics* (at the piano) with her friend, Jamie (tenor). How very Edinburgh. How very poignant.

She thought to herself – and smiled at the thought – if one followed the well-ordered life one would start each day with the writing of one's letters of apology . . . She wondered for a moment who else might be expecting an apology from her. Perhaps she had been a bit harsh in her rejection of that article on vice from that vicious Australian professor; perhaps he was gentle and sensitive and was in favour of vice only in the most theoretical of senses; perhaps he wept by whatever shore it was when he received her rejection – more likely he did not. All the Australian professors of philosophy she had met had been fairly robust. And she had not been rude to him – a bit brisk perhaps, but not rude.

She went through to the kitchen, thinking of form and friendship and how letters – and gifts – were the only vestiges of form which remained to us in the conduct of our friendships. Other cultures had much more elaborate forms for the recognition and cultivation of friendship. In South America, she had read, two men becoming friends might undergo a form of baptism ceremony over a tree trunk, symbolically becoming godchildren of the tree and therefore, in a sense, brothers to each other. That was strange, and we were just too busy to arrange ceremonies of that sort; meeting for coffee was easier. And in Germany, where form is preserved, there would be linguistic milestones in the development of friendship, with the change to the familiar *du* address. Of course one should not too quickly start to use the first names of friends in Germany; in some quarters a good few years might be required. Isabel smiled as she remembered being told by a professor from Freiburg of how, after several years of knowing a colleague, they were still on formal terms. Then, one evening, when the colleague had invited him to his house to watch an important football match on television, in a moment of great excitement he had shouted out 'Oh look, Reinhard, Germany has scored a goal!' and had immediately clasped a hand to his mouth, embarrassed by the solecism. He had called his colleague by his first name, and they had known one another for only a few years! Fortunately, the visitor had taken a generous view of this lapse, and they had agreed to move to first-name terms there and then, drinking a toast to friendship, as is appropriate in such circumstances.

Isabel had been intrigued. 'But what happens,' she asked, 'if two colleagues agree to address one another as *du* and then they fall out over something? Does one revert to the old formal usage and go back to *sie*?'

Her friend had pondered this for a while. 'There has been such a situation,' he said. 'I gather that it occurred in Bonn, amongst professors of theology. They had to go back to the formal means of address. It caused a great many ripples and is still talked about. In Bonn.'

She switched on the coffee percolator in the kitchen and

looked out of the window while the machine heated up and entered upon its programme of gurgles. The next-door cat, arrogant and self-assured, was on the high stone wall that divided her garden from its own – not that he recognised these human boundaries. The real boundaries, the feline lines of territory, were jealously guarded and supported by a whole different set of laws that humans knew nothing about, but which had every bit as much validity – down amongst the undergrowth of cat jurisdiction – as did the law of Scotland. The cat hesitated, turned round, and stared at Isabel through the window.

'That cat knew I was looking at him,' said Isabel, as Grace came into the room. 'He turned round and stared at me.'

'They're telepathic,' said Grace, simply. 'Everybody knows that.'

Isabel thought for a moment. 'I had a discussion with somebody yesterday about heaven. She said that one of the reasons for not believing in heaven – or indeed in any after-life – is that there would be so many animals' souls. It would be a terribly crowded place. Administratively impossible.'

Grace smiled. 'That's because she's still thinking in con-crete terms,' she said. And then, with the air of authority of one explaining New York to someone who has not been there, 'Those physical things don't apply on the other side.'

'Oh?' said Isabel. 'So cats and dogs cross over, if I may use your term. Do you . . . do you *hear* from them at the meetings?'

Grace stiffened. 'You may not have a high opinion of what we do,' she said, 'but I assure you, it's serious business.'

Isabel was quick to apologise – her second apology of the

morning, and it was not yet ten thirty. Grace accepted. 'I'm used to people being sceptical,' she said. 'It's normal.'

Grace went out to the hall to check for mail. 'No postie yet,' she said when she came back, using the Scots familiar term for the postman. 'But this has been pushed through the door.' She passed over a white, unstamped envelope on which Isabel's name had been written.

Isabel laid the envelope to the side of the percolator while she poured her coffee. Her name had been written in an unfamiliar hand, *Miss Isabel Dalhousie*, and underneath the words a flourish of the pen like one of those on Renaissance manuscripts. And then she knew; it was an Italian hand.

She took her cup of coffee in one hand and the letter in the other. Grace glanced at her and at the letter, clearly hoping that Isabel would open it in the kitchen and she would find out the identity of the sender. But this was private business, thought Isabel. This was to do with their trip, and she wanted to read it in her study. The envelope had that *charged* look about it, something which was difficult, if not impossible, to identify, but which hung about love letters and letters of sexual significance like perfume.

She stood by the window of her study while she opened it. She noticed that her hands were shaking, just slightly, but shaking. And then she saw from the top of the note-paper, *Prestonfield House*, that she had been right in her assumption.

Dear Isabel Dalhousie,

I am so sorry that I have had to write, rather than

259

to call on you personally. I have some business in Edinburgh today that will make it difficult for me to see you before I leave.

I had very much hoped that we would have been able to make that trip together. I had found many places that I wished to visit, and you would have been a good guide, I am sure. I even found on the map a place called Mellon Udrigle, up in the west. That must be a very fine place to have a name like that and it would have been very nice to have visited it.

Unfortunately I have to go back to Italy. I have ignored my business interests, but they are not ignoring me. I must return tomorrow. I am taking the car on the ferry from Rosyth.

I hope that we shall have the opportunity to meet again some time, perhaps when you are next in Italy. In the meantime I shall remember our dinner together most fondly and remember, too, the trip that we never made. Sometimes the trips not taken are better than those that one actually takes, do you not agree?

Cordially, Tomasso

She lowered the letter, still holding it, but then she dropped it and it fluttered to the carpet. She looked down. The letter had landed face-down and there was nothing to be seen – just paper. She bent down, picked it up, and reread it. Then she turned away and went to her desk. There was work to be done, and she would do it. She would not mourn for those things that did not happen. She would not.

She read through several manuscripts. One was interesting, and she placed it on a pile that was due to go out for refereeing. It was about memory, and forgetting, and about our duty to remember. Its starting point was that we have a duty to remember some names and some people. Those who have a moral claim on us may expect us to remember at least who they are.

How long would she remember this Italian? Not long, she decided. Until next week, perhaps. And then she thought: It is wrong of me to think that. One should not forget out of spite. All he did was flirt with me, as Italian men will do almost out of courtesy. The fault, if any, is mine: I assumed that he saw me as anything other than that which I am. I am the editor of the *Review of Applied Ethics*; I am not a femme fatale, whatever that's meant to be. I am a philosopher in her early forties. I have male friends, not boyfriends. That is who I am. But it would be nice, even if only occasionally, to be something else. Such as . . . *Brother Fox*, who was looking at her from the garden, although she could not see him. He was looking at her through the window, wondering whether the head and shoulders he saw behind that desk were attached to anything else, to legs and arms, or were a different creature altogether, just a head-and-shoulders creature? That was the extent of Brother Fox's philosophising; that and no more.

22

Ian had expressed doubts, as she expected he would, but finally he agreed.

'It's simply a matter of going to see him,' she said. 'See him in the flesh.' She looked at him and saw that he was not convinced. She persisted. 'It seems to me that there is an entirely rational explanation for what has happened to you. You have received the heart of a young man who died in rather sad circumstances. You have undergone all the psychological trauma that anybody in your position might expect. You've been brought up against your own mortality. You've . . . well, it may sound melodramatic, but you've looked at death. And you've harboured a lot of feelings for the person who saved your life.'

He watched her gravely. 'Yes,' he said. 'All of that is right. That's how it has been. Yes.'

'These emotions of yours,' Isabel went on, 'have taken their toll. They have to. They've been translated into physical symptoms. That's old hat. It happens all the time. It's nothing to do with any notion of cellular memory. It's nothing to do with that at all.'

'But the face? Why should the face be that of his father? *His* father – not *my* father.'

'The father of the heart,' mused Isabel. 'That would be a good title for a book or a poem, wouldn't it? Or, perhaps, *The Father of My Heart.*'

Ian pressed her. 'But why?'

They were sitting at one of the tables in Cat's delicatessen during this conversation. Isabel looked away, to the other side of the shop, where Eddie was handing a baguette to a customer. He was sharing a joke with the customer and laughing. He's come a long way, thought Isabel. She turned back to face Ian.

'There are three possibilities,' she said. 'One is that there really is some sort of cellular memory, and frankly I just don't know about that. I've tried to keep an open mind on it, but the more I've thought about it, the more difficult it becomes to pin much on it. I've looked at some of the literature on memory and the general view is that there just isn't any convincing evidence for it – what there is seems anecdotal at best. I'm not New Age enough to believe in things for which there's no verifiable evidence.' She thought for a moment. Was this too extreme? Some qualification might be necessary. 'At least when it comes to matters of how the human body works. And memory is a bodily matter, isn't it? So where does that leave us?

'The next possibility is sheer coincidence. And that, I think, is a more likely possibility than one might at first think. Our lives are littered with coincidences of one sort or another.'

'And the third?' asked Ian.

'The third is an entirely rational one,' said Isabel. 'Some time, somewhere, after you had your operation, you saw something which pointed to the fact that the donor, your benefactor, was a young man called Gavin Macleod. Then, perhaps at the same time, you saw a photograph of Gavin's father. You may not even have been aware that your mind was reaching these conclusions.'

'Unlikely,' said Ian. 'Very unlikely.'

Isabel raised an eyebrow. 'But isn't the whole thing completely unlikely? Isn't it unlikely that you would have had these symptoms . . . these visions? Yet that is all very real to you, isn't it? And if something that unlikely can happen, then why shouldn't there be further levels of unlikelihood?' She paused, assessing the effect of her remarks on him. He was looking down at his feet, almost in embarrassment. 'What have you got to lose, Ian?'

For several minutes he said nothing, and then he had agreed, with the result that now they were making their way out to West Linton, with Isabel at the wheel of her old green Swedish car. She rarely drove this car, which smelled of old, cracked leather and which, in spite of being largely neglected, never once in all its years had refused to start. I shall keep this car until I die, she had decided, a decision which had made her feel bound to the car in a curious way, as life partners are bound to each other.

Ian was silent, tense beside her. As they negotiated their

way out of the Edinburgh traffic, he stared out of the window, balefully, thought Isabel, like a man on his way to punishment, a prisoner en route to a new, remoter jail. And even as they passed Carlops, and the evening sky to the west opened up with shafts of light, he did not respond beyond a murmur to Isabel's remarks about the countryside. She left him to his mood and his silence, but just before they reached West Linton itself, he pointed to a house some distance off the road, a large stone house with windows facing a stretch of moor. The last rays of the sun had caught the roof of this house, picking it out in gold.

'I stayed there,' he said casually. 'I spent three weeks there when I was recuperating. It belongs to friends of ours. They invited us to come and stay.'

Isabel glanced at the house and then back at Ian.

'You stayed in that house?'

'Yes. Jack and Sheila Scott. They're friends from university days. Do you know them?'

She steered the car over to a small patch of grass at the side of the road and drew to a halt.

Ian frowned. 'Is there something wrong?'

Isabel turned off the engine. 'I wish you'd told me, Ian,' she said.

He looked puzzled. 'About Jack and Sheila's house? Why should I have told you about that?'

'Because it provides the answer,' she said. She felt angry with him, and there was an edge to her voice. 'Did you go into the village itself?'

'From time to time,' he said. 'I used to go and browse through the bookshop. You know it?'

Isabel nodded impatiently. 'Yes, I know it. But tell me, Ian, would you have seen people while you were there?'

'People? Of course I saw people.'

She hesitated for a moment. They were near, so near to the solution. But she did not know whether she dared to hope that it could be so neat and tidy.

'And spoke to people?'

He looked out of the window at the grey-stone dyke that followed the side of the road. 'It's difficult to find dry-stane dykers,' he remarked. 'Look at that one. The stones on the top have fallen off. But who can fix them these days? Who's got that feeling for stone?'

Isabel looked at the dyke. She did not want to talk about that now. 'People,' she repeated. 'Did you speak to people?'

'Of course I spoke to people,' he said. 'I spoke to the man who runs the bookshop. He's a composer, isn't he? I spoke to him and sometimes I spoke to people who came into the shop. He introduced me to some of the customers. It's very villagey, you know.'

Isabel knew that she could not expect the answer she wanted to the next question, but she asked it nonetheless. 'And did you meet a vet?' she asked. 'A vet who lives in the village, quite close to the bookshop?'

'I have no idea,' he said. 'I might have. I can't remember it all that well. I was still a bit fuzzy round the edges then, you know. It was not all that long after I had left hospital.' He turned and looked at her, almost reproachfully, she thought. 'I'm doing my best, Isabel. You know, this isn't very easy for me.'

She reached out and took his hand in hers. 'I know you

266

are, Ian. I'm sorry. It's just that we're very close now. So let's not talk about it any further. Let's just go and see him. He's expecting us round about now.'

He had just returned from work and was still wearing his jacket, a green waxed-waterproof. One of the pockets in the front was bulging with what looked like a bottle of tablets. Beneath the jacket she glimpsed a red tie which she recognised: the Dick Vet in Edinburgh, the university veterinary school.

He opened the door to them and gestured for them to come in.

'This place is a bit of a bachelor establishment,' he said. 'I mean to tidy it up, but you know . . .'

Isabel glanced about her. It was not unduly untidy, she thought, but it was spartan, as if nobody really lived there. She stole a glance at Euan Macleod: there were the high forehead and the eyes; yes, he was not unlike Graeme. But his was a kinder face, somehow, a gentler face.

'You said that you wanted to see me about Gavin,' he said, as he motioned for them to sit down. 'I must confess, I was a bit surprised. You know that I am separated from my wife? You know that we're divorcing?'

Isabel nodded. 'I know that.'

Euan looked directly at Isabel as he spoke, but there was no note of challenge in his voice. 'So that meant that I didn't see the children very much. In fact, my wife made it more or less impossible for me. I decided not to make a fuss. Only the youngest is under eighteen. The other two could decide for themselves in due course.'

Isabel caught her breath. This was a different story from his wife's, but of course one expected very different accounts of a marriage ending in an acrimonious divorce. Both parties could rewrite history, sometimes without even realising that that was what they were doing. Both could believe their own accounts.

'I'm sorry about what happened to your son,' she said.

He lowered his head in a gesture of acknowledgement. 'Thank you. He was a very nice boy. But that illness . . . well, what can one say? Such a waste.'

'Yes,' said Isabel. 'But there was something salvaged from the tragedy. And that's what we came to tell you, Mr Macleod.'

He started to speak – something she did not catch – but lapsed into silence.

'Consent was given by your wife to the use of your son's heart,' she said. 'He was the donor in a transplant. And my friend here is the person who received it. This is why he is alive today.'

Euan's shock was visible. He stared at Isabel, and then he turned to Ian. He shook his head. He put his hands over his eyes.

Isabel rose to her feet and approached him. She put a hand on his shoulder. 'I can imagine what you're feeling,' she whispered. 'Please, I do understand. The reason why we came to see you is that Ian, my friend, needed to be able to say thank you. I hope you understand that.'

Euan took his hands away from his eyes. There were tears on his cheeks. 'I didn't see him,' he said quietly. 'I couldn't face it. I couldn't face the funeral. I just couldn't. I couldn't go . . .'

Isabel bent down and placed her arms about him. 'You mustn't reproach yourself about that. I'm sure that you were a good father to him, and to the others.'

'I tried,' he said. 'I really did. I tried with the marriage too.'

'I'm sure that you did.' She looked at Ian, who rose to his feet and joined her beside Euan.

'Now listen to me very carefully,' she said. 'Please listen. Your son is living on in the life of this man here. And this man, who owes your son so much, has come to you because he needs to express his gratitude. But there's another thing – he can say to you that farewell that you and your son did not exchange. Look. Look.' She reached out and took Ian's hand and turned it over, to expose his wrist. 'Put your hand there, Euan. Can you feel that pulse? Can you feel it? That is your son's heart. Your son would forgive you, you know, Euan. Your son would forgive you anything that you felt needed forgiving. That's true, isn't it, Ian?'

Ian began to say something, but could not continue, and so he nodded his assent and clasped the hand above his, firmly, in a token of forgiveness and gratitude. Isabel left them together for a few moments. She crossed the room to the window and looked out on the village, at the lights and the darkening sky. Rain had set in, not heavy rain, but a gentle shower, drifting, soft, falling on the narrow village street and her green Swedish car and the hills, dark shapes, beyond.

'I see that it has started to rain,' she said. 'And we must get back to Edinburgh soon.'

Euan looked up. She saw that he was smiling, and she

269

knew from this that she had been right; that something had happened in those moments, something which she had thought might happen, but which she had not allowed herself to hope for too much, for fear of disappointment. I am often wrong, thought Isabel, but sometimes right – like everybody else.

23

Grace put the mail on Isabel's desk.

'Not very many letters this morning,' she said. 'Four, in fact.'

'What matters is the quality,' said Isabel, shuffling through the envelopes. 'New York, Melbourne, London, and Edinburgh.'

'Edinburgh is the fish bill,' said Grace. 'Smell the envelope. They write the bills out in that funny little office they have at the back of the shop. Their hands smell of fish when they do it. One can always tell the fish bill.'

Isabel raised the plain brown envelope to her nose. 'I see what you mean,' she said. 'Of course, people used to send perfumed letters. I had an aunt who put a very peculiar perfume on her letters. I loved that as a child. I am not sure whether I'd be so keen on it now.'

'I think that we come back to these things,' said Grace. 'I loved rice pudding as a girl. Then I couldn't touch it. Now I must say that I rather look forward to rice pudding.'

'Didn't Lin Yutang say something about that?' mused Isabel. 'Didn't he ask: What is patriotism but the love of the good things that one ate in childhood?'

Grace laughed. 'Grub first, then ethics. That's what I say.'

Isabel began to say, 'Brecht . . .' but stopped herself in time. She picked up the envelope which bore the New York postmark. Slitting it open, she extracted a letter and unfolded it. For a few minutes she was silent, absorbed in the letter. Grace watched her.

She was smiling. 'This is a very important letter, Grace,' she said. 'This is from Professor Edward Mendelson. He's the literary executor of W. H. Auden. I wrote to him and this is his reply.'

Grace was impressed. She had not read Auden, but had heard him quoted many times by her employer. 'I'll get round to reading him,' she had said, but they both doubted if she would. Grace did not read poetry – Grace's razor.

'I wrote to him with an idea,' said Isabel. 'Auden wrote a poem in which he uses imagery which is very reminiscent of Burns. There are lines in "My love is like a red, red rose" about loving somebody *Till a' the seas gang dry*. You remember those, don't you.'

'Of course,' said Grace. 'I love that song. Kenneth McKellar sings it beautifully. He made me fall in love with him. But there must be so many people who fell in love with him. Just like they all fell in love with Placido Domingo.'

'I don't recall falling in love with Placido Domingo,' said Isabel. 'How careless of me!'

'But Auden? What's he got to do with Burns?'

'He taught for a short time in Scotland,' said Isabel. 'As a very young man. He taught in a boarding school over in Helensburgh. And he must have taught the boys Burns. Every Scottish schoolchild learnt Burns in those days. And still should, for that matter. You learnt Burns, didn't you? I did.'

'I learnt "To a Mouse",' said Grace. 'And half of "Tam O'Shanter".'

'And "A Man's a Man for a' That"?'

'Yes,' said Grace, and for a moment the two women looked at one another, and Isabel thought: This is one of the things that binds us together – in all the privilege of my life, in all that has been given to me through no effort of my own, I am bound to my fellow citizens in the common humanity that Burns spelled out for us. We are equal. Not one of us is more than the other. We are equal – which was the way she wanted it; she would have no other compact. And that is why when, at the reopening of the Scottish Parliament after those hundreds of years of abeyance, a woman had stood up and sung 'A Man's a Man for a' That', there had been few hearts in disagreement. It was the rock to which the country, the culture, was anchored; a constitution, a charter of rights, written in song.

'I wrote to Edward Mendelson,' Isabel went on, 'because I thought I could detect Burns – the influence of Burns – in one of Auden's lines. And now he's written back to me.'

'And said?'

'And said that he believes it possible. He says that he has some correspondence in which Auden says something about Burns.'

Grace's expression suggested that she was not impressed. 'I must get on with my work,' she said. 'I'll leave you to your . . .'

'Work,' said Isabel, supplying the word that Grace might have uttered in quotation marks. She knew that Grace did not regard the hours she spent in her study as real work. And, of course, to those whose work was physical, sitting at a desk did not seem unduly strenuous.

Grace left her, and she continued with the rest of the correspondence and with a set of proofs that she had neglected over the last few days. She did not regret the time she had spent away from her desk, particularly the previous day's trip to West Linton. As far as she was concerned, she had done her duty by Ian and had brought the whole matter to its resolution. On the journey back from West Linton Ian had been loquacious.

'You were right,' he said. 'I needed to say thank you. That was probably all there was to it.'

'Good,' said Isabel, and she had mused on how strong the need to thank may be. 'And do you think that will be the end of those . . . what shall we call them? Experiences?'

'I don't know,' said Ian. 'But I do feel different.'

'And we've laid to rest all that nonsense about cellular memory,' said Isabel. 'Our faith in the rational can be reaffirmed.'

'You're sure that I met him, or had him pointed out to me, aren't you?' Ian asked. He sounded doubtful.

'Isn't that the most likely explanation?' replied Isabel. 'It's a small village. People would have known about the death. They would have talked. You probably heard it, even if indirectly, from your hosts – a chance remark over breakfast or whatever. But the mind takes such things in and files them away. So you knew – but didn't know – that Euan was the man you wanted to thank. Doesn't that sound credible to you?'

He looked out of the window at the dark fields flashing by. 'Maybe.'

'And there's another thing,' said Isabel. 'Resolution. Musicians know all about that, don't they? Pieces of music seek resolution, have to end on a particular note, or it sounds all wrong. The same applies to our lives. It's exactly the same.'

Ian said nothing to this, but thought about it all the way back to Edinburgh, and continued to think about it for the remainder of that evening, in silence and in gratitude. He was not convinced by Isabel's explanation. It could be true, but it did not seem true to him. But did that matter? Did it matter how one got to the place one wanted to be, provided that one got there in the end?

Jamie was invited for dinner that evening and accepted. He should bring something to sing, Isabel said, and she would accompany him. He could choose.

He arrived at seven o'clock, fresh from a rehearsal at the Queen's Hall and full of complaint about the unreasonable behaviour of a particular conductor. She gave him a glass of wine and led him through to the music room. In the kitchen, a fish stew sat on the stove, and fresh French bread

275

was on the table. There was a candle, unlit, and starched Dutch napkins in a Delft design.

She sat down at the piano and took the music which he handed to her. Schubert and Schumann. It was safe, rather *gemütlich*, and she felt that his heart was not in it.

'Sing something you believe in,' she said after they had reached the end of the third song.

Jamie smiled. 'A good idea,' he said. 'I'm fed up with all that.' He reached into his music bag and took out a couple of sheets of music, which he handed to Isabel.

'Jacobite!' exclaimed Isabel. '"Derwentwater's Farewell". What's this all about?'

'It's a lament,' said Jamie. 'It's been dredged up out of Hogg's *Jacobite Relics*. It's all about poor Lord Derwentwater, who was executed for joining the rebellion. It's all about the things that he'll miss. It's very sad.'

'So I see,' said Isabel, glancing at the words. 'And this is his speech here – printed at the end?'

'Yes,' said Jamie. 'I find that particularly moving. He delivered it a few minutes before they put him to death. He was a loyal friend to James the Third. They had been boys together at the Palace of St Germain.'

'A loyal friend,' mused Isabel, staring at the music. 'That greatest of goods – friendship.'

'Yes, I suppose so,' said Jamie. He leant forward and pointed to a passage in the printed speech. 'Look at what he says here. Near the end – minutes from death. He says, *I am in perfect charity with all the world*.'

Isabel was silent. *I am in perfect charity with all the world*, she thought. *I am in perfect charity with all the world*. Resolution.

'And over here,' said Jamie. 'Look. He says, *I freely forgive such as ungenerously reported false things of me*. Then he goes to his death.'

'They acted with such dignity,' said Isabel. 'Not all of them perhaps, but so many. Look at Mary, Queen of Scots. What a different world.'

'Yes,' said Jamie. 'It was. But we're in this one. Let's begin.'

He sang the lament and at the end of it Isabel rose from her piano seat and closed the cover of the keyboard. 'Fish stew,' she said. 'And another glass of this.'

At the table, the candle lit, they used the French bread to soak up the fish stew at the edge of their plates. Then Jamie, who was facing the window, suddenly became still. 'Out there,' he whispered. 'Just outside the window.'

Isabel turned in her seat. She did so slowly, because she had guessed what it was, who it was, and did not want a sudden movement to scare him off.

Brother Fox looked in. He saw two people. He saw them raise their glasses of wine to him, liquid that for him was suspended in the air, as if by a miracle.